W9-BVO-353

STACKS

WITHDRAWN

SUDDEN
BILL DORN

**Center Point
Large Print**

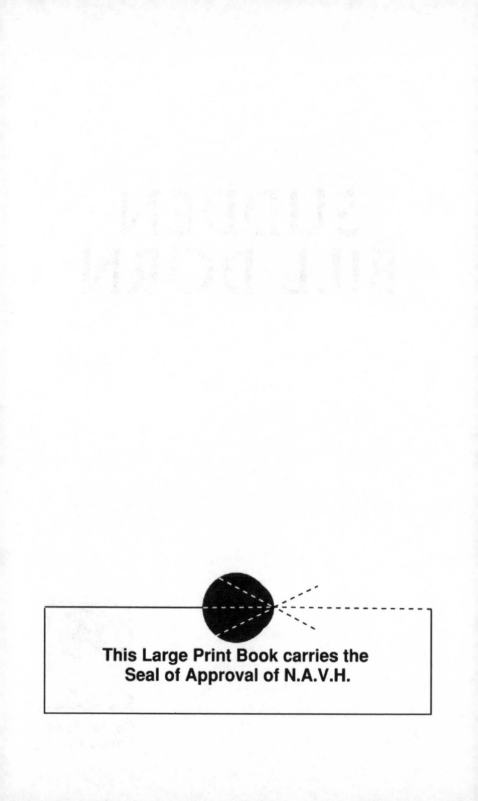

**This Large Print Book carries the
Seal of Approval of N.A.V.H.**

SUDDEN
BILL DORN

Jackson Gregory

CENTER POINT PUBLISHING
THORNDIKE, MAINE

This Center Point Large Print edition
is published in the year 2010 by arrangement with
Golden West Literary Agency.

Copyright © 1937 by Jackson Gregory.
Copyright © renewed 1965 by
the Estate of Jackson Gregory.

All rights reserved.

The text of this Large Print edition is unabridged.
In other aspects, this book may vary
from the original edition.
Printed in the United States of America
on permanent paper.
Set in 16-point Times New Roman type.

ISBN: 978-1-60285-781-0

Library of Congress Cataloging-in-Publication Data

Gregory, Jackson, 1882-1943.
  Sudden Bill Dorn / Jackson Gregory.
     p. cm.
  ISBN 978-1-60285-781-0 (library binding : alk. paper)
  1. Large type books. I. Title.
  PS3513.R562S83 2010
  813′.52—dc22

                                        2010001373

I

IF BILL DORN had ever doubted that the sheriff was a true friend he would never doubt again. Dorn rose slowly from his table, littered with papers, and stepped to his open door, his face dead white, the muscles corded along his lean jaws, his dark eyes burning ominously. For a time, motionless and silent, he stared out across the billowing grazing lands sloping gradually up to the far pine-timbered mountains, yet saw nothing of the wide expanse. The sheriff watched him shrewdly, never batting an eye. Nothing of the rigidity of the still form escaped him, nor did the scarcely perceptible tensing and stiffening of the broad shoulders.

When Bill Dorn spoke it was tonelessly, almost under his breath and without turning.

"You've been mighty square with me, Bart," he said. "I'll be apt to remember."

The sheriff, relaxing nothing of his vigilance, asked bluntly:

"Well? What are you going to do, Dorn?"

The rancher made no immediate answer. After a while, when he faced about, his eyelids drooped so low that he looked sleepy, but the sheriff, still seated, saw and read aright the hot flash of his eyes. Bill Dorn, about to speak, thought better of it; instead he filled his lungs slowly to a deep intake of air, then crossed the rude plank floor, bare save for its scattering of local Indian rugs, passing out of sight in an adjoining room. He returned almost immediately wearing his coat and broad-brimmed old black hat. Sheriff Barton MacArthur, not the man at most times to overlook details, certainly not today, marked the bulge under the coat at Bill Dorn's hip.

"So that's the answer, is it?" he demanded. As he stood up he gathered the papers from the table, snapped a rubber band about them and put them into his wallet.

Dorn glanced at the clock on its shelf over the fireplace.

"I've got me some riding to do, MacArthur," he said casually. "The afternoon's half gone and I'd better be on my way."

"You said just now I'd treated you white, Bill Dorn," said the sheriff. His own eyes narrowed and the lines about his mouth hardened. "You said you'd be apt to remember." He shrugged heavily. "Buckling on your gun now and starting for a ride—well, it ain't going to make things any easier for me, is it?"

"I guess we've about talked this thing out, Bart," said Dorn. "I'm on my way."

"Into Nacional?" demanded MacArthur. "Have it your way, you hot-headed fool. I'm riding with you."

"No. I'm riding alone this time. Tomorrow, if

you want me, or maybe tonight, I'll take orders. I'll never pull a gun on you, Sheriff, and you know it. But for a few hours I am my own boss."

Under one of the big live oaks was a saddled horse, its reins grounded, its dark hide stained with travel. Bill Dorn passed it on his way to the corral, selected one of the half dozen animals there and led it into the barn to saddle up. When he rode out into the open, ducking his head through the doorway, the sheriff had already mounted the horse under the oak.

"You'd do well to take anyhow a day to think things over, Bill," he called, and for the first time sounded angry.

"Thinking won't mend matters now," returned Dorn. "So long, Bart."

He struck into the dusty road leading south, heading, as the sheriff had expected, to Nacional just over the Mexican border. Already the sun was dipping westward; the shadows ran out from the little hills making an early dusk in the barancas. It would be sundown by the time he reached the Mexican border town.

At first he rode with his head down, brooding, his hat drawn low, his somber eyes taking no stock of the country through which he rode. He did not glance back to see whether the sheriff followed; it would make scant difference what MacArthur chose to do. But presently he straightened in the saddle and swept the wide landscape

7

with eyes which, still hard and bleak, yet were no longer unseeing.

"Wonder if I'll ever come back to it?" he asked himself.

Here was a spot which he loved, one that had held him in rich contentment for the greater part of his life. The wide grassy valleys, the narrow, shady passes through the hills, the black, pine-clad slopes in the north and the silver-gray, sage-mantled reaches in the south and west—all this constituted an eternal, living, ever changing familiar scene which had come to mean very much in Bill Dorn's life. He looked at it now as a man might regard a friend at time of a last hand-clasp. But it was for only an instant that his eyes softened; again they grew hard with the bitterness within him.

Only when two or three miles from the ranch house, as he rode up into the first low line of brushy hills, did he turn to look back. The sheriff was nowhere in sight; evidently he had gone on about his business, leaving Bill Dorn to his own affair, even to carrying it out in whatever way he chose. After all a sheriff's work generally began only after the other fellow had said his say.

He struck into a dim trail affording a short cut through the hills and for the first time noticed a flock of buzzards wheeling low, dipping almost to the ground; the *whoosh* of their great wings was loud in his ears. He saw two or three of the ugly scavengers already on the ground; at his approach they eyed him balefully, took their few awkward hops and rose into the air with flapping wings, grown graceful only when sailing aloft, circling with their companions. They'd wait now with their desert-bred patience until the man moved on.

Any man would have tarried to discover what it was that had invited the red-headed nauseous birds down to their ghoulish feast. Despite the grim nature of Dorn's errand, despite its obvious urgency, he forced a snorting, rebellious horse down into the brushy hollow where he expected to find a dead coyote, shot by some cowboy, or perhaps an old pensioner of a horse which had stretched out here for the last time. Instead he saw through a thin screening of sage brush that it was a man's body lying there.

Dorn withdrew a hundred yards or so to a small scrub oak, tethered his horse and returned on foot. The man was but recently dead; the cause of his death was written clear; his hat was off, lying within reach of outflung fingers, and in his fore-head, dead center, was the bullet hole.

"It's Jake Fanning," muttered Dorn. "You'd almost say he killed himself; anyhow the gun was shoved right up close to his head."

But he knew that Fanning never carried any weapon except his old double-barreled shotgun, and neither was this a shotgun wound nor was the weapon anywhere in evidence. Nor were Fanning's horse and pack mule. Their scuffed tracks were at hand all right; they had brought him this far, had gone on, heading toward the road.

Bill Dorn squatted on his high heels and pondered. Jake Fanning, a man for whom he had never had any use, had been an ugly devil in life, and death had done nothing to beautify him. One of a special breed in the wide Southwest that harbors so many types, he was a desert rat, a shiftless prospector, a border town burn when in funds, a beggar or a thief when down to his last silver dollar. Maybe he deserved killing? Dorn was not concerned with that. The question was what to do with him now? Circling shadows still drifted over the ground when the black wings sailed low against the westering sun. Bill Dorn, impatient to be on his way, regretted that he hadn't let MacArthur accompany him; here was another job for an already overworked sheriff. In the end he shrugged heavily, got up and gathered the dead man into his arms. His horse was going to make a terrible fuss over it, but you couldn't very well go off and leave even a dead Jake Fanning like this. Had there been a shovel, had there even been a blanket or tarpaulin—

There was no house within miles, other than his own ranch house; so, when he had subdued his blue roan, desperate as the beast was with terror, he heaved his unlovely burden up across the saddle, roped him there and started back on foot.

"Funny thing," he thought somberly. "Here I set out to find Michael Bundy; here dead Jake stops me, and Michael was the last man that ever grub-staked Jake. It's as bad as if he'd hired a dead man to hold me up for a spell."

He found no one at the ranch house, but looking off across the ranch to the north where the cursed oil derricks lifted their dirty skeletons against the clean backdrop of the mountains—derricks which had started all the trouble, which had ruined something very fine, which had smashed a sort of dream and had made mockery of an ideal of friendship—he saw two home-drifting cowboys and with his old sombrero waved them the command to step along. They came racing in, wondering what the boss wanted.

"What did yuh kill him for, Bill?" they wanted to know. "An' why drag him home with yuh?"

They carried dead Jake Fanning into the house, stretching him out on the floor with an old sheet over him.

"Seen the sheriff, either of you boys?" Dorn asked. They shook their heads. "One of you come along with me then; I'll show you where I played it low on the turkey buzzards today—"

"Me, I'd think yuh done 'em a favor," grunted one of his hearers, young Bud Williams, who like most others had small liking for the late Jake Fanning.

"Later you can look up the sheriff, if I don't run into him in Nacional, and can show him the spot; there's a chance, though mighty small, he might do some tracking from there. Somebody after killing Jake led his live stock off.—By the way, boys, I guess you're not working for me any longer."

They stared incredulously; slowly both tanned faces reddened and the eyes bent so frowningly on him hardened.

"Fired, huh? Jest like that! Why, damn your eyes—"

"Not exactly fired," said Bill Dorn coolly. "I'm off for a ride and it looks as though I'd not be riding back here."

"What about Mike Bundy? Where's he at?"

"I'm not sure, but hope to see him real soon."

"Say, Bill! Yuh ain't sold out to that—"

"That what, Bud?"

Bud shrugged and spat as he led the way outside. "Sold out to him, have yuh?"

"Not exactly. But in effect I'd say it's the same thing."

He swung up into the saddle of the blue roan, more eager than ever to be on his way. Bud Williams, frowning, was kicking up dust with the toe of his boot. He exclaimed, "Here, what's this?" and stooped for something lying close to the threshold. Dorn turned, wondering what it was that the cowboy peered at so intently. "Quartz rock, by thunder, all shot full o' gold!" exclaimed Bud. "Say, where'd it come from?"

No one knew whence it came. Spilled from Jake Fanning's coat pocket as they dragged him down from the saddle? *Quien sabe?*

"Tell the sheriff about that, too," said Dorn. "He's the man hired to do all the tall guesswork, times like this. Let's go."

He had lost upward of an hour because of Jake Fanning, and long before coming to the Mexican village, blossoming like a noxious flower on the international border line, he was riding in a violet twilight. Down into old Mexico the sun sank, flaring up a hot red before it melted into the low bank of clouds, then vanishing in a fanfare of colors. Thereafter came the purple night, far mountains swimming mistily and dissolving into the dark, the first big white stars flaring out across the white miles of desert between the southernmost confines of the erstwhile Dorn Ranch and the north rim of Mexico. A ridge of low-lying hills drew the line pretty fairly between a region of good stock land and one of aridity. Behind him was a grassy country; he rode now through vast sweeps given over to cactus and greasewood. Being a man not without imagination he wondered whether this sort of progress might be symbolic.

He crossed the border long before he came to the village, slipping from one country to another in a bit of rugged terrain which, some years before, when smuggling Chinese into the States went merrily on, had come to be called La Puerta de los Chinos. By now the sky was all purply-black velvet with brilliant stars strewn across it for glittering spangles, and the earth beneath was a silver-gray sea, lonely, untenanted save by himself, and without a beacon light anywhere. Then at last he rode up out of a hollow where desert willows grew higher than his head, and mounted a gentle rise of land; suddenly the few lights of that mad, bad little lost town of Nacional flared out at him, beckoning impudently through the big shady cottonwoods.

Now, Nacional drowsed in its shade through most days of the year, like a lean, hungry coyote keeping a low-lidded eye just enough open to be ready to leap and attack and rend at the proper moment; and though it stirred and awoke from its lethargy a little after sundown, still it went for the most part on padded feet, did its murdering with a quiet knife in a dark alley, and was outwardly inert until late enough for men to get drunk on as bad liquor as even a border town ever poured blisteringly down its ravening red throat. Tonight, however, early as it was, Bill Dorn heard the beast's growl almost as soon as he saw its eyes. Something out of the ordinary was afoot. But then there was the old saying which, translated from the Spanish, avers: "In little Nacional it is the usual thing for the unusual to happen."

But whatever it was that Nacional was bestirring itself about did not in any way interest Bill Dorn. His eyes and ears told him that more men were in town than was usual, and that they gave the impression of being in some sort of gala mood; his thoughts, however, did not bite into the fact. An earthquake or a conflagration, though forcing themselves on his notice, would not have concerned him. He was here looking for Michael Bundy. Nothing on earth mattered except the one consideration: He was going to find Bundy and kill him.

He left his horse at the stable, the first building at the end of the street, when one rode in, as he did, from the east. Then, walking with purposeful long strides, his boot heels echoing on the board sidewalks, he made his way between the two rows of squat adobe houses, headed for the nerve center of this place—what they called the Plaza, a mere irregular widening in the road with a drinking fountain and a flagpole in the middle of it—looked out upon by the doors and windows and balconies of half a dozen two-storied adobe saloons and gambling hells. If Bundy were in town, Bill Dorn would find him somewhere along the Plaza. If Bundy were not here, some word might be had of him. So Dorn moved swiftly along, peering to right and left, seeing the men who thronged the street but making nothing of them save that so far none of them was Michael Bundy.

Before he had gone two squares, which is to say half the journey from Ramiro's stable to the Plaza, a dozen men had accosted him. His responses were curt, indifferent; he scarcely noted the men themselves beyond realizing each time, "That's not Bundy." As he drew nearer the Plaza he began shouldering his way, and even then he did not so much as ask himself what it could be that had caused the crowd to gather. Here were not only the scant handful of denizens of Nacional which housed scarcely more than seven hundred swarthy, lower class Mexicans and Indians, but men from ranches and mines and other settlements on both sides of the dividing line. There swelled in front of him, in a compact mass, a churning eddy of sombreros, blue jeans, hairy *chaparejos*, serapes. He, taller than most, looked over their heads for another taller, bulkier man, a big blond, handsome, dynamic, roistering man whom the border for five hundred miles knew as Mike Bundy.

Bill Dorn began to lose some of the paradoxically calm quality of his murderous rage, which had been somehow like a queer cold flame steady within him. It irritated him that today of all days of the year so many men should clutter the street of Nacional and so make difficult the simple task of finding a wanted man here. When someone whom he knew caught his arm and said excitedly: "Say, Bill! What's the inside dope? You've got it, ain't you?" Dorn shoved him away so violently that he crashed into the thick of the crowd from which he had emerged. Other men, spotting him, followed him; they asked him questions which were like stinging flies plaguing his impatience. All these fellows seemed to take it for granted that he knew something that they would have given their ears to know. Some, seeking to be tactful, invited: "Hi, Bill! Come have a drink." He muttered at them; he lifted his shoulders at them; he shook his head; and before he was done he damned them out of his way. He didn't take the trouble to try to figure out what they had in their minds. At every step he hoped to come on Bundy.

From the first saloon to the last he looked in at every one. He would enter the front door, pass slowly through the long room, return slowly, his head pivoting, his burning-bright eyes searching out every face in the shadow of every broad-brimmed hat. He saw men gathered in small, tight, eager knots; he didn't care the snap of his big hard fingers what they were discussing so earnestly.

After the first hour he unlocked his lips enough to begin asking, "Have you seen Michael Bundy?" No one had seen Bundy; many, it appeared, were asking about him, saying among themselves, "If anyone's got the straight of this, be sure it'll be Mike Bundy." Bill Dorn had his first drink at the old adobe cantina leaning crazily away from the border line as though fearful of it. He was not a drinking man; none of those who watched him so speculatively had ever seen him step to a bar alone and pour down his liquor as he gulped it tonight, his face hard, his eyes giving an impression of small hot fires glinting through smoke. They began to nudge one another and point him out.

"He ain't like Bill Dorn," one said, and many thought. "It's like some other hombre had slipped inside his hide while ol' Bill was away."

By eleven o'clock Bill Dorn's dark eyes were red-flecked and all who saw him coming gave him a wide berth. They had other things on their minds tonight than quarreling, and all any man could look for from Bill Dorn was trouble.

II

THERE are those men who go through life never known by any name except that wished upon them in their cradles. On the other hand, there are men who gather nicknames as inevitably as a magnet draws convenient steel filings. Speaking now of Bill Dorn: His name—fond parents concurring after a forceful mother had dictated the terms and an easy-going father had agreed, "Sure, why not?"—was William Stockney O'Shaunnessy Dorn. Now, twenty-seven years old, six feet four in his customary two-inch-and-a-half boot heels, he was known along the border as Sudden Bill, as Roll-Along Dorn, as Long Horn Bill, as Here-We-Go Dorn, as Daybreak, as Aces. How names did stick to him! One day a lean old chestnut-hued cattle man, a great friend of Bill's, chanced to say in the presence of Bill's Chinese cook, "Shore he's a heller, that boy. Born a Dorn, ain't he?" And the Chink had giggled and said, "Born-a-Dorn, damn good name. Me call him Born-a-Dorn Bill now." That's the way it went. His father, violently removed from the mundane scene some years before, was Early Bill Dorn.

And it was the father, Early Bill, who had carved out the original Dorn Ranch close to the rim of cattle country, on the edge of the desert. He was buried with his boots on, a forthright gentleman of the old school with Kentucky blood and proclivities in his staunch veins, leaving behind him a wife who still adored him, knowing him to the depths though she did; leaving also a single son and an unencumbered ranch of six thousand four hundred acres, together with a tobacco tin heavy with gold coins under a stone in the hearth. Bill's mother lost interest in life, pottered about listlessly for three or four years, told young Bill that he'd never need her half as much as old Early Bill did, and died happily. Young Bill sat all night by the two graves. Then he hitched up his belt, looked life square between the eyes and tied in to his job.

He built the ranch up to sixty thousand acres. And he lived like a king—a barbarian king, to be sure—in the same old ranch house. It was close to a hundred years old—at least the kernel of it was—an imperishable affair of good honest adobe mud reinforced with honest straw, of field stone and cedar timbers hauled forty miles from the Blue Smokes Mountains. And now, all of a sudden, circumstances over which young Bill Dorn had not maintained control up-ended him.

He had been given what folk call "advantages"; that was because Bedelia Dorn, his mother, insisted. He had even had "schooling," though old Early Bill guffawed. He had had money to jingle at the age when jingling is sweet in the callow ear, so he had jingled it with the best of the Jinglers. He had knocked about a bit; he had "been places"; he was like the bear that went over the mountain. After his mother fluttered him a good-bye and slipped away to see if she could find the place where Early Bill would need somebody to see that his socks were dry, young Bill did some pretty precipitate knocking about. He was mighty glad and grateful to get back to the old Dorn Ranch.

During his prowlings he met many people, many kinds. One of them, encountered no farther away than Los Angeles, a city well known in Southern California at that time, which was long before Hollywood absorbed it, was a man who seemed to fit into Bill Dorn's life like a finger in a glove. That was Michael Bundy. The two clicked the first time they met.

They locked horns in a poker game in La Puebla de Nuestra Señora la Reina de los Angeles, which happens to be the proper name of the city now so pertly called Los or L.A. It was at a club in La Primevera Street, which the gringos have chopped down, for speed of all things, to Spring Street. The two plunged, but they plunged with method in their madness. The other players dropped out one by one; foregathering at the adjacent bar they were unanimous in their expressions of satisfaction at getting out with their skins intact. It was that sort of roofless game.

Bill Dorn was lean and dark, like a well oiled spring ready to explode into expression of power released; Mike Bundy was blond, red-haired and dynamic, a favorite with women, also with men until they came to know him down to the boot heels, and Bundy was acute enough to make sure that few knew him as far as that. He was an adventurer and said so; he had knocked about as much as Dorn, and more; he was, as he himself said, a pioneer in black gold. That meant oil, at which most men, lacking Mike Bundy's vision, twitched their noses.

The two became inseparable. They became Damon and Pythias. Bill Dorn would have gone to hell for Mike Bundy. Mike Bundy would have gone to hell for an option on the devil's coal, sulphur and brimstone mines. That was how it was. And many outsiders realized it; some even tried to make it clear to Bill Dorn. One man, well-intentioned, had opened his mouth on the subject only to have Dorn, in sudden fury, knock him cold.

"Come out to the ranch, Michael," Bill had invited one day. Bundy came and he stayed. He had money; he gave people the impression of having all the money there was. He nosed around for oil. The very first well he drilled on a near-by property brought in his damned black gold. The well never paid—that is, it never paid anyone but Mike Bundy. He spread out; he fished for suckers, at first with a hook, then with a net. He "promoted," lovely word. On paper, where it's as cheap to set down a long string of ciphers as it is to dot an i, he made money for many a credulous and suddenly avaricious, hitherto contented land owner. On paper—that was Bundy for you. Witness all those papers this afternoon on Bill Dorn's table, gathered up at the end and snapped together in the sheriff's rubber band.

It was another cutthroat poker game with Bill Dorn, only Dorn didn't know it. He went in with his friend; he'd back his play to the limit. He did just that. And he did more. What else he did was the thing which stung him, now that the dead cards were spread out face up. He had gone to his own friends, and they were many, men who trusted Bill Dorn as some of them had trusted

Early Bill before him, in the day when they had the quaint old saying, "His word is his bond." Bonds were worth something then, and so was the word of a Dorn. When Bill Dorn said to his friends, "It's absolutely safe; I give you my word for it," they dug up their buried hoardings and plunked down all they owned, all they could borrow. They saw themselves on the high road to becoming millionaires. Now they were ruined. So was Sudden Bill. But he wasn't thinking of his own losses; a poker player of the old school, he could shrug at them. But he couldn't shrug away the looks he knew he was bound to see in the eyes of his friends to whom he had said, trusting Mike Bundy to the limit, "It's abolutely safe; I give you my word for it."

His had ever been a light touch on life; he was Roll-Along Dorn; Here-We-Go Dorn; he had never known what it was to brood. But tonight he brooded. Those eyes of his, grown red-flecked, when not sharply focusing on some newcomer into his ken who might be Michael Bundy, gloomed bleakly into vast distances. More than one bartender who served him, and thus came under those smoke-dark eyes, experienced a creepy feeling and stood aside as soon as he could.

He entered, one after another, all the swinging doors facing the Plaza. Throngs continued to swell on the street, in the saloons and dance halls and gaming places, and he would have needed to be deaf and blind as well as preoccupied not to come early upon the explanation. When he understood, he merely made a wry face and went on, immediately forgetful of the cause of this latest Nacional mob scene. Men were damned fools, always chasing after the same thing—

"There's a new señorita who dances, and she sings, too, over at the place of One Eye," said the bartender in the border argot which passes as Spanish. "Don Bill, he has seen her, no?"

"Where in hell's Michael Bundy?" growled Don Bill.

So when at last he went to the place of One Eye, a burly, bulky Mexican bandit of the name of Pico Perez who boasted of the fact, if fact it were, that his lost eye had been gouged out by none less renowned than that immortal bandit El Toro Blanco, it was still seeking a man and without the remotest thought of a new señorita who danced, and sang, too.

But there was no escaping that girl. Not a man of the many who thronged the place escaped her. She was as vital as life itself, as merry-mad in her dance act as a leaf blown along a March wind, as gay and triumphant, one would have said, as tossing banners of a victorious army—a girl, in a word, to strike any susceptible male square between the eyes. It was not that Here-We-Go Dorn was in the least susceptible on this night of all nights for him, but he did have two eyes and he could still see what was before him; and so he, like many another, saw the girl who danced at One Eye's place. But where others stared, Bill Dorn glared.

She disturbed him and he did not want to be disturbed. She wore a damnable little black mask which only made her beauty the more piquant. He worked up a sneer; with a glance, as though it were any affair of his, he as much as accused her of seeking to make a mystery of a trite, commonplace and altogether sordid bit of business. Hell take her and all her kind; he was looking for Michael Bundy.

He leaned back against the sixty foot bar, one high heel hooked on the foot rail, both elbows hooked on the bar, and gave the barnlike room a pretty thorough onceover. He overheard what two men, desert rats like the late Jake Fanning by the look and talk of them, were saying. The word to rivet his attention was a man's name. They were talking about Mike Bundy.

"Shore," said the first man, and took off his drink garglingly, the way that old-timers, with desert alkali in their throats, knock off the first one. "Mos' folks think this is One Eye Perez's place; hell, it's Bundy's now. Bundy'll be showin' up here 'fore the night's over. An' if any man in Nacional has got the low-down on this last play, well, Mike Bundy's real apt to be that man."

"Shore," said the second man, who had throated his drink while the other spoke. Then he recognized Bill Dorn standing next to him and gave his partner a prod with his elbow. He added something in an undertone; that done he said for anyone to hear: "Shore, she's a cute trick. Wonder where Perez picked her up? Say, I'll pay that gal's rent any time."

Bill Dorn looked down his nose at the man who had first spoken, looked at him with all the amiability of a man regarding another over the sights of a rifle. He demanded curtly:

"You say this is Michael Bundy's place now? You say he'll be showing up here?"

"Why, hello Bill," said the other. "I didn't see you. I—"

"This place used to belong to One Eye Perez," said Dorn. "How come it's Michael Bundy's now?"

"Perez needed money—he borrowed from Bundy—Bundy took a mortgage—Oh hell, Bill, you ought to know—"

Bill Dorn left the bar and went to a small table, to sit alone. He was hungry but didn't know it. When a white-jacketed Mexican waiter with a damp towel in the crook of his arm came up and gave the table a swipe, thereafter giving his towel a flick like a blacksnake, Bill Dorn ordered a drink. Then he shoved his hat back and rolled a cigarette and permitted his eyes to flick to the girl

26

making a show of her pretty self on the platform at the end of the room. Three young gentlemen of confused Latin and Indian extraction, pianist, violinist and guitarist, made the music which lapped her movements in soft Durango airs.

How Born-a-Dorn Bill did resent that girl! She ought to have her pink and white face slapped, that's what she ought to have. She was the most graceful thing he ever saw, and hers was not the cheap stereotyped grace of the usual dance hall girl. She danced not as though trying to show her body to men, rather as one who so loved dancing that she couldn't help it; she gave the tremendously disturbing impression of having forgotten that she was being watched, of fancying herself quite alone somewhere in the woods, or on a seashore in the dawn or twilight. "Hell," snorted Dorn, and gulped his drink. He vowed he'd keep his eyes off her. There were too many like her— like her, that is, under the dainty white and pink exterior. He muttered sneeringly to himself: "Gilded tombs do worms enfold." He thought: "The world grows rotten, peopled with folk like Michael Bundy and this flip. *Muchacho! Un otro aguadiente!*"

He wasn't drunk. Don't get Sudden Bill Dorn wrong. But he was in a savage mood and his unaccustomed savagery had been nicely promoted along to a brutal stage by the fiery cargo he had taken aboard. He had not forgotten Mike

Bundy; the only reason he was here was that he awaited with all the patience of a hungry tiger which, even starving, can control itself and wait—and wait. But meantime he experienced an urge to spring up on the low stage and pull that girl's silly mask off and slap her face.

He grew conscious of three things: First, that the men all about him were talking excitedly about the stirring event which had brought the mob surging into Nacional; second, that now and then one or another of them would nudge his fellow and point Dorn out; third, that that damned dancing girl was watching him pretty nearly all the time now.

Now, Bill Dorn, down underneath the outward layers of him, was far more of a poet than he'd ever come to suspect; and with a great, soul-troubling love he loved beauty itself. Dawns and dusks and twilights over the desert, the wind in the mountain piñons, the satiny sheen of a thoroughbred's flank, the falling of water in a pool, a sudden unexpected strain of music—these and their kindred had the trick of putting a knot into his lean brown throat. He felt with the philosopher poet, whom he had once read, that if you get simple beauty and naught else you get about the best thing God invents. Here, in this girl, in the ripple and flow of her sweet young body down the current of music from hushed piano and whispering guitar and muted violin, was—perhaps he *had* had too much of the cursed border liquor!—beauty ineffable. Why, damn the cheap little wench, she looked like sweet sixteen pirouetting on the spray-misted crest of the rainbow-tinted wave which carries sweet sixteen along toward the inexorable years. Her voice, too, had reached him; she had sung just a few bars of a little old Mexican love song, a song as old in the South as La Cachucha itself, and her voice had been like the rest of her—all youth and innocence and lilt and loveliness.

She started to withdraw. There was a burst of applause. A flimsy curtain, more or less under the control of a grinning Chinese boy at the side, jerkily shut off the stage.

Bill Dorn stood up. He had been holding himself in check today, but after all he was Sudden Bill Dorn, Roll-Along Dorn, Here-We-Go Dorn, Born-a-Dorn Bill. At the side of the stage was a narrow passageway leading to the three rooms at the rear of the long adobe building, kitchen and dressing room and sanctum of One Eye Perez, former owner, present manager. Bill Dorn, wearing his hat perilously far back and walking on his heels, strode purposefully down that restricted hallway. He knew just where he would encounter her, coming down the three steps to the dressing room.

He intercepted her coming down. She saw him, read the purpose in his eyes, and made a dart in the murk of the three-foot passageway for the first door, that leading to One Eye Perez's office. Bill Dorn stepped swiftly in front of her and she brought up, frightened, her back to the wall and her hands lifted before her breast as if to fend him off.

"You make me sick," said Bill Dorn.

She gasped; he could hear the sharp intake of her breath. He glared; she could see even in this dim light the scornful anger in his eyes. He wanted to storm at her. Later, thinking things over, he rather guessed he did storm at her. She flattened herself against the wall, looking smaller and daintier, more fragile and fairylike than ever. He felt then that he could crush her between finger and thumb as easily as a silly butterfly; he felt also that he'd relish the job. Still he did not touch her as he started in to scold her.

"You're no Mexican girl, no half-breed, no rag-tag of hell such as the border breeds," he snarled at her. "You're American, and to begin with you were damn fine American, of the finest stock in the world. Can't I tell? And now, look at you! You cheap little gutter-snipe! Dancing in a place like this! Dragging loveliness in the muck! You've got no business here; you have no right to make your loveliness as cheap as a few dirty coins in some man's pocket. Get out! Get the hell out of here—and keep going! Hear me? Beat it! And keep yourself decent—as decent as you are now, anyhow—or I'll break your damned little neck!"

"You—you—" Breathless, choking up, her face scarlet under her sketchy little black mask, she got only that far when her voice left her. He saw the flash of her eyes; he didn't know then what color they were; blue? violet? It was just that her anger, as hot as his own, darkened them.

"I tell you—" stormed Bill Dorn.

Just then her voice came back to her. She went straight on from where she had left off:

"You—you big ugly beast! The nerve of *you,* talking to me like that! You are out to do murder tonight, Mr. Bill Dorn; all keyed up to shoot a man—in the back, I suppose!—and you stand up and lecture me! You'd do better to slink off in your own slime and hide your ugly face in the good clean desert sand! You—you—you make *me* sick!"

Down here at the end of the hall they were out of sight of any in the barroom, out of hearing, too, since the men at the tables and strung along the bar were drowning with their own voices all other sounds. Bill Dorn lifted his hands as though to choke her. But he did not touch her. He said:

"How do you know I am here to commit murder?"

"Every man, woman and child in Nacional knows! I've heard it a dozen times. And if I doubted—Oh, go look into a mirror! Your eyes are full of it! You are here to kill your own

31

partner—and then, you drunk fool, you dare—*you dare!*—to read me a lesson in human behavior! Ugh! Go away; get out of my sight!"

"You are going to clear out of this dive," he told her in still fury, not caring the snap of his fingers whether he spoke in reason or out of it. To hell with reason anyhow. "And you're going to get out now."

She said curiously: "You're a big unimaginative beast—like a plow horse—or a sick lion! Did you ever see a dead man? A man who had been alive a little while before, then suddenly dead? Ever see a man recently murdered?"

"You little fool!—Well, yes. Not longer ago than this afternoon."

"You killed him!" She shrank still tighter back against the wall, her eyes large with horror.

"No. I found him."

"Was it—Was he nice to look at?"

"Are you crazy?"

"Maybe I am. But not murder-mad like you. Now tell me, Bill Dorn: Will you ever forget how that man looked, dead this afternoon? And after you have killed Mike Bundy, and have looked at him, turned all of a sudden into a senseless lump—"

"Shut up!" he stormed. "If you think for a split second—"

"Sh! What's all the commotion in the barroom? Do you suppose that Bundy has come at last?"

She tricked him into swinging about, for an

instant shifting his eyes from her. An instant was all that was required by that girl, as swift as a leaping deer, for her escape. Out of the corner of his eye he caught the flash of her flight; she was at One Eye's private door, had snatched it open and shot through, before Bill Dorn could say damn.

That commotion in the barroom? There wasn't any more uproar than there had been pretty consistently for an hour. Anyhow Bill Dorn disregarded it. Of a sudden he took the bit between his teeth; of a sudden he was wholly himself again, which is to say he was a man whom you might readily call Sudden Bill Dorn. He had heard the girl shoot a bolt on the inside of the door as she sped through. He hurled himself at the door, going in his accustomed fashion, headlong. He had heard also an exclamation which he knew came from One Eye Perez.

"Open your damn door or I'll smash it off its hinges," said Sudden Bill Dorn.

III

BEYOND the bolted door the girl was vehement in her demands.

"I want my money now. Now, do you hear me?" she cried excitedly. "You promised yesterday—"

One Eye Perez spoke sneeringly to her. He said in that oily voice of his which could grow ugly as rancid oil grows ugly:

"I pay you, *seguro*. But when I get ready. Now with a big crowd in town for maybe two-three day—"

"No, no, no! Now, I tell you—"

Then there was Bill Dorn at the door. Perez called sharply:

"*Quien es?* Who is there? What you want?"

"Open up, and get a move on," said Bill Dorn. "It's Bill Dorn, and I'm coming in."

Perez promptly shot the bolt back and Dorn came surging in.

"Hello, Bill. *Caramba contigo!* What's wrong?"

Bill Dorn bestowed only a fleeting glance at the girl, then looked scowlingly upon the swart, squat, one-eyed figure.

"What's the row in here?" he demanded angrily.

"He promised me yesterday," the girl began, flushed and all but breathless, her eyes blazing.

"I'm talking to Perez," snapped Bill Dorn. "Speak up, Perez."

Perez shrugged. Also he bristled. He had been rough-handled of late by Dorn's partner, the Michael Bundy who had taken up his papers, papers which One Eye Perez little understood, in exchange for what looked like generous loans. He had no stomach for further brow-beating; he meant to stand nothing more from anyone connected with Bundy. So he flared out, catching fire in a heated atmosphere:

"This dirty little road-runner, this little scrap of

garbage that I fed when her belly was empty—"
He was speaking fluently in border Spanish, so the girl didn't get it all, which was just as well. But Bill Dorn did catch all the implications, which was not just as well for One Eye Perez. When Dorn's fist cracked into the Mexican's jaw it was like an explosion. Perez didn't fall, but that was only because the smallness of the room favored him; reeling backward he brought up with the breath jolted out of him, his thick shoulders against the wall. He made a gesture toward the gun worn low on his left hip.

"Reach for your wallet instead," roared Bill Dorn, towering over him. "Pay her and let her go."

Perez' hand went first to his jaw, feeling it gingerly. "Some day, Señor, I get you for this," he said almost inaudibly.

"Then you'll shoot me in the back, you scum!"

No man in Nacional or in all shrugging Mexico, for that matter, could shrug more eloquently than One Eye Perez.

"The back is a good place, Señor," was all that he said. But he moved, all obedience, to his table, unlocked and opened a drawer and extracted a small box containing coins and bank notes. "There you are," he said to the girl. "There's your pay. You're through." And he shoved it into her hand.

She didn't stop to count; she flashed him a look

of terror; she sped a bright, undecipherable look at Bill Dorn, and vanished into the corridor where they heard the light patter of her running feet.

Dorn backed to the door, making his exit as from the presence of royalty, his eyes bright and hard on Perez' unlovely face, a face just now so twisted with rage that it was as though the hate within him were a poison, himself in convulsions because of it. Once through the door, Dorn drew it shut and turned toward the long barroom. He kept looking back, half expecting at every stride to see the rear door open, to have a stream of lead poured after him by the enraged Perez.

He returned to the front room and saw that every man there was watching him, had been awaiting his return. He ignored them now as before, looking not at them but among them, through them, beyond them, hunting for Michael Bundy. Failing to find Bundy anywhere, he returned to the bar. As he did so a small knot of men, four or five of them, moved purposefully toward him from somewhere near the front door. At their fore was a young fellow whom Bill Dorn knew well and liked, a lean gangling chap of not more than twenty-two or twenty-three, his hair a windblown, straw-colored mop, his eyes a shining, fearless, good-humored blue. He wore two guns tied down at his hips, he walked with an unaffected swagger and he was doing his level best to summon up a casual grin. This was young

Ken Fairchild, a small rancher from the desert rim of Antelope Valley.

" 'Lo, Bill," he said.

Dorn nodded with a curt, "Howdy, Ken." He looked beyond young Fairchild to the men who had followed him and had come to a halt only a few feet away; three of them he knew well, all from Antelope Valley; Stock Morgan, old man Middleton and John Sharp. All were eying him. He said to Ken Fairchild: "Looks like a delegation."

The Adam's apple went up and down in Ken's brown throat.

"Dammit, Bill," he burst out. "You're lookin' for Mike Bundy, ain't you?"

Bill Dorn lifted his thick, ragged black brows at the young fellow and that was all the answer he made. Ken Fairchild, under his thick tan, flushed up. Also those steady blue eyes of his hardened. Young was Ken, but a man whom already other men banked on. He liked Bill Dorn, and there was a genuine warmth in his liking, and a certain respect went along with it; but he wasn't taking anything off Dorn or anyone else. He said, with an edge to his voice:

"You got to look here, Bill! You came in town to kill Bundy. Well, us fellows don't want him killed. Not today. Get it?"

Dorn did get it, and for a moment Ken Fairchild held his interest. Still, though wondering, he kept his silence. He knew that Fairchild and Bundy hated each other like poison; he couldn't understand Fairchild going out of his way to protect Michael Bundy.

Fairchild went on crisply: "We don't know what he's done to you, Bill, though we can guess, knowin' the two o' you. But that's none of our give-a-damn."

"Give him the straight of it," called out Stock Morgan, grown impatient. "Looky, Bill Dorn, word's got out that gold has been found. A bonanza they say it be! Well, you know that much, seein' ever'body does. But do you know they's only three men knows the rights o' the whole thing, only three men knows where the new strike's been made? Them men is, firs' an' las', Jake Fanning——"

"Jake's dead," said Bill Dorn. "Somebody shot him through the head today."

"Then," shouted Morgan, "that leaves only two men knowin'; one of 'em is One Eye Perez, who keeps out'n sight an' won't talk until his new pardner shows up; an' the las' one is that pardner, Mike Bundy. An' us boys has an int'res' in keepin' them two alive until we know as much as they do."

It was right then, while Morgan was striving to make his point emphatic in the only way he knew, roaring lustily, that the pistol shot startled the roomful of men and created a deep hush. The shot was muffled and came from no one knew exactly where; just the one cryptic crash of sound, dying away echolessly. Men started pouring out through the front doors; someone cried out that the shot came from the street. But a half grown Mexican boy came running from the rear where the kitchen was.

"It's One Eye Perez!" he shrilled in a jibbering sort of fashion. "In his room—somebody shot in from outdoors, through the window. He's dead already—a bullet in his head. And, Jesus Maria, blood all over everything!"

The frightened boy began to grow incoherent. Stock Morgan caught him by the shoulder, shook him until his teeth rattled, then yelled into his ear: "Who kilt One Eye? Did you find him like that, or did you see the shootin'? Talk, or I'll bat your brains out! Who kilt him?"

"I don't know," stammered the boy. "Somebody outside. Maybe it was that girl, the new one that came yesterday. She and Perez had trouble. I saw her run outside just before the shot. She had something in her hand, I don't know what. Maybe it was a gun. I tell you—"

"Dry up an' blow away," said Morgan disgustedly, and flung the boy from him. Then he turned to confront Bill Dorn, his face grim, his eyes stone-hard. "An' now they's only *one* that knows whether there's been a bonanza turned up or whether some johnny-come-lately has jus' got his pick in fool's gold. An' the one that knows is Mike Bundy. *Sabe*, Dorn?"

While other men hastened to the rear room to look in on the dead saloon keeper, and while others ran outside and quested up and down, hoping to come on some trace of his slayer, Bill Dorn and the small group gathered about him held their ground. Dorn looked at these men curiously.

"Are you boys crazy or am I?" he demanded. "If there is a pot of gold somewhere, if Michael Bundy knows where it is—and if he is the only man living who does know!—do you count on having him take you by the hand and lead you to it?"

"Bundy's close-mouthed, all right," grunted Stock Morgan, "but no man is as mum alive as he is dead. What's more, there's been rumors about Jake Fanning, grubstaked by Bundy, finding gold somewheres up in the Blue Smokes. And there's other rumors. Bundy, the hawg-for-money that he is, won't be hangin' back, doin' nothin', leavin' it to chance for some other feller to back-track along Jake's trail an' spot the place. You know damn well, an' Bundy'll know it jus' as well, that either Jake Fanning or One Eye Perez might have talked before they got kilt. Give me a grab on Mike Bundy's coat tails, Bundy bein' alive, an' I'll get a sniff o' this new bonanza anyhow—an' maybe I'll stake me a claim. That ain't too hard for you to understan', is it, Bill?"

"I see," said Dorn.

He went back to his table and sat down, insistent on being left alone. So there were three, Bundy and Jake Fanning and Perez, who knew all about the new gold strike—and now, with Fanning and Perez shot to death, there remained only Michael Bundy with the golden key in his possession. That was Bundy's luck for you!

But was it just luck? Bill Dorn, the last man in the world to grow circuitously suspicious, frowned into the glass slowly twirling between his sunbrowned fingers. Funny, he accounted it; funny that today those three alone had known the answer to the question which at this moment was making a turbulent maelstrom of Nacional—that now, of the three, two were dead with bullets through their brains—that only Michael Bundy still lived!

"I see," said Dorn to himself, and did feel like a man who had been blind for a long time and now had his sight restored. He thought that belatedly he began to see other things as well. Take this place of One Eye Perez, for instance. It had long been a favorite resort of Michael Bundy's; he had dropped in here more and more frequently of late and had gained a fresh reputation for plunging at the gaming tables. He had brought Bill Dorn with him more than once, and Dorn knew that Bundy had steered others of his "friends" into pretty lively games here. There was the mining man from Colorado, the big sheep man from Nevada, a couple of strangers, good spenders both, from Los Angeles. They, along with Bundy, had lost of course; men like them, knowing their ways about, knew how to lose at such dives and could take their losses with less of a grimace than they made when downing the border's forty-rod whisky. Bundy was always the best loser of them all—but now when Bill Dorn muttered, "I see," it was with the realization that perhaps Bundy hadn't lost a red cent. If the One Eye Perez house belonged to Bundy now, perhaps he had had a major interest in its winnings all this while.

Always Bill Dorn had sensed that Michael Bundy was a man of large caliber, a man who could do big things, and some day, when he got good and ready, *would* do them. Now it dawned on him that Bundy was by far the biggest man on the border, if you gaged a man's stature by his financial accomplishment and weren't concerned with the ethics of his methods. Bundy began to loom as a sort of border colossus; he functioned like a gigantic, well-oiled, crushing, merciless steel-entrailed engine. He was hitting his stride, was Michael Bundy; he was operating like a steam roller. A steam roller doesn't grow sentimental, doesn't shed tears no matter what it presses back into the earth whence all things come anyhow.

When there arose a sudden commotion, as

abrupt as an explosion, in the street just outside the swinging doors, Bill Dorn cocked an alert ear, thinking, "Here comes Michael Bundy at last!" In fact Bundy was close at hand, yet the flurry had not arisen about him, since he had not yet been glimpsed. Dorn, starting to his feet, heard a rustle of voices all about him, heard and hearkened to a gust of exclamations, got the drift of it. "They've got the man that killed Perez. They've caught him red-handed. They're bringing him in here."

Dorn reached out for his forgotten glass and started settling down into his chair again. Then like a rising wind came voices again bearing another burden: "Mike Bundy's coming! He's in the crowd outside. It's Bundy! Mike Bundy!"

By now every man in the room was on his feet and Dorn had a tight-packed mob to plow through, but plow through he did, getting himself cursed at every step. He broke through into the outer night that was palely lit by the stars, rather more warmly illuminated by the lamp with its huge reflector hung over the narrow hell-gates of the Perez swing doors. He saw two men—he knew them both, gunmen of a sort he had small liking for, lean, Cassius-eyed Hank Smith and the bleak, cold, reptilian Mex Fontana, a pair of desert coyotes with the trick of hunting in pairs, men who of late had been so often doing chores for Mike Bundy that they began to be known as his bodyguards. He saw too, in that swift first photographic glance, that Hank Smith and Mex Fontana held prisoner between them, one by each jerking wrist, a slight, frightened familiar figure.

But he scarcely noted that it was the señorita who danced and sang, too; and he marked not at all that her terror-widened eyes flashed him a plea that was like a summons. For beyond this small group a handsome blond head and a pair of stalwart shoulders loomed above the crowd. Bundy! As Bill Dorn tore along, one half his brain had to register impressions though he cared nothing for them. The tight knot of men about Smith and Fontana and their white-faced prisoner were muttering: "She killed Perez. These two saw her shoot; they ran her down."

Bill Dorn shook his head like a young bull annoyed by summer flies. He made straight, crashing through the crowd, for Bundy. Bundy saw him in the lamplight and read aright the message of the red fires in eyes grown smoky with long smoldering rage. As though a storm wind had blown an open pathway through a cornfield, men fell away to right and left.

Not a man in Nacional that night cared to stand between the two.

"What the devil's happened to you, Bill?" shouted Bundy. "You're crazy—you're drunk—"

Bill Dorn came grimly on. He hadn't anything to say. He knew at last, past all doubt, the sort of man Michael Bundy was; and he knew that Bundy understood that the inevitable moment had come. There was no use saying in words what could be said so much more forcefully another way.

They came together, body to body, in the human lane which had opened up a good ten feet wide in fear of flying lead, and the thing which bewildered all onlookers was that neither man reached for his gun. Presently that was understood. Bundy, it happened, didn't have a gun on him, and as for Bill Dorn, his fists balled and his muscles crawled—and he forgot all about the weapon banging at his hip. He had never known such a murderous fury as the one gripping him now, and his whole urge was to get his hands on Bundy, to beat him to a bloody pulp with the good honest tools nature had given him.

Bundy, with a muffled angry roar, had sprung forward to meet the avalanche bearing down on him, so the two men came together with an impact which jarred both to their bootheels. But at the outset no such wild unleashed motive power drove Bundy as that which impelled Bill Dorn. The two went down, Bundy toppling backward, Bill Dorn coming down on top of him. A shout of approval went up from the churning crowd; some few voices were raised to cheer Bundy on, but for the most part they were yelling: "That's the stuff, Bill! Knock hell out'n him."

That was exactly what Bill Dorn was striving to do. His rage, now that he had actually come to grips with the man he hated so newly and so violently, burst all bounds. He took a blow in the face which rocked his head, and did not feel it.

"Damn you—if ever a man needed killing—" he panted, and got Bundy's burly throat in the grip of both hands.

A man standing close by muttered: "Look at Bundy's eyes! They're damn near poppin' out! Dorn's killin' him shore."

The man scarcely overstated the fact. There was froth on Bundy's gaping mouth, and in his eyes, starting from their sockets, a glaze of horror.

Stock Morgan clawed his way through the crowd, getting himself heartily cursed yet making swift progress. He came to stand closest of all to the two battling men. He shook his head and pursed a long lower lip. Then, adroitly and with neatness and dispatch, he put an end to the fight. In a quiet, matter-of-fact way he drew out his belt gun, a big cumbersome black-barreled Colt, and rapped Bill Dorn smartly over the head with it. Dorn, to all intents and purposes, simply folded up and went to sleep.

"Couldn't have you gettin' hurt tonight, Mike Bundy," Stock Morgan said quite pleasantly. "Hell, no!"

IV

Until a long time after midnight Nacional was as hectic as a man tumbling in a high fever. But in the pale lemon dawn, with a sweet warm spring wind redolent of sage blowing up from the South, Nacional was hushed almost beyond imagining. Had a stranger chanced along, he might have mistaken the place for a ghost town.

Bill Dorn felt the soft southern breeze in his face, shook his head, winced and fell to scowling because of the headache which awoke along with him and from a queer sense of not knowing where he was and what had happened to him. Then he remembered and sat up with a jerk.

He discovered that he was on a bed in a bare room surrounded by adobe walls none too clean, the plaster cracking on them. There was a rickety table with a tin wash basin, a dirty towel on a peg over it, a tin bucket on the floor. He turned slightly, put his head into his hands with a groan, and thought: "Somebody cracked me over the head with a telegraph pole just as I was choking the life out of Bundy."

He heard a faint sound, lifted his head again, saw the one window through which the scent of sage-in-the-dawn came to him—and then discovered the girl sitting on a stool by the window.

"You! But I thought—"

"Sh! Please!" Her whisper began with a command and ended with pleading. Bill Dorn got his feet on the floor—they hadn't taken his boots off—and sat staring at her. She rose swiftly and came to him. She looked rather boyish just then in her boots and riding breeches and loose coat and big hat pulled down over her curls.

"What's it all about?" muttered Dorn. "I don't get this. How'd I get here? How'd you get here? Where's everybody?"

"Somebody hit you on the head while you were fighting Mike Bundy," she explained hurriedly, still whispering. She paused to glance apprehensively over her shoulder at the closed door. "They brought you here. You are in the old hotel right next door to the Perez place. And they—I think they're all gone."

"Who hit me?"

"I couldn't see."

"And you? I thought Hank Smith and Mex Fontana had you in tow—"

"When they heard somebody yell out that you were killing Mike Bundy they seemed of a sudden to take more interest in that than in me. I felt their hands relax on my wrists. Then the crowd was surging every which way—and I broke loose and ran! I hid—and then I came here. I was sure nobody would look for me here with you."

He pondered heavily; he wondered dully whether his brain ever would grow clear again.

He said, puzzled: "What do you mean by saying they're all gone? All who? Gone where?"

"There's hardly a soul left in Nacional. They went storming out of town—Oh, it must have been an hour, two hours ago; maybe longer. They went like a lot of crazy drunken creatures, not men even. Mike Bundy and the two men who had held me and a few more like them were in the lead. It was like—like the Pied Piper of Hamelin! I couldn't hear everything; I was hiding. But they had gone crazy with the hope of gold! Gold! As though they were going to roll and wallow in it."

"Where?" demanded Bill Dorn. "Which way did they go?"

"I don't know. But I heard, over and over, 'Blue Smokes.' I wondered what and where the Blue Smokes were."

"Mountains," he told her. "Off yonder, north, sixty-seventy miles from here. Back in the States. But you? Why are you still here? A man would think that you'd have grabbed your chance and skipped out of town."

She looked at him in such a strange fashion that he could not begin to make her out. She was wearing a pair of gauntlets; she began stripping them off, began putting them on again. She said slowly, not looking at him: "You stood my friend tonight, Mr. Bill Dorn, though you did so like the brute it is in you to be. I thought that maybe you were dying; I wanted to help you. Now I'm going."

"Where?" he demanded, and stood up.

She shrugged. "Out of Nacional. As fast and far as I can. Before they accuse me again of murder."

"Going south or north?" he asked. "Down into Mexico or up into the States?"

"North. Do you think—"

"Back home?"

"No. Not back home."

"You haven't any home. I'd bet a man!"

"I doubt that he'd take your bet. If he did— you'd win."

"Got a horse here?"

"No."

"How'd you get here? What have you got?"

"Nothing, Mr. Nosey Bill Dorn."

"You've the money Perez gave you—"

"But I haven't. Either those thugs got it when they grabbed me or I dropped it. What I do have is a sunny disposition, a pleasant smile—and the clothes I stand in. Any more questions?"

"None." He stood up, found his hat lying on the floor, jammed it on, noted that they hadn't taken his gun—that gun with which he was going to kill Bundy; funny how he had forgotten it—and said: "You're coming with me. We ride together this morning."

"I—I was hoping you'd ask me," she said, and smiled just a little. "As a matter of fact I am scared stiff."

"You'd better be," he snorted. "With Smith and

Fontana swearing they saw you shoot Perez, this is no place for you. Let's go."

They went out through the window and into a cluttered alley, that seeming the simplest way. From the corner, peering out, Bill Dorn saw a deserted village, the adobe houses ghostly pale in the first daylight.

"Not a soul in sight, except seventeen Injun dogs, two Mex babies and one lame burro," he reported. "Here we go."

He led the way to the stable at the far end of the street, and she had to run to keep up with him. Not that she minded running! It was such a glorious morning, it was so glorious to be alive and free, and the glory of glories was the hope of being out of wicked little Nacional in a short time.

At the stable they found a ten year old boy left in charge; that was because the boy was a cripple and could not follow the gold rush, and because his father had put him here. Dorn, going to saddle his own horse, asked to hire a nag for his companion. The boy shrugged and grimaced; all horses had been taken, except that one in the stall yonder, the big black. That was Señor Bundy's horse, left here because he had ridden it hard yesterday—

"I'll take it," said Dorn. "You can tell Señor Bundy that I've got it."

"Sure, Señor Beel," said the boy.

51

So Bill Dorn and his companion rode out of Nacional before it was yet full day, both of them glad to be out of the place. At first they rode south, Dorn leading the way, then eastward through the desert willows, and finally northward again through Puerta de los Chinos. Thus none saw them cross the border.

"I'm heading up to the Blue Smokes," Dorn said. "I've an unfinished job of work to get done. And you, Miss Stranger?"

"I told you that I didn't have any home. But maybe I have. Anyhow I hope to know in a few hours, if I can find the place. Perhaps you can help me? Do you know where the Palm Valley Ranch is?"

"I'll tell a man," said Dorn, and regarded her from a fresh angle of interest. "Know anybody up there?"

"My aunt—"

"Mrs. Kent! So Nellie Kent is your aunt. Well!"

"You know her? Well, I am—I am Lorna—Lorna Kent. And what is so strange about my being Nellie Kent's niece?"

"Somehow," said Dorn drily, "I can't quite figure Mrs. Nellie Kent's niece being a border dance hall girl."

"Oh! You make me sick," said Lorna.

"Seems to me I've heard you say that before."

"Will you tell me where her ranch is? I expected her to meet me in Nacional. She didn't come; she didn't send any word. I can't understand that. And I'm so anxious to find her."

He extended a long arm, pointing northward. Far off across the billowy sweep of desert and grass lands beyond she saw the hazy blue mountains standing up into a brightening sky.

"Those are the Blue Smokes," he told her. "Up there somewhere, it would seem, they've found gold; the spot might be sixty, seventy or even eighty miles from here. That's where I'm heading. And about half way to the Blue Smokes is one of the loveliest and loneliest oases that you ever saw. That's the Palm Valley Ranch. And if my company doesn't make you too darned sick, Miss Lorna, I'd be glad to ride along that far."

"You're a dear," said Lorna and beamed at him. "Let's go, Here-We-Go Dorn! About thirty or forty miles before breakfast—nothing at all for two old-timers like us."

"By thunder, I never thought a word about eating!" he said ruefully. "I didn't wake up with any hungry wolf's appetite this morning."

"Who cares about eating anyhow?" said Lorna Kent. She lifted her chin; he saw the stretch of her soft round throat, saw how her breast rose to a deep intake of the clean morning air. "Who wants food when there's life and freedom, and a gorgeous morning like this!"

So they rode into the north with the day brightening all about them, with the sun soon rolling up as genial as a florid guest at a banquet. The sky from a deep velvet blue turned a steel gray and the sun grew hot and the desert stretches of sand grew whiter and whiter, a burning glare in their eyes.

Sand rustled faintly under the horses' hoofs, Dorn's spurs and the bridle reins jingled, softly musical, and there was at times a half-heard creak of saddle leather; these were small sounds shut in by a vast silence. As far as they could see nothing on earth moved except themselves; the dawn wind had sighed itself away and the world was breathless. High above, spiraling in the sky, were a few turkey buzzards. They made Bill Dorn remember Jake Fanning.

They came to a ragged, rocky hill standing up emphatically and seeming all out of reason in the flatness all about. "Let's ride up there and see what we can see," he invited. From the barren crest they looked back; Nacional had vanished in the earth's folds and creases; the way they had come stretched empty, sun-smitten. They peered, eyes squinting, into the northern distances.

"There they go!" said Lorna. "See yonder? Way off—"

"Yes." Scarcely more than dots in the distance, yet not to be missed by a keen eye in all this brilliantly clear country, a string of mounted men pushed on toward the barrier of blue mountains in the still farther distance. "They're going by way of Palm Valley, too. Most folks go that way, headed for the Smokes. There's water there and shade, and as much hospitality in the heart of that aunt of yours as there is water in the ocean. They're a good many miles ahead of us; we wouldn't even have seen them but for the sun being just right."

She asked suddenly: "Aren't you interested in the discovery of gold? You don't act like it. You seemed the only man in Nacional who wasn't half mad over it."

"Let's ride," said Dorn. "It's getting hot and we'll be getting hungry and thirsty too. We didn't even bring a canteen along! That shows the sort of addlepates we are."

But he knew where water was to be found even in these arid wastes, brackish, almost steamy-hot water, to be sure, but welcome enough to man and maid and beast when they reached it. Also he showed her how a hungry man can knock a young jack rabbit over with a lucky pistol shot. He made a tiny fire of brushwood; he spitted the fore and hind quarters of his game and turned them over blaze and coals; he dusted the meat over with dried sage leaves ground powder-fine between his palms, and they dined sumptuously. Then Bill Dorn lay back and had his cigarette—and grinned at her. It startled her, the way of a sudden his white teeth flashed at her and his dark eyes crinkled at the corners and the hard line of his mouth vanished in a humorous quirk.

"It's a darned fine old world after all, huh?" challenged Bill Dorn.

For some queer reason, or for none at all, she found herself flushing. Under her breath, not for him to hear, she said, "Darn you!" Here of a sudden, all without warning, her brute of Nacional showed himself a downright human, likable young man.

"It's the finest world there is!" said Lorna, and started digging in the sand with a bit of dead stick.

"If your aunt expected you," he said meditatively, not exactly calling her a liar yet making clear that he was open-minded, "it's kind of darned funny she didn't meet you or send someone. She knows what Nacional is like." He began sifting sand through idle fingers. "Unless, of course," he added coolly, "she planned to allow you time for your bit of fun, dancing at One Eye's!"

"I was in Nacional three days," said Lorna. "My aunt had written, saying she would meet me. I came down from the East; I wrote ahead, telling her when I would arrive. I got to Nacional with a dollar and ten cents left. I tipped a boy a quarter for carrying my bag; I lived like a queen for an hour or two, spending royally. Then when no word came from Aunt Nell I began to get scared. I've been scared ever since."

"You couldn't find a better little town to get scared in," he conceded her.

"I couldn't even pay for my hotel room. I kept telling myself that at any moment I'd have word from my aunt. That didn't keep me from getting hungry. And there weren't any nice young men bringing me barbecued rabbit, either."

"So you went to work, dancing for Perez?" His hat was pulled low down, against the sun, but she knew without looking that one eye was on her.

"Yes," she said shortly. "You think I'm lying, don't you? All right. Let's start on, shall we?"

"Sure." He stuffed his cigarette butt down into the sand. "About that suitcase of yours: did you forget it?"

"As soon as you made that man give me my money I ran to my room and changed, stuffed my things into my suitcase and started to go somewhere, anywhere out of Nacional. I heard the pistol shot; I started running; those two thugs grabbed me. Whatever happened to my suitcase, I don't know, Mr. Will Dorn. Anyhow there were no pearl necklaces and diamond brooches in it."

He stood up and went for the horses. He offered her his hand to help her up; she slipped her toe into it and rose lightly into the saddle.

"It's kind of too bad you lost your black mask," he said as he mounted. "You did look like a real bandit woman wearing it."

She whipped it out of her shirt pocket and fluttered it before his eyes, a mere scrap of black silk with scissored holes for the eyes.

"The badge of my profession," she warned him, and pocketed it again.

"Why did you wear that thing?"

"Do you suppose that I'd want it ever known that I had had to dance in a place like that?"

Climbing up out of the hollow in which the pool was, they struck into a wagon road thick with fresh sign of many horses passing recently. But the riders themselves, whom they had glimpsed once, had vanished in the more broken country leading up to the foothills of the Blue Smokes and were not seen again. It was a couple of hours later that from a gently swelling eminence they saw the lower end of Palm Valley.

It was a place of beauty, all the lovelier for its setting in the heart of desolation, an expanse of green pastoral beauty, quiet and gentle and smiling when one first caught sight of its broad level lowlands bright with alfalfa like a carpet of emeralds. For there was gushing water in plenty in Palm Valley.

They came to a gate in a barbed wire fence; on the gate post was a sign, looking as fresh as though written yesterday, big black penciled words on a piece of cardboard: "Private Property. Keep out."

"That's funny," said Bill Dorn as he stooped from the saddle to open the gate. He had spoken of Mrs. Nellie Kent's hospitality, as boundless as the sea. "I've been here many a time; rode this way less than a month ago; you'd think she'd be the last one to put up a sign like that. Wonder what's come over her?"

"It isn't very welcoming, is it?" said Lorna, with a queer little twitch of her mouth. "Maybe that's for me to read; maybe she changed her mind about my coming to stay with her, and so, instead of meeting me, she put it up for me to read!"

They rode on into the valley and presently came to the winding creek slipping whisperingly along between its low banks along which trees had been planted—broad leaved poplars and swift growing weeping willows for the most part. A mile farther on the meadow lands narrowed and the hills began to encroach on both sides, rocky brushy hills baking in the sun. Then the hills pinched in closer and closer, so that the creek came tumbling through a narrow, steep-walled cañon—and beyond that lay that section of the ranch which gave its name to all, Palm Valley. Here was a tiny, narrow, elongated, crooked valley, hardly more than a deep dusky ravine, only wide enough at its upper end for the farmhouses and corrals and some twenty acres of land, and all along the watercourse and on the slopes of the sheltering hills were groves of shady native palms. The air was fresh and cool and sweet; there was an orange orchard behind the house and the scent of orange blossoms was like honey in the air. "It's the most wonderful place in the world, I think," said Lorna softly.

The house was a tiny, tidy place in a flower garden; its walls were a grayish-white, its windows blue-trimmed.

"Well, here we are," said Dorn, and of a sudden found that the journey had been short. "I'll stop a moment and say howdy to your aunt."

She was out of the saddle and ran up the steps ahead of him. There was a screen of morning glory vines veiling the front porch; for an instant he lost sight of her. Then she came running down the steps again, calling: "Bill Dorn!"

She couldn't see him anywhere. There stood her horse, but there was no sign of Bill Dorn or his blue roan.

"The great big dunce! If he's gone off and left me—"

But he hadn't gone far, only a couple of hundred yards to something he had glimpsed on a hill slope, something that he had never seen there before. Now as she hurried to the corner of the house she saw him riding back, up near the barn; his head was down and he seemed deep in thought. She called to him and at the queer tense tone of her voice he came spurring.

She led him up the steps to the door. Here again was a fresh sign, heavily penciled on cardboard like the other. This one read like a slap in the face. It said: "This Is My Place. Keep Out." And it was signed by Mike Bundy.

"Let's go inside," said Bill Dorn. "I've something to tell you."

"B-but this sign! Can it be that Aunt Nell sold to Mike Bundy and left—without a word to me? And how can we go in—if it's Mike Bundy's now!"

"To hell with Mike Bundy," snapped Bill Dorn. He began hunting a way to enter. The front door was solid oak; the windows were shuttered. At the rear he found a window boarded up from the outside. He pried the boards loose, got the window up and crawled in. Making his way through the darkened, gloomily hushed house, he was wondering how he was going to break the news to her of the new-made grave on the hillslope, of the plain headboard whose message would explain to her why her aunt had not met her in Nacional.

V

WHEN he had unsaddled and watered and stabled the horses, Bill Dorn came loafing down from the corral, allowing the girl in the house a few moments alone. He was thinking of the consternation written large on her expressive face, and his eyes clouded as he recalled how of a sudden hers had grown wet. He had hurried out to the horses before the first tear could spill over.

But there was not a tear, not even a trace of one when he returned. She had opened the little house wide to sun and air, every door and window open;

she had hurriedly bathed her hot face in the cool water that came gurgling down the pipe from the spring; she met him at the door and said, sounding quite gay:

"Welcome to my poor adobe, Mr. Sudden Bill."

"Thankee, lady," said Sudden Bill, and grinned at her as he had grinned once before, back there by the desert pool. He added lightly as he came in, "You seem to have all my names and titles." And then he demanded, suddenly serious: "Now what? What are you going to do next—after the horses are rested a bit?"

"I am going to stay right here," said Lorna.

"But—"

"Will you sit down? I'll have some coffee ready and a snack of sorts in a jiffy—thank heaven no one has raided the larder. And I want to ask you a question or two."

"Shoot," said Bill Dorn.

"Tell me about Mike Bundy. You and he were friends. You're not friends any longer. You meant to kill him last night! Tell me about him. What sort is he, square or crooked?"

He frowned at her. Somehow he didn't care to talk about Michael to anyone. Then he shrugged a weakness aside. "Crooked as hell. But what about it?"

"I don't believe this place belongs to him!" she cried hotly. "Oh, listen, Bill! You say that—that the grave out there was dug about a week ago—

62

and it's only about ten days ago that I got a letter from her. She said that she felt she was getting old, that she couldn't last forever, that she was lonesome for one of her own stock, that I was to come and stay with her, if I could stand the stillness of these hills, for always. And she said something else—that she was making her will, that she was leaving whatever she had left, Palm Valley included, to me! Then just a few days later she was found dead. Do you think that during that time she would have sold the ranch, after inviting me, after what she had said in her letter? Hmf!" said Lorna eloquently. "I know better! And when it comes to just plain *thinking* things, if you want to know what I think, it's that Mike Bundy murdered her and is trying to steal the ranch!"

"Whoa!" said Bill Dorn. They regarded each other soberly a moment. Then he shook his head slowly. "No; you can't tie murder to Bundy. He's not a man to make a misstep like that. Certainly not to steal an outfit like this which, at the outside, couldn't be worth more than ten or twelve thousand dollars."

"What did kill Aunt Nell then?" she demanded. "And how does it happen that Mike Bundy claims the ranch?"

He shook his head again. Then, "Have you still got that letter?" he asked.

"It's in my suitcase."

"Too bad. Good-bye letter. Did your aunt say

that she was going to make her will in your favor—or that she had already done so?"

Lorna Kent wrinkled her little nose up, a trick of hers when meditating and fearful that she wasn't going to find facts to turn out exactly as desired.

"I'm afraid I can't remember her exact words; whether she said, 'I am leaving you everything,' or, 'I have left you everything,' or 'I am going to leave you everything,' I just don't know. But somehow I have the impression she had already made her will. I—I didn't like to think of it; honestly I didn't! For you see, Aunt Nell was so g-good to me, even though she quarreled with my mother and never liked my father; and she did everything she could for me, sending me to school, remembering me at Christmas time—I didn't want to think of her ever dying—"

"If she did make a will," he suggested, "likely she had it witnessed. Likely too that it's some-where about. She might have sent it to a bank or a lawyer; but it's just as likely that it's somewhere about the house. It wouldn't be a bad idea to look."

"Later; not now," said Lorna. She glanced about her through the hushed house. The place, small as it was, had two bedrooms with bath between, a long, cool, Indian-rugged living room, a cozy dining room looking out under wide overhanging eaves to the hills, a gay, spick-and-span kitchen. She added: "I promised to feed you. Also it seems

64

to me that I invited you to sit down. Make yourself at home, Mr. Bill Dorn," she concluded, and went into the kitchen.

Promptly he followed her. While she was hunting the coffee he said bluntly, "You can't stay out here all alone very well."

"I'd rather be alone here than in Nacional! Or out in the desert listening to the coyotes. So, until I'm thrown out, here's where I am going to be."

She found the coffee, lighted a coal oil stove, put the pot on and began an inspection of the tins on a pantry shelf.

"By the way," he asked, as though a pertinent thought had just struck him, "are you sure that you really are Lorna Kent and Mrs. Kent's niece?"

"What do you think?" she said over her shoulder.

"Well," said Dorn, "I'm not paid to think. But seems as though, when you told me your name back there, you sort of hesitated. How about it?"

"Hmf!" said Lorna. She went on to add, "If you take canned milk with your coffee, here's the can."

She brought the tin to the oilcloth-covered table, and he started operations with a can opener. Frowning over his task, while she still rummaged, he said: "Your aunt never lived here all alone. There was generally a young girl; not always the same girl. Then there was always one man on the job outside, sometimes two, tending to stock, running the ranch. Today the place reeks with desertion."

"That's queer." She too started frowning. "I saw some horses out in the field."

"There's a handful of chickens, too. There's always a string of white ducks going down to the creek or swimming or coming back from the creek. And some turkeys and anyhow two geese. Not a man in sight to take care of anything. Sure, it's queer."

"Mike Bundy chased them off; I know!" She said it as though she did actually know. "He had some reason. Oh, I'm going to hate that man!"

Dorn got the can open and she brought some tinned green peas and string beans and, for dessert, sliced pineapple.

"If this should turn out to be Mike Bundy's property," she said, quite gay about it, "I suppose he can send us to jail for theft on top of house-breaking. So we better make a good meal while we're at it."

"Right," agreed Dorn.

"Won't that frown ever come off?" she asked. "You're looking gloomier and gloomier. What now?"

"Thinking," he muttered. "I told you I saw your aunt less than a month ago. I've known her four or five years; we got along, she and I. She sent for me and I came. Now I wish to thunder I had

66

stayed away! You see, she had asked my advice two or three times; once about buying the lower end of the valley, then about some stock, then about selling a bit of property she had down along the border. Any man likes to give advice, and I guess I spread myself. In each case she played it my way, and in each case it came out right. Then this last time when she sent word to me to stop in some time, she asked me some questions which I wish now I hadn't answered."

"Something about Mike Bundy!" she exclaimed swiftly.

He stared at her. "How do you know? Well, yes, that's what it was. She said Bundy wanted her to chip in on one of his oil projects. And I told her, making it as emphatic as I knew how, that Bundy was absolutely the safest, soundest man in the world. From what I know now—Well, I suppose he bled her for every cent she had lying around loose. And maybe somehow, through the deal, Bundy got title even to her ranch. That sort of thing, I discovered only yesterday, is what he has been doing." He made a wry face. "I know he did that to me."

"What a fool you must have been!"

"Sure. I trusted him."

"And when you give your trust—"

He shrugged. "You don't call it trust, do you, if it doesn't go all the way? And now do we eat all these victuals cold? Where are the pots and pans?"

Both were thoughtful, little given to words, as together they prepared their meal and as they ate it. Lorna was spooning up her pineapple juice when she said abruptly, "You said there was one thing you wouldn't put at Mike Bundy's door, murder."

"He makes too sure of every step. He's a crook, yes, but within the law. He's too cautious for murder."

"I heard a lot of chatter in Nacional," she went on, "men chattering like parrots, pouring out twice as much gossip as women. More than once, when they were on the common topic, I heard it said that just three men knew all about the new gold strike. They were Mike Bundy and Jake Fanning and One Eye Perez. And now? Well, Mike Bundy's the only one of the three alive!"

"Look here! If you mean—"

"The two others were murdered, weren't they?"

Harder than ever did he stare at her, looking down that long nose of his like a man sighting a rifle.

"Do you realize, young woman," he rasped out, "that there were two men last night who told the world that they saw you pull down on Perez?"

"They were liars!" she flared out. Then she asked, "Just what do you know about them?"

"They're gunmen, killers of the worst sort even the border ever bred. Hank Smith and Mex Fontana. And just now they're—" He broke off and a queer look widened his eyes. "By thunder, they're new henchmen that Michael Bundy has taken on!"

"You see?" said Lorna, and it meant, "Well, didn't I tell you so?"

"I'm off to look at the horses," he said, and went out.

Before he came back he saw a lot of things besides the two stabled animals which he scarcely noted at all. There were signs for him to read in the road that went by the barn and to the Upper End, and they told him that many men had ridden this way today, the crowd rushing on to the Blue Smokes, who would naturally come through Palm Valley. It would seem then that the mob, led no doubt by Stock Morgan, Ken Fairchild and their hangers on, had talked turkey in such fashion with Bundy that they had made him see wisdom in having them ride with him to the new Golconda in the Blue Smokes.

"There were more than a hundred men, two hundred maybe," mused Bill Dorn, "that rode through here today hell-for-leather. And there's bound to be ten times that many pounding the trail inside the week. Men swarming like flies to the honey pot."

He grew conscious of a gathering about him of a lot of barnyard fowls, chickens, turkeys, a couple of guinea hens. They looked hungry. He went into the barn, found a grain bin and fed them. "If Michael does own this place, why hasn't he left a man here in charge?" Perhaps he had; perhaps the hired man, like all the rest, had rushed off after gold, dropping and forgetting all commonplace chores.

"If that girl is Nellie Kent's niece—hang it, who's going to vouch for her? She might be the devil's stepdaughter, for all I know."

He looked down the palm-studded ravine opening up into the broadening green valley; it was as pretty as a picture. He turned toward the thirty-miles-distant Blue Smokes Mountains; they always veiled themselves in purples and violets and smoky grays, withdrawing behind shimmering transparent curtains, somehow hinting of mysteries even in broad daylight. He thought: "I've loafed here long enough. My horse is rested by now."

When he went back to the house Lorna was in the hammock on the front porch, gazing far off through the screening of morning glories, her eyes trafficking with the all but limitless southern distances. At his step she roused herself and on the instant was as brisk as a cricket. But it was Dorn who spoke first.

"How could you prove that you're Lorna Kent?"

"Mercy, Mr. Bill Dorn! I haven't the least idea!"

"Anybody around here who could identify you?"

"Only you," she said serenely. He cocked up his ragged eyebrows, and she laughed at him. "Didn't I tell you that I was none other than Lorna Kent?"

"Sure. That would help a lot, wouldn't it? Where are the nearest persons who do know you?"

"Baltimore. How far is that? Three thousand miles?"

"Your geography's first class."

"You asked me where I was going from here. May I ask you the same question?"

"To the Blue Smokes."

"When?"

"Pronto."

"Look me in the eye, Bill Dorn!" He did so, his eyes low-lidded, revealing nothing. She exclaimed impatiently: "You say you wished that you hadn't advised Aunt Nell. You feel morally responsible for her losses—if she did lose, and we both fancy she did. It becomes my loss now, doesn't it? And I gather that there are other people of whom you think well, people who think or thought well of you, that you have also helped along in the general direction of ruination?"

"That's what's eating me up!" said Dorn, and glared at her.

"And so you'd step along and kill Mike Bundy!"

"Yes, I'll kill the skunk."

If a girl as pretty as Lorna Kent ever actually sneered, the sneering was done right then. There was nothing but contempt in her expression as she remarked with a sort of italicized sarcasm: "That will be so nice of you, Mr. Dorn! Oh, it will help a lot, won't it? All the people who have been robbed by Mike Bundy, a lot of them through your connivance, will get all their money back that way, won't they? With Mike Bundy nice and dead and buried, and you in jail or hung or on the jump to save your precious skin, they'll have every chance to make up all their losses, won't they? Oh, I could bite you!"

"What the devil are you driving at?" snapped Dorn. She jerked her head up like a skittish colt tossing its young mane, and started to go into the house only to have him catch her by the arm. "Let's have the rest of it while you're in just the right mood to warm up to it."

She jerked free but stood where she was, her breast rising and falling swiftly, her eyes now as hot as his. But when she spoke she held herself in check, her voice low but tense.

"Mike Bundy is a crook; you say so. He has robbed many, you among the rest. If you kill him, or if he has the better luck and kills you, there is an end. If he is kept alive, and if you're half the man he is, you can somehow—don't ask me how! *Somehow!*—you can square your debt with your friends, and make Mike Bundy dig up every single cent that his dirty claws stole. And there you have what's on my mind, Mr. Headlong Blind Bull Bill Dorn, while I'm exactly in the mood and all warmed up to it!"

"Whew!" said Bill Dorn. She slammed the door as she went in.

He turned and went down the steps and to the barn for his horse. He did not look back, did not see her face at a window, did not even think about her. His swift stride grew more and more purposeful before he came to the corral.

He went into the stable, saddled his blue roan and rode out, his spurs jingling softly, his hat cocked at an angle, a lazy cigarette dangling from his lips. He rode straight northward, toward the Blue Smokes, did not look back.

It was not quite an hour later—but there are times when an hour can seem longer than a blue moon—that a lively rat-tat-tat sounded on the door of the little house in the Valley of Palms. The girl who said that she was Lorna Kent had heard hoof beats, had peeked out from behind a curtain, her first guess being that here returned Bill Dorn. He hadn't even said good-bye. When she saw it wasn't Dorn she ran to fasten every door and window. Again she peeked out. And when the knocking came, she went to the door. For she had seen the man's face and she wasn't afraid of him. She even smiled friendliwise at him as he beamed in on her.

"Howdy, Miss," he said. "Me, I'm Cap'n Jinks, an' I'm come along to say howdy."

She thought he must be a hundred years old; his face was all puckers, he was as ugly as a superannuated monkey, his skin might have been old saddle leather, dried and wrinkled and cracked in the sun, and he had as roguish a pair of blue eyes as ever twinkled on land or sea. Somehow, so did the old fellow's lively good nature effect her that the ancient sawed-off shotgun tucked under his arm looked no more offensive than a little boy's toy. When she had taken him all in, her smile flashed out twice as friendly.

"You see, Miss Lorny," he ran on, "I jus' rid down from the Blue Smokes where the boys is breakin' their fool naiks over gold huntin'." He had to stop and cackle at all the fuss-and-feathers those fellows were making over the new strike—just mere gold, stuff you dug out of the ground. "I meets my ol' *compadre*, Will Dorn, an' me an' Will palavers. He tells me about you."

"Won't you come in, Captain?" she invited, and did want him to come in; his presence only accentuated the loneliness of the last hour, and made horrible the thought of the loneliness to come—a whole long black night of it, with coyotes howling from the hills, and strange noises bubbling up in their eerie fashion out of the silence's void.

He shook his head, then nodded it.

74

"Not now, bein' in a hurry, but shore I'm comin' in. Me, I'm stayin' here with you, Miss Lorny. Them's Will's orders. Only firs', I got me some more ridin' to do. Will says I'm to scare up the Injun gal, Florinda or her sister or some other gal, to stay with you. Soon's I do that I'm to toddle back an' visit with you. Don't cry fer me, Miss Lorny, while I'm gone; I won't be more'n three-four-five-six hours. *Adios.*"

She called after him: "I suppose Bill Dorn is on his way to the Blue Smokes?" He stopped and turned, and she saw how bow-legged he was.

"The dang fool!" he barked. "Mos' likely he'll be dead nex' time we see him. He's on his way to a meetin' with Mike Bundy, an' Bundy's ready for him, an' has tol' ever'body he'll shoot on sight, claimin' he's got to. Se'f defence, he'll make it, the murderin' pup!"

"But—but Bill Dorn can shoot as fast and as straight as Mike Bundy any day!"

"Hell's bells, I mos' forgot your present," said the old fellow, and came back up the steps. "Will says you, bein' alone an' scared, ought to have it. Reckon you ought." He dragged it out from his trousers belt and handed it to her. "Will sent it," he said. It was Bill Dorn's gun.

VI

RIDING along to the Blue Smokes on a blue roan that could strike a gait between a pace and a rack, and could keep it up all day, Bill Dorn met within the first three miles the kicker-up of the puff of dust he had noted from the ranch. With an old friend, Cap'n Jinks, he paused to talk a while, gathering an inkling of what was going on ahead and in the end sending the old fellow along with an errand or two.

"You ever was a dang jackass, Will Dorn," said the Cap'n at the parting, "an' I reckon you ever will be, amen. Jus' the same, after Mike Bundy shoots you up from hat to heels, don't come aroun' sayin' I didn't tell you."

Several miles farther along, in a region of hot, rocky hills and sparse grass and splotches here and there of cactus, Dorn met the second man. This time it was his friend, Sheriff Barton MacArthur.

"I just burglarized a house, Bart," said Dorn. "Any law against it?"

"I'll look it up some time, Bill," said the sheriff. "What are you riding this way for? Why aren't you up in the Smokes staking a claim with the rest of 'em?"

MacArthur, looking tired and dusty, eased himself sideways in the saddle, hooked a knee about the horn and started to work rolling a meticulous cigarette.

"Not me, Bill," he said, when he had licked his paper. "I moseyed up to get a lay o' the land, got it and am going home. Mike Bundy's top dog up yonder. I guess he's got a mine, all right; he's staking his claim and he's got fifty hired men staking theirs all around him. Then he lets the rabble in."

"All quiet and serene up there?"

"So far, sure. But you'n me have seen crowds like this before, huh, Bill? They always blow up trouble, give 'em time."

"And time's what you're giving 'em? Time and a lot of room?"

Across MacArthur's weary face a hint of a smile flitted like a glint of winter's sun on a rock.

"Know where Silver Creek is, don't you, Bill?"

"Same as I know where my hat is," nodded Dorn.

"Well, it's right in there that Jake Fanning, grub-staked by Mike Bundy, found him his gold. It's right in there that the boys, going pretty darn wild-crazy with the sort of expectations that used to stir folks to lively deeds up in the Yukon, already have got it figured out they're going to build 'em a town! All in a handful of hours! Well, it's me, taking an outsider's friendly interest, that persuades 'em to the exact spot where they ought to pitch their camps now and, later on, raise the walls of their fair city. They're bedding down, Bill, in that little flat with the scrub pines all around it—on the north side Silver Creek Canyon!"

He was chuckling when he got through. Bill Dorn frowned at him, mystified.

"The county just north of us is Rincon County," grinned MacArthur. "Ever hear of it, Bill? Ever hear who's sheriff up in Rincon County?"

Of course Dorn knew the Rincon sheriff, a fat, oily and good-humored individual, known far and wide as Slobby Martinez.

"Go ahead; you make me wonder," he said.

"The thing is," grinned MacArthur, "that the county line runs right through there. Where I've got 'em sot is up in Rincon County, sure as mud, and when the fracas blows the lid off hell, as sure she'll blow, Bill, it'll be over the line, an' in Slob Martinez's county. Which is all haw-haw-haw with me!"

"Dodging trouble, you wily old son-of-a-gun," said Dorn. "Same as usual, having all of that commodity that I can use handy always on tap. Well— so long, Bill."

"So long," said Bill Dorn.

Yet neither made the first move. They looked at each other like a couple of stolid Indians, their faces expressing about as much of their emotions as did the elongated countenances of their horses just now rubbing noses.

"I reckon you know, Bill," said MacArthur, "that as soon as Bundy sees the whites of your eyes he's going for his gun? He won't have to wait for you to make the first play; he's got a dozen and more witnesses to swear you're out to kill him."

"I'm not even carrying a gun, as you can set for yourself."

The sheriff did see, and marveled. "That won't stop Bundy from killing you, Bill, and you ought to know it. And when he does it will be self-defense even if you don't happen to be armed. Better do one of two things; steal a gun off me while I'm not looking, or swap your horse around end for end and ride some other way."

"No." Dorn who had it in him on occasion to be as stubborn as an old army mule, shook his head. "I'm going on; I want a talk with Bundy; and I mean to keep him alive."

"*Adios* then," snorted the sheriff, "I'll send flowers." But before he could ride off Dorn's voice arrested him, demanding: "Did you know old lady Kent was dead?"

"I heard."

"Then you'll know when she died—and why she died—and who buried her?"

"Not exactly. I heard it mentioned that she had passed along; some sort of accidental fall, I understood; fell off the porch while she was reaching out to water her flowers. About a week ago, I got the idea. I didn't pay any particular attention. Why?"

"Haven't heard anything about her selling Palm Ranch to Bundy, have you?"

"News to me," said MacArthur.

This time when Bill Dorn said, "So long," he meant it, and started on his way. But over his shoulder he called back at the sheriff who had not moved but was looking after him: "There's a girl at the ranch now. You're going that way, so better stop in and say howdy."

"Hey, Bill! What the devil—"

"Adios, Viejo," Dorn called back and rode on.

This was forlorn country, a land of desolation extending from the oasis to the base of Timber Mountain, a rugged old out-post of the Blue Smokes. Under foot was a sort of road, for teams at times came down from the ranches lying off to the northwest, cattle country there, freighters bound for Nacional or for America City, a lusty young town on the right side of the border line, or for the thriving new settlement at Liberty Springs. From a long rocky elevation that was like the petrified fin of some antediluvian sea beast, Dorn could see, very far in the north distance, a smudge of trees against the skyline, and fancied he saw the quiet gleam of white adobe walls; up there was the old Spanish grant, still held by the Villagas who had had their patent from Don Carlos way back in 1769. Bill Dorn drew rein a moment, and his eyes grew dull with unhappiness.

"I ought to go back and get my gun," he muttered. "I ought to kill him after all."

Those Villagas, what a fine old anachronistic family they were! Don Francisco and his wife, growing old now, and their daughter Diana and their two sons, Juan and Ramon, poor bewildered lost babes in the wood of modern money manipulations. They didn't belong to this place and time; they should have lived a hundred years sooner. Even their glorious old home with its sturdy walls and flowery patios would be reft away from them soon. Mike Bundy's shadow, which seemed to Bill Dorn to be spreading out in monstrous proportions, as black as ink, reached even up yonder, making dark the Villagas' mid-day. They were mortgaged right up to the hilt, and Bundy held their mortgages—and Bill Dorn had been the man who had introduced Bundy to Don Francisco and his family, saying simply, "Michael is a friend of mine."

Still Dorn rode on. He recalled all the things that girl had said. She had asked at the very beginning: "Did you ever see a dead man? One who had been alive a few minutes before—then suddenly dead?" He remembered Jake Fanning, a focal point for the concentric circles of drifting buzards. Jake had finished now. He'd do no more evil deeds in a world where there were evil deeds enough without him; equally he'd never make restitution for any of his wickedness. Bundy, dead, would be like that. "Alive," that confounded girl had said, "somehow you can make him square the deal. You can—if you're as good a man as he is."

Again in the open country and on higher ground he looked the world over in all directions. Straight ahead rose the barrier of the mountains, slashed deep with their purple gorges eternally thick with shadows. It was already late afternoon; he was allowing some five hours for the ride from the oasis ranch, and it would be sundown by the time he got to the new camp on Silver Creek.

When he chanced to see, off to the north in the general direction of the Rancho de Villaga, a cloud of dust which might have been stirred up by a frolicsome whirlwind or by horses' hoofs, he merely thought: "Here come some more of them. When a gold strike is made men drop in like those damned red-headed birds to visit with Jake Fanning." When, off to the south, he saw dust again he had no way of knowing that it wasn't only riding men who came on from that quarter, but that his fate or destiny or good luck was about to speak up. But for what lay under that filmy dust cloud Bill Dorn would have been a dead man in another twenty minutes. The dust cloud swept on with men under it, and so today young Dorn, not so young now, is still riding bucking broncos.

They were like lazy banners, those streamers of dust, three of them, counting that which the blue roan kicked up, and they indicated lines of direction converging at that spot in the Blue Smokes where Silver Creek bickered out of its little pocket valley and started boldly into the desert only to dry up like the hopes of weak-hearted men. The creek for two miles was bright and lively and full of courage; it snaked its way through a crooked cañon before it shot out into the open. It was in the jaws of the ravine where the cañon walls overhung the trail like beetling eyebrows, brushy with mountain shrub, that Bill Dorn came so close to the end of his earthly career.

He was doubly watchful now, having been twice warned and having come to believe that at last he knew Michael Bundy and his methods pretty well. When he saw two horsemen coming down the trail he was swift to recognize them though the light was failing and their hats were low on their brows. Hank Smith and Mex Fontana, that's who they were, Bundy's pet gunmen. He saw too that they were as quick to make out who he was; in a flash they dropped their hands to the guns tied down at their thighs.

The two rode abreast, the trail being just wide enough. Dorn approached them steadily, the blue roan racking. He thought, "Here's as nice a spot for a quiet bit of murder as a man could want." There was no turning to right or left; it would do no good to turn back. He thought, further, with a flick of resentment, "That confounded girl!"

The Mexican, the impatient one, fired first. The pistol shot crashed into the ravine's silence like a young cannon and the flash of fire was a tiny orange flame in the shadows. Bill Dorn promptly toppled out of the saddle, struck earth on all fours and scrambled behind a trail-side boulder, while the blue roan ran wild, whirling and dashing back down trail. Fontana, as he and Hank Smith came on, fired the second time, his bullet singing off angrily after contact with the rock behind which Bill Dorn lay.

Then it was that three riders responsible for the cloud of dust Dorn had noted in the north, cut into the ravine only a hundred yards below him, and came first to the frightened riderless horse, then next to a fuller explanation of the two shots they had heard.

They were the two Villaga boys—twin insepa-rables not yet twenty-five, one as dark as his father, the other as blond as his mother, two wild young devils who rode full tilt now as they did at life in general—and with them their sister, Señorita Diana Villaga, a boy like them to look at as they swept into view, wearing black *chaparejos* and wide-brimmed black hat like theirs except for its enormous silver buckle—a rarely lovely girl to stare at when she came close. Their abrupt arrival checked the gun play.

"Valgame!" shouted Ramon, the dark one, a man every bit as impatient as the Mexican Fontana and perhaps even more so. "What is all this? You have killed a man and still keep on killing him some more?—Ah! It is you, Fontana? You and Señor Smith?"

Bill Dorn stood up. He reached for his fallen hat and put it on so that he might take it off in the presence of his rescuers, especially the bright-eyed Diana.

"You three Villagas are most welcome," he said, and gave the señorita the bow which she, a regal slip of a thing somehow as bright as the slender curve of a new moon, would expect. "Always welcome, especially so today."

Hank Smith, slower to shoot but quicker to think straight than Fontana, explained, and was as pleasant as a starved coyote snarling over a bone.

"We jus' met this Dorn guy like you see right here in the trail. Lately he's gone crazy with some sort of a killin' idea in his head. Tried to kill Mike Bundy las' night down to Nacional. Saw me an' Fontana, an' went for his gun. Fontana let him have it."

Diana Villaga, spurring closer, the pale light dancing on the silver buttons of her little Spanish jacket, said solicitously: "You're not badly hurt, Bill Dorn?"

Only, as she pronounced it it was "Beel" and

she put a ripple into the solitary *r* in his name. Dorn had once told her: "Say, if there were two or three *r's* in my name, when you said it it would sound like an angel playing on a harp!" Now he said, rubbing his shoulder: "Hurt? Not any, Diana, except where I hit the ground. You see, not having a gun on me, I figured my one best bet was to roll out of the saddle pronto and hide behind a rock like a rabbit going under a bush."

"What have you got in your hands, Bill?" said Juan Villaga curiously.

Bill Dorn glanced down at his two hands rather grimly. In each he clutched a stone about the size of a baseball. He was going to let Hank Smith and Fontana have all he had when they came close to make sure they had potted him. He said, "Well, you see, Juan—"

The mercuric Diana burst out excitedly:

"Went for his gun, did he? You—you—you murderers! Why, he hasn't even got a gun on him! Get out! Get out, get out, you—you two dirty murderers!"

Both Fontana and Smith bristled. But their bristling didn't amount to much for, before they could make clear that it must have been a mistake, that they had thought Bill Dorn was filling his hand to burn them down, those other riders who had come along under the dust cloud from the south arrived. They were three cowboys from the Dorn Ranch, Bud Williams and Duke Jones and Curly

O'Connor. They plucked their running cow ponies in on bunched feet sliding in the trail, their hats beaten back by the breeze they made, their eyes alike in that they ran like quicksilver over the entire situation. Under their stares Hank Smith turned a sickly white and Mex Fontana a sort of diluted dirty purple.

"Let's call it a sort of mistake all 'round, huh?" suggested Bill Dorn. He tossed away the two stones he had held until now, dusted his hands together and added, "If somebody'll sling a rope over my horse, why shouldn't all of us ride on to the new camp on Silver Creek? That is," he amended, "all but Smith and Fontana who're riding the other way."

Hank Smith, a lean leathery Texan, said drawlingly: "Hope there's no harm did, Bill. It was, like you say, sort of a mistake. Glad Fontana didn't poke a bullet through you. Say, would he turn red when he found out you wasn't carryin' no hardware! Har, har!" He gave Fontana a look and the two rode on down trail.

The three Dorn Ranch cowboys gawked. But also they bestirred themselves, heading off the frightened blue roan over whose neck Bud Williams' rope settled skillfully. Bill Dorn, dusty and somewhat bruised, otherwise carrying no mark of his recent run-in with Bundy's gunmen, swung back up into the saddle. It was good to be riding again!

Diana Villaga spurred to his side, and he and she led the way on toward Silver Creek.

"Tell me, Bill!" she commanded. "Tell me about everything."

VII

TAKE it from one who knows, Diana Villaga was a girl to hit you in the eye at forty paces. Spoiled? *Seguro que si, Señor!* Spoiled from her cradle, *Valgame!* Pampered, if you like, even before birth, when the whole Villaga family, having two boys already, prayed to all their saints that it be a little daughter this time. The little daughter obsessed them before her arrival, making them wait their long impatient hours at the last quite like a grande dame coming late to the opera. She was as lovely as the golden springtime sunshine.

She wore a big black hat like her brothers, but its band carried a silver buckle as big as your hand, polished bright by an old servitor at the Hacienda Villaga. She wore black *chaparejos* like her brothers, and in the belt another buckle to flash in your eyes. Like them, too, she wore two pistols; their grips were mother-of-pearl. Her cheeks were delicately tinted, ivory with a flush of old rose, and her hair broke into little curls that were somehow like Spanish laughter, and her eyes seemed so deep that the wary sensed danger, and her lips were as red as the pomegranate seeds.

"Don Bill," she said for first words, "who was that girl who danced last night in Nacional?"

Dorn looked at her wonderingly. "That's Señorita Diana for you," he thought. "She's like a nice young leopard in a jungle. You know she'll pounce but you don't know from where." Any other girl would have wanted to know about what had happened just now with Hank Smith and Mex Fontana trying to kill him.

"You weren't in Nacional too, were you?" he asked.

She treated him to an eloquent southern shrug. Her whole body could talk for her when she was interested, as she seemed to be now—as she had a way of being most of the time. She exclaimed impatiently: "*Uf!* Did I have to be there? Don't I hear what is going on? I want to know about her. Who is she and why did she wear a mask and what made you take such an interest in her and is she the one who killed One Eye Perez?"

"Of course she didn't shoot Perez," said Bill Dorn stoutly. "She is a nice girl. Her name is Lorna Kent, and she is the niece of Mrs. Kent of Palm Ranch. That's all I know about her."

"Is she as pretty as they say?" Diana wanted to know.

He gave her a shrug as good as her own. "*Quien sabe, Señorita?* A man can look at her without getting a headache."

"*Uf!*" said Diana. "Already you are in love with

this one, no? And Don Michael too, does it not make his head ache to look at her? You go often to see Mrs. Kent, don't you, and—"

"You hadn't heard that Mrs. Kent was dead?"

"Don Bill!" Her gauntleted hand gripped his arm. She gasped. "But that cannot be! I had tea with her—she was so bright and gay for such an old, old lady. She even showed me an old dance step, a polka. Dead?" She shuddered. Death, to Diana the bright, was unthinkable. She murmured under her breath: "Oh, but I am sorry. And the niece, the Lor-r-r-na Kent? What of her?"

"She's down there at the ranch house. Pretty much alone. And—"

"*La pobrecita!* The poor little thing! I shall go to her. Now. Today. Anyhow tomorrow."

Then they came out upon the lower end of the flat, where the base of the mountain let Silver Creek escape, and saw the new camp. On a bit of bench land beyond the creek were gathered a hundred, perhaps two hundred men. Dusk was deepening; here in the embrace of the mountains which rose loftily about the spot it was already nearly dark. A camp fire burned brightly; near by a red glow went up into the air from a freshly contrived barbecue pit. Down the air drifted the scent of beef broiling. Two men squatted by the pit, their faces red like devils over one of hell's open furnaces, slowly turning their long green willow poles with their chunks and slices of browning meat. A couple of hungry cowboys had found a fat young steer that had strayed, had hazed it into the little valley—and now supper was almost ready.

"There is Señor Bundy!" cried Diana, sounding eager as she rose in her stirrups and lifted her riding quirt, pointing. "He is easy to see, eh, Don Bill?"

Bill Dorn only nodded. Sure, Michael was always easy to see in any crowd. Not only was he a striking man physically, tall and blond and handsome, but he had a way of dramatizing himself. You could hardly say that he was affected; it was just that he was Michael Bundy who was what they called in those days a "big gun"; a man to mix with any crowd yet somehow to stand apart and above it. He even dressed with a flourish; his shirt was white, a heavy silk, and about his muscular throat he wore a flaming red silken handkerchief. He struck a note anywhere— among his lady friends, and they were legion; among hard, two-fisted men no less. This gathering in the Blue Smokes was Michael Bundy's party, and not a man of them was foolish enough to dream otherwise. The best they could look for were such scraps as the hyena picks up after the lion's kill.

The latest riders up the trail to Silver Creek Flats came rocketing into the gathering, Bill Dorn and Diana Villaga at the fore, the two Villaga boys just behind them, the three cowboys from the erstwhile Dorn Ranch crowding them close. Diana came down out of her richly ornamented Mexican saddle like a feather. Bill Dorn struck ground, his boot heels solidly planted, his big spurs jangling. He and Michael Bundy almost rubbed noses, so close did Dorn's sliding blue roan bring him.

Bundy without stopping to think, without needing to stop to think, sped a hand down to his belt where his gun rested loosely in its old blackened leather holster. But both of Diana's quick guantleted hands extended toward him stayed him a moment. And then Bill Dorn spoke.

"Hello, Bundy," he said casually, though his voice sounded thin and hard.

"Hello, Bill," said Bundy. With one hand, the left, he imprisoned both Diana's gloved ones. His other hand remained on the grip of his belt gun. "I hear you're looking for me."

It was Diana who spoke up then, laughing as though the funniest thought in the world had just struck her.

"Don Michael," she gasped, "would you like to laugh with me? Then laugh at this: This funny Don Bill Hop-Along Dorn has lost his gun—and a while ago he was going to start fighting like a little boy—throwing rocks! It is so true, Don Michael! Tomorrow you can ask your friends, Hank Smith and Mexico Fontana; they will tell you. They tried to shoot Don Bill out of his saddle; they thought he was going for his gun to shoot them; they were so red in the face when we all found out that he didn't have any gun! Isn't that funny, Don Michael?"

"Look here, Bill," began Bundy angrily, but Diana broke in: "Oh, Michael! Tell me! They say you have found so much gold here that you and all the rest of these men can't use it all! Is that true, Michael? You aren't going to forget the Villagas!"

Bundy squeezed the two little hands which he held such willing prisoners, and the lines of his face softened fleetingly as he looked down into Diana's eyes, which seemed to yearn upward through the fire-flushed semidark.

"There's anyhow one Villaga no man on earth could ever forget," he told her, and sounded earnest and sincere; one would have said that he was fully aware of the appeal of the mercuric girl, and that something deep down within him responded to the challenge which was Diana. Then he returned his gaze, intent and watchful, to Bill Dorn's face, ruddy in the fireglow.

"Right now," Bundy continued, "there may be a bit of unfinished business between Dorn and me; business before pleasure you know, Señorita." After staring a moment longer at Dorn in that arrogant, high-headed way of his, he demanded curtly: "Well, Dorn? What's on your mind?"

"Mike Bundy," said Bill Dorn, "killing is too good for you."

"So your murder-mania of which I've heard so much, was just a flash in the pan?"

"Last night I wanted to kill you," said Dorn. He spoke quietly and steadily yet there was in his voice a queer quality which made perfectly clear to all who heard him that he was holding himself in check only with the greatest difficulty. As he had flown at Bundy last night down in the border town, so did every instinct and blind purpose within him drive him toward doing now. But at this particular moment a clear thought in a cool brain over-mastered rebellious instincts, whipping them like snarling beasts back into their cages.

"You interest me!" Bundy mocked him, a flash coming up into his hard steel gray eyes.

"Last night I would have killed you, but when I saw you I forgot my gun!" retorted Dorn. "And now I thank God that I did."

"Let's not drag God into this," jeered Bundy. "But just why the change of mind, why the softening of heart?"

"You deserve killing," said Dorn sternly. "You're a crook and a cheat and a damned traitor, but I'd rather have you alive than dead, and I'll tell you why. You have robbed right and left, you have gutted those who trusted you; you have shown the world that you're as crooked as a dog's hind leg. And instead of turning you into a lump of carrion I am going to make it my job, if I never get another chore done, to see you alive long enough to make restitution for at least the bulk of your robbery of my friends."

"You rat," said Bundy, slow and deliberate and angry yet controlled as was his erstwhile friend. "I've heard you out, and now you're free to tuck your tail between your legs, like the yellow dog you are, and run. If you want me to beat you to death with my hands, why just tuck in! If you want me to fill you full of lead, just get you a gun and say the word. Outside of that I'm done with you."

"No," said Dorn a trifle huskily, "you're not done with me, Bundy. Rather, we're just starting. I'm not going to get a gun, and if I'm found shot to death—well, there'll be no trouble for the crowd to guess who did it! Jake Fanning's dead; One Eye is dead; someone shot the two of them. Better go slow about making me the third, Bundy!"

"Why, damn you!" Bundy roared out at him. "If you mean—"

Bill Dorn had to lift his own voice to a shout for his words to cut across Bundy's.

"I've got a question to ask which you can answer or not as you damned please! Did you—"

"To hell with you and your questions!"

"About Palm Ranch. There was a sign on the

door saying, 'Keep Out.' I went in. Does Palm Ranch belong to you?"

"Yes! And by God, if you trespass there again—"

"Did you buy the ranch from Mrs. Kent?" demanded Dorn, sharp and eager. "If you did, you'll show the deed. If you didn't—well, I've an interest in that place myself."

"I warn you to keep away from that place, you fool Dorn!"

"That's all I wanted to know," retorted Bill Dorn, sounding cool, and turned away. "If you had bought it, you'd have said so."

"I've warned you!"

Bill Dorn went on his way through the crowd that had formed a tight ring but which now opened up to let him through. He was thinking: "He didn't buy the place or he would have said so. He has got a strangle grip on it somehow, but he's lying when he says that it's his. His he means to make it, like everything else, but he can't know about Lorna and—By thunder!"

Maybe Mike Bundy *did* know about Lorna Kent! Maybe that was why Bundy's two hellions, Smith and Fontana, had grabbed her in the border town and yanked her into full notice, swearing that it was she who had shot Perez. Conceivably their act, ordered of course by Bundy, could have had a dual purpose—to pin the murder on someone, to get rid of the Kent heiress for good and all.

At some little distance from the barbecue pit yet in the full glow of the camp fire, seeking someone to tell him of what had happened out here in the day, Dorn came to a small knot of friends. They were young Ken Fairchild, old Middleton and Stock Morgan. Before he could speak Stock Morgan took a step toward him, saying crisply: "Well, there ain't no hard feelin's, is there, Bill?"

Bill Dorn stared at him, failing to understand.

"Between you and me, Stock?" He shook his head. "Not on my part. Why should there be?"

"Know who hit you last night, Bill?"

"No. Hadn't thought about it."

"Well, I did. With the end of my gun. If you wanted to beat hell out of me now, I don't know's I'd hold it ag'in you. It was a kind of a low down trick, sneakin' up on you from the rear an' hammerin' you. But you see, Bill, I'll swear to gran'ma I sure thought you was chokin' Mike Bundy to death an'—Well, us boys didn't want him dead right then."

Bill Dorn looked him over as though of a mind to tie into him. Then a slow good-humored grin broke up the bleak sternness of his face into pleasant lines. He put out his hand.

"Thanks, Morg," he said. "I'm throwing in with you boys on one thing anyhow: Between us, no matter what hell breaks loose, as it's apt to do before long, it's up to us to make sure that Bundy is as safe as a man in jail. Might as well let the world know that any man that wants to do Mr. Bundy any harm has got us boys to reckon with. It's closed season right now on Mike Bundy. Now tell me. What's the line-up here?"

Stock Morgan drew a deep breath and began hunting for his pipe. "I feel sort of better, your takin' it that-away, Bill," he said, and there that matter was closed. "As for today's activities up here, well you might guess how they went, Mike Bundy bein' top dog as usual."

Bundy, he explained, had consented to lead the pack to the new gold strike, but things must be done Bundy's way. Well, that was fair enough. So Bundy designated some forty men who were to be first to stake claims after him. The spot was on the rim of the meadow, where the shaggy cliffs were based in a broken talus. And only after Bundy and his selected men had staked were the rest permitted to crowd in.

"An' already," said Ken Fairchild, "Bundy's had not only his picked lot but another dozen or so sign papers. Some sort of a pardnership racket, they think it is. Pardnership, hell, with Mike Bundy! Like a herd of muttons signing up with a mountain lion. An' he's told the world he's goin' to build him a high fence around what's his'n, an' the crowd of claim-hunters can keep out."

"You stakin' yourse'f a claim, Bill?" asked Morgan.

"Not any," said Dorn. "No more kicking in with Bundy."

"We heard you doin' some pretty wild talkin' to him, Bill. How in blazes do you figger you can make a man like him cough up anything he's swallered?"

"Talk to you later, Morg. I'm beginning to get myself a couple of notions. Maybe you knocked 'em into my head last night, or anyhow sort of opened it up so a new idea could sneak in. Tell me, did you boys know that old lady Kent, down at Palm Ranch, was dead?"

"We rode by that way today, of course. Somebody said as how she was dead, the place deserted. What did she die of, Bill?" he demanded curiously.

"I'd like to know! Maybe sometime the sheriff'll want to know too! Bundy claims the place is his."

"Shucks, Bill, you can't go tyin' everything to Mike Bundy! If you got him figgered goin' aroun' murderin' folks, Jake Fanning and Perez an' now ol' lady Kent—Well, I must of knocked all the sense out of that head of yours that was ever in it. Bundy's got a lot of fox mixed up with the gorilla blood that's in him."

Bill Dorn nodded. "Yes, guess you're right, Morg; I'm beginning to see things crooked. But all round it's a damn funny mess."

It was perhaps twenty minutes later that Duke

Jones, hunting everywhere for Bill Dorn, ran him down.

"Say, Bill," he said, "after you walked out on Bundy he did a lot of loud talkin'. He's pretty damn' sore, Bundy is; jumpy, kind of, too, an' that ain't like him. What was on his mind was that you had your warnin' to keep off Palm Ranch. He says, so you c'n hear him a mile, the place is his an' that already he's sent his two killers, Mex an' Hank, down there to guard the place, an' that they're to throw out anybody that tries to nose in—an' that if you get funny with 'em they're apt to finish what they started on the trail this afternoon. I kind of thought you might as well know."

"Lorna Kent is there," muttered Dorn, as much to himself as to Duke Jones. "Bundy doesn't know that, but—"

"The hell he don't! I heard that Villaga pullet tell him; I thought he was goin' to jump clean out'n his boots."

"Good God!" said Dorn. "They'll grab her the way they did last night—they'll rush her back across the border—she'd never have a chance—"

"Not a Chinaman's. Hey, Bill—"

But Sudden Bill Dorn was no longer with him.

VIII

MIKE BUNDY lost not a single unnecessary moment turning back to Palm Valley Ranch. He had brought two led saddle horses with him up from Nacional, and riding a fresh mount which he had no thought of sparing he was out of camp and on his way ten minutes before Bill Dorn heard what Duke Jones had to tell him.

When at the end of the ride he came down stiffly out of the saddle his horse stood with legs trembling, its nose almost brushing the ground. There was a light in the house; Bundy started toward it, his big roweled spurs clanking. Two figures rose up out of the shadows to block his way.

"Hey there," said a voice. "Who're you? What do you want?"

Bundy snapped, "That you, Smith? That you, Fontana? What in hell are you doing out here? Where's the girl? Inside?"

"Yes, she's in there," said Smith.

"If you two had a grain of sense between you," stormed Bundy, "she would be on her way to the border. Get your horses ready; you're riding with her in two shakes."

He started on toward the steps, but Smith's voice stopped him. "She's got company," said Smith. "That's why we're leavin' her be for a spell. It's bad luck killin' sheriffs, Bundy. Me, I know."

"You mean MacArthur is here?"

"*Seguro* for sure," said Fontana, and one guessed from his voice that his lip was lifted after the snarling fashion he had, so that his teeth showed. "Thees sheriff, she's gettin' pretty damn nosey, Señor. Bad luck to keel?" He spat audibly and you knew that he shrugged.

Already Mike Bundy was rapping for entrance. A voice called out heartily, "Come along in," and Bundy entered to find Sheriff MacArthur sitting alone in the living room, his boot heels up on a bench before a small blaze in the fireplace, his hands clasped behind his head, the stub of a cigar turning slowly in the corner of his mouth.

"Hello, MacArthur," said Bundy curtly. "What are you doing here?"

"Hello, Bundy," said MacArthur. "Take your spurs off and make yourself at home."

"I am at home! Maybe you didn't know? Well, this place is mine now."

"Nice place," said MacArthur.

"Maybe you saw my sign nailed to the door." Bundy's eyes bored into him. "The sign isn't there now."

"Maybe that's it," said the sheriff, and used the toe of one boot to point. "I noticed a while ago some words printed on a piece of cardboard; burnt, mostly, now though."

"There's a girl here," said Bundy. "She *is* here, isn't she?"

"What girl?" asked MacArthur.

"A cheap scrap of calico who calls herself Lorna Kent; she says she's old lady Kent's niece. She's the girl, by the way, who killed One Eye Perez last night. You might take her in, MacArthur, and hand her over to the Mexican authorities."

MacArthur shrugged. "Me, I've got plenty jobs of my own without working for the boys on the other side the line. I'm still sort of puzzled about the sudden taking off of Jake Fanning—not that he didn't need the same. Haven't any ideas on that, have you, Bundy?"

"No. And I don't give a damn about it one way or the other. Where's that dance hall filly?"

"Squat and rest your bones," invited the sheriff. "And tell me how you know this girl killed One Eye? She don't look much like a killer."

"Smith and Fontana saw her shoot through the window and plug him in the back of the head."

"Where were you?" asked the sheriff. He tossed his cigar stub into the fire where it should have gone long before and started building himself a cigarette.

"I'd just got into town. I didn't see it."

"And then you and that hot-head, Bill Dorn, had what you might call an interrupted fist fight. You didn't have any gun on you, did you?"

"I don't always carry a gun," said Bundy. "What about it?"

"Nothing. Say, here's something funny! Bill Dorn didn't have any gun on him this afternoon; I met him on the trail and he showed me. It was because he wanted it known he wasn't out gunning for you any longer. And your not carrying hardware last night—well, it showed folks, I guess, that anyhow it wasn't you that shot One Eye."

Bundy's jaw hardened and his steely eyes blazed dangerously. "Put a name to it, MacArthur, if you've got anything to say!"

"Nary a word," said the sheriff pleasantly. "I was just thinking."

Bundy moved to cross the room toward a closed door. MacArthur pulled his feet down from the bench.

"Where are you going?" he asked, suddenly businesslike.

"If that girl is here—"

"Wait a shake. I heard what was on that sign. Whose place is this now, no joshing, Bundy? Yours or the girl's?"

"It's mine. And in my own house I go where I please, open what doors I want open, even if I have to smash 'em off their hinges. Is that clear?"

"It ought to be. But wait a shake again. If this place is yours out and out you must have bought it, or anyhow got a deed to it. If so, you've got the deed in your pocket or somewhere, or you've placed it on record. There seems to be a sort of mix-up about this, Bundy. Any objection to putting me straight?"

Bundy came back slowly and stood leaning against the chimney. The scowl remained on his brows while he spoke deliberately.

"When I say that Palm Ranch belongs to me I mean it. No; I didn't buy it and I haven't any deed. But I loaned the old woman a lot of money on it; it's mortgaged to me for twice as much as anyone on earth would ever pay; she's dead intestate; there are no heirs, for she was a widow all alone in the world. This little snip that calls herself Lorna Kent is a nervy little fake, and I'll soon show that. So the place is as good as mine, and I mean to protect my interests. It's a way I have, MacArthur," he ended drily.

"I thought it might be something like that. But how come, Bundy, that you loaned twice as much as the place would be worth to anyone else?"

"Suppose you figure that out for yourself? Maybe I just got soft-hearted all of a sudden! Maybe my reason is my own particular business. And now, sheriff or no sheriff, to hell with your questions, MacArthur."

"Sure," said the sheriff. "Sure." He lighted the cigarette he had rolled so carefully. Then over his shoulder he called toward the closed door: "Better come along in, Miss Lorna. There's a gent here to see you."

The door opened instantly and Lorna came in and with her came old Cap'n Jinks, his leathery face puckered, his bright eyes harboring their habitual look of roguishness. He was first to speak, chirping cheerily: "Why hello, Bundy! Ain't run off an' left them fellers to steal all your new gold, have you?"

Bundy ignored him, his attention fully given to the girl. There was a first flick of fear in her eyes as they rested on his face which, despite its handsome blondness, was just now like a pleasant landscape made ominous by shadowing black clouds. That glint of fear in her eyes went as swiftly as it had come. She stiffened her slight figure and walked to the bench at the fire, sitting close to the sheriff.

In a flash too the scowl fled from Bundy's face; he stared at her in a strangely intent sort of way. His brows went up, his eyes opened wide and then over his face played an expression not in the least hard to read, one which certainly would not have displeased most girls. Bundy, in surprised admiration, was paying her beauty full tribute.

After Cap'n Jinks' words died away there had been an utter silence so far as human tongues were concerned, only the faint crackle of the fire and the sudden, startling hoot of an owl nearby ruffling the stillness. Then suddenly Bundy spoke out:

"I never really saw you until now! Why didn't

somebody tell me? There was never a girl like you! *You* kill a man, murdering him in cold blood, shooting him in the back?" He laughed at that. "They're fools or liars to say so. And if you tell me you are really Lorna Kent and Mrs. Kent's niece, by the Lord I believe you!"

Lorna bestowed on him a rather superior smile; her lips remained unparted, but the corners came up ever so slightly.

"Then I'm not just a soiled scrap of calico after all? Not just a little dance hall—what was it?— oh, yes; a dance hall filly! No little—let me see— no little snip that calls herself Lorna Kent? You're being terribly kind to me, you know, Mr. Bundy!"

If she counted on upsetting his aplomb she failed utterly. He put back his head and laughed heartily. Then he said, grown sober again: "Forgive me please, Miss Kent. I tell you I hadn't had a good look at you. I take back every word and I crave your pardon. I thought—No, I won't say what I thought or I'll have to apologize again. You see, I listened to Hank Smith and Mex Fontana, and I'm hanged if I know whether they're bigger fools than liars or vice versa."

"You ain't makin' love to her, be you, Bundy?" cackled old Jinks. "Soun's kinder like it, an' I don't think the moon's up yet. Besides which you'n her ain't all alone in a hammick swingin' under the pa'm trees."

Bundy only chuckled good-humoredly. To

Lorna he said quite pleasantly: "Shall we talk this thing out in friendly fashion, Miss Kent? I am afraid that I've done you an injustice. I want to make amends if you'll let me. And also," and he smiled disarmingly, "I admit that I'm pretty keen on acquiring this property. Suppose we discuss the entire proposition?"

"I'm not at all sure that I'd care to dispose of Palm Ranch," said Lorna. She had to fight with herself to remain frozen toward him; the man was disturbingly fascinating, somehow, a bold, piratical devil whose sheer arrogant assurance carried him far. "I simply fell in love with the place the instant I saw it."

He nodded his understanding; he said quite soberly: "Love at first sight, eh? Well, the thing is possible; I know that." He remembered his spurs, removed them and then drew a chair up to the hearth, sitting opposite her. "I hope, even against my own interests, that you can keep your ranch, Miss Kent. But can you? Pardon the intrusion, but this is apt to turn into a business talk before we are through. Can you raise twenty thousand dollars to take up the mortgage which I hold? And if you can raise that amount do you deem it wise to sink it in this desert ranch?"

Lorna gasped. "Twenty thousand dollars? Mercy! I didn't know there was that much money!"

MacArthur, looking puzzled, broke into the

conversation. "You don't mean, Bundy, that you advanced twenty thousand dollars on this outfit?"

"I had my reasons," said Bundy. His attitude was that of a man suddenly determined to be frank. "You know, MacArthur, for it is certainly no secret, that over a period of years I have been gathering in lands. Some I have bought, some I have taken in on mortgages. Have you ever taken the trouble to check my various holdings and note their strategic values? Of course you haven't and no one else has. If you took a map of this part of the world and blocked out on it all those lands which I now control in one way and another, I think you'd open your eyes. Pretty soon if anyone wants water, and that's what everyone has to have hereabouts or go to the wall, he'll have to come talk with Mike Bundy, and damned little good his talk is going to do him." He cocked up his brows at Lorna and smiled his engaging, quizzical smile. "You'll forgive an occasional damn, Miss Kent?" Then, stern faced as he again fronted MacArthur, he continued: "You'd find, working over that map of yours, that I was in position to own outright or to control, without the trouble and expense of ownership, a tract approximately fifty miles square. It's a small empire, Mr. MacArthur, and I'm by way of becoming a small emperor, and not so damned small at that! Now with a gold strike falling into my hands in the Blue Smokes—"

He broke off there dramatically; he extended a

forceful muscular hand, the fingers open. Slowly he closed the fingers, at the end clenching them tight.

Lorna was swift to see his vision; her own eyes caught fire.

"It's big," she said. "Tremendous."

"So am I," said Bundy quietly, and those clear, bold eyes of his challenged her to convict him of being a braggart. "And this ranch—"

"What with its location and, most of all, its water," returned Bundy sounding franker, were that possible, than ever, "it is of considerable value to my project. I won't say it's essential; it would be bad business on my part, wouldn't it, to say to its owner that Las Palmas Rancho was a necessity to the forwarding of my plan? But it's worth a good twenty thousand to me; yes, more; and it isn't worth that to anyone else. And now you know why I advanced that sum and why I consider this ranch as good as mine."

"You were pretty sure you'd get the ranch?" said MacArthur. And he added sharply, "What did Mrs. Kent want with all that money?"

"She invested it. With me. It went into a separate venture which I am sorry to say failed. She made her bet the same as I did; she lost every cent, the same as I lost the money I put in with hers. One can't win every time, you know."

"That's a fact a good many folks has learned recent," put in old Cap'n Jinks, and demonstrated that on occasion he could look dreamily innocent as a full-fed cat.

No one knew better the trick of ignoring a man in whom he wasn't interested than Bundy. He had been speaking to the sheriff; now he turned direct to Lorna Kent.

"I did not know that your aunt had any relatives living," he said. "That's why I was so cocksure of already being as good as owner here. If you inherit this property, Miss Kent, you also inherit a mortgage of twenty thousand dollars. Do you have the slightest idea of redeeming Palm Ranch at that figure?"

Lorna looked helpless. She hadn't twenty thousand dollars; she hadn't twenty cents.

"You will of course," said Bundy, "take time to think it over. Also I hope you'll advise with your friends. The place isn't worth anything like that amount of money to anyone on earth but me. Just the same I'll make you a proposition. I'll give you five thousand right now for your interest as it may appear in your aunt's ranch."

Lorna gasped. She simply couldn't help it. To her, five thousand was a fortune! What couldn't she do with it? A trip to Europe even, and money left over to do all sorts of wild and lovely things. But after the involuntary intake of air she said shrewdly: "But you don't even know that I do inherit! You don't even know that I am her niece at all!"

"I am reputed to be something of a gambler,

111

Miss Kent," said Bundy smilingly. "And if you will just give me your word that you are Lorna Kent—it's a lovely name!—and that you are Mrs. Kent's niece and sole heiress, why I wouldn't consider it a gamble at all. As a matter of fact, with your big eyes looking at me like that, I rather think that I'd believe you if you told me that you'd found the moon where it had fallen down a well and that it was made of green cheese!"

"I'll consider your offer, Mr. Bundy," said Lorna, as sober as a judge. "I'll advise with my friends, as you recommend; my new friends," and a quick smile touched her lips as she laid her hand on the sheriff's arm and from him glanced at Cap'n Jinks. "When you come again I'll let you know."

She hesitated there and looked searchingly at Bundy. She began to fear that perhaps she had been doing him injustice. Ruthless in business matters he might be, a man who drove his way along mercilessly to some golden goal of his own; yet she sensed that all captains of industry were like that perforce, and she realized that at the same time they might remain warmly human, real and understandable and likable. Certainly it seemed that Mike Bundy was being fair with her.

He sat there watching her, almost yet not quite smiling, sensing on his part that she had not altogether finished, patiently awaiting her final word.

"Thank you, Mr. Bundy," was what she said,

feeling his personality like an enveloping warmth about her. "We misunderstood each other, didn't we? I'm glad that's over."

"That's great!" cried Bundy and stood up and put out his hand to her. She slipped hers into his; she had never before thought that she had a tiny hand, but now it felt infinitely small in his. "And I'm glad we're not closing any deal tonight; I'll have an excuse to come back, won't I? And if at any time I can be of service—"

It was just then that Bill Dorn arrived. They heard the rush of hoofs where he pulled his horse in at the front steps, and Bundy broke off short. Dorn had had no such luck as Bundy, with his fresh horse at his command, and, unwilling to ride his blue roan thirty miles after already having ridden it sixty since morning, had to cast about for some other, unfatigued animal. One of the boys from Antelope Valley supplied his need, and thus he arrived this short time after Bundy's coming. He didn't stop to knock; he flung the door open and came hurrying in, a look of concern on his face. That look passed swiftly when he saw that both MacArthur and old Jinks were here.

But Lorna saw that first look and guessed what caused it; she rose and went impulsively to greet him.

"I'm so glad you've come back, Bill," she said. He seemed like an old friend she had known all her life. Well, they had begun their acquaintance

113

last night quarreling! That sort of thing ripened friendship like a warm wind from the south!

"I wasn't sure that MacArthur was here," said Dorn. "I wasn't even altogether sure that the Cap'n had stayed with you. I came as soon as I learned that Mike Bundy's killers were headed this way."

"Hero stuff!" laughed Bundy. He hitched up his belt, making a point of drawing attention to his loosely holstered gun. "By the way, I see you're toting a gun again, Bill. Not for me, is it?"

"No," said Bill Dorn crisply. "That's out, Bundy, as I told you. It just happened that I knew Smith and Fontana were here."

"And they let you ride by without knocking you over?" jeered Bundy. "What can those boys be thinking of!"

"Mr. Bundy has just offered to buy out my interest here," said Lorna quickly, anxious to turn the tide of talk. "He says that—"

"Don't sell," said Dorn. "Not to Mike Bundy. Not until you've talked with me anyhow."

"One of these days, Dorn," said Bundy, his voice cold and deadly, "you're going to dig yourself a grave with that tongue of yours." To Lorna he said, thoroughly businesslike: "Remember that the place is mortgaged to me for twenty thousand dollars and that I've offered you five thousand spot cash for your interest. If Dorn here wants to help, remind him that talk is pretty cheap but that to see my bet will cost him twenty-five thousand. I think you'll find him tucking his tail between his legs. Good night, Miss Kent. I'll be running in again soon."

He took up his spurs from the floor and went out. Dorn, puzzled as MacArthur had been before him, stared frowningly after the departing, stalwart figure. Bundy carried himself into the outer night with his characteristic near-swagger, like a conqueror.

"You would say off-hand that twenty-five thousand is more than Palm Ranch is worth," he said thoughtfully.

Cap'n Jinks exclaimed explosively: "If Mike Bundy offers twenty-five, Lorny here's got a right to ask fifty! Mike Bundy's a skunk an' a t'rant'ler an' a egg-suckin' houn' dawg that never spent a dollar yet that he didn't figger he was cheatin' somebody out'n his eye teeth. I don't git this play of his; soun's crazy to me; but you c'n bet all you got that he's spreadin' himself to cut Lorny's throat. Take it from Ashbury Jinks, that knows."

"I've got an idea," began Bill Dorn slowly, only to be cut short by Cap'n Ashbury Jinks.

"Say!" He smote his bony old thigh, beating out a puff of dust that looked ghostly in the lamplight. "I got it! Bundy's foxed 'em ag'in! Ain't he forever doin' it? He's led the crowd o' sackers 'way off to the Blue Smokes to stake their claims, an'

I'll bet a turkey gobbler ag'in an empty jug that the gold's right here on this ranch!"

They looked at him soberly. But Bill Dorn shook his head.

"No go, Cap. The gold's up there all right. He might fool a big part of that mob, but there are men there who know, and they're sure. No, it's something else. And I think maybe I've got it figured out. If Miss Kent were in a position to spend some money—But let's lay the question over for a bit. Tomorrow's another day, and I want to sleep on this thing before I say anything further."

"Sleep's always a good idea," observed the sheriff, and stood up. "Lorna must be clean tuckered. She's had quite a house warming and we better call it a day. I'm drifting along." He glanced at the two other men. "Staying here, Jinks?"

"Shore I am. Firs', I've sorta adopted Lorny; she minds me fine already. Nex', she needs some sort of chappyrone; me, I'm it. I tried to scare up an Injun woman for comp'ny, like Bill said, but no luck for tonight. Josefa Morales'll be over mañana, but tonight I'll stick."

Lorna looked gratefully at Bill Dorn.

"I'll be so glad to have another woman here with me. You think of everything, don't you?" she said smilingly.

"Speaking of house warming, also of another woman here," said Dorn, "I think there are still other folks coming pretty pronto. The young Villagas rode into camp at the Blue Smokes just when I did. They were staking their claims in the half dark when I left. From something which Diana said, and from what I know of that young lady's impulsive temperament, I fancy she and her brothers are on the way, following me pretty close."

"The young Villagas?" repeated Lorna questioningly.

"They're your next door neighbors, and fine folks, *muy caballeros*. Rancho Villaga is only about fifteen miles from here, off to the northeast. There are the two brothers, Juan and Ramon, and their sister Diana. You and she are bound to be friends."

"I have felt so utterly friendless these last few days," said Lorna in a small voice. "And now it seems that all of a sudden I am being blessed—"

"There they come now," said the sheriff.

They listened to the clop of horses' hoofs breaking the outside silence abruptly when they hammered on the packed ground about the corrals. The hoofbeats ceased suddenly when the horses were pulled in, and voices replaced them. Then the voices died away and again it was very still on the Rancho de Las Palmas.

"They met Bundy, no doubt," said Dorn. "Bundy and Smith and Fontana."

Several minutes passed before there was any

sound, then the hoofbeats came on and ringing out above that drumming sound rose young voices.

"It's the Villagas all right," said Dorn.

"Will you open the door for them?" asked Lorna. "You know them."

As gaily jingling spurs came up the steps, Dorn opened the door. First to come in was the vivid Diana Villaga. Her big black eyes sparkled in the lamplight, the enormous silver buckle in the red band of her wide black hat gleamed like a jewel. Close behind her came her two good looking brothers, their eyes drawn swiftly to the new girl.

"Oh, hello, Don Beel!" cried Diana, and as though she hadn't seen him for a long time gave him both her gauntleted little hands. For a space of perhaps two seconds she regarded him strangely; he could make nothing of the midnight mystery of her eyes, and yet found her glance queerly disquieting. Then she hurried toward Lorna, her two hands again outstretched. "You poor dear!" she said sympathetically in that warmly husky voice of hers. "I am so sorry for you. Your aunt, oh, I loved her! And to have her gone away from us, if it saddens me so it must break your heart. Will you please—"

Dramatic in everything she did, Diana Villaga was never more dramatic than now. She jerked away from Lorna, whipping back as from a scorpion.

"She is not Lorna Kent!" Her voice rang out as clear as a bell, resonant with accusation. "That one? No. No, I tell you, and no and no and no some more! The dancing girl from Nacional, no? Well, she is not Lorna Kent at all but a—What do you call it? An impostor."

"Diana!" said Dorn out of an electric silence. "What the devil are you driving at? How do you know anything about her? What do you know of Lorna Kent anyhow?"

Dark Diana made a piquant face of distaste.

"La Señora Kent, I liked her and she was my friend," she retorted. "I came sometimes to spend an afternoon with her. She had a niece, yes. The last time I came, only two weeks or three ago, she told me much about her. She showed me even her picture. I said, '*Pero*, Señora, how dark she is! Dark like me!' And this one?" Diana laughed coolly and went to the door. "Open it for me," she commanded her brother Juan who stood nearest. He, like Ramon, was looking at the girl who had said she was Lorna Kent, and in his expression as in Ramon's was only frank admiration of beauty.

Juan started and opened the door. Diana ran through, calling back, "Good night, everybody. Oh, what great big fools men are! Come, Juan; come, Ramon; it is late."

The two boys bowed, suddenly grown stiff, and withdrew. The door closed after them; spurs jingled down the steps. The three men left in the room turned to the girl. She seemed struck speechless.

"Look here!" snapped Bill Dorn. "Are you an impostor impersonating Lorna Kent? Or is Diana Villaga crazy?"

"If you say another word to me I'll bite you!" the girl flared out.

"Dammit!" said Bill Dorn.

"Oh, darn!" said the girl, and fled the room and slammed the door good and hard.

Dorn, puzzled as ever a man was, looked as though for help to Sheriff MacArthur, from him to old Cap'n Jinks. MacArthur's face was like a blank wall; Jinks was grinning like a withered old apple on a shelf in the winter sunshine. Dorn promptly stalked to the closed door and rapped on it good and hard.

"Lorna!" he called commandingly. "Open up. You've got to tell me whether you are Lorna Kent or not!"

There was a silence, then a voice as tense as the taut quivering string of a violin:

"I'm Lady Macbeth and the Mother of Monsters, and you can g-go to—to thunder!"

"She forgot to put in the Queen o' Sheeby," chuckled old Jinks.

"G'night, boys," said the sheriff hurriedly, and grabbed his hat. "I'm getting out of here. I've got enough on my hands as it is." Out he barged, and closed the door as emphatically as the girl had done.

"Why don't you all go and leave me alone?" came her voice in a muffled sort of way.

"You come out here," commanded Dorn. "I want to talk to you."

"I won't," she retorted. "I don't want to talk to anybody. You can go talk to yourself."

"I'll smash your damned door down and drag you out!"

"That's the way to talk to 'em, Bill," said Jinks, and nudged him in the ribs with a bony elbow. "They like it an' come a-runnin'."

She didn't come running, but after a brief pause, she did open her door and stood on the threshold. Queen of Sheba? Jinks would have come closer to it had he said Ice Queen.

"Well, Mr. Dorn?" she inquired loftily.

Dorn reached out, caught her by the arm, led her back to the fireplace and plopped her down on her bench.

"You make me sick!" stormed Bill Dorn.

"You—you great big brute! If you think for a minute—"

Then all of a sudden she burst out laughing. She laughed as though she'd never stop. Dorn, amazed, stared at her as at a mad woman, and Jinks, his brows puckered, began plucking at his lower lip.

"We're carrying on from where we started last night!" the girl cried half hysterically. "How did the rest of it go? You offered to break my damn' little neck—and I cordially invited you to slink off in your own slime! Shall we go on with it?"

"Will you answer me?" said Dorn, very stern.

"Are you Lorna Kent? If you are, why did Diana say that?"

"I am the witch's daughter, and I dine off a brew made of toads and noisome herbs picked at midnight at the dark o' the moon. I—"

"Oh, hell!" said Dorn.

"Echo!" she retorted.

"Will you tell me or won't you?"

"I won't!"

He went to the mantel, leaning where Bundy had leaned a little while ago, staring down at the dying coals on the hearth. Presently, without looking up, he said in the sort of voice a man might use communing with himself:

"I don't know that I blame you. If you are Lorna Kent, well you've already said so, and once ought to be enough. And if you're somebody else, well, it's your affair. But maybe you'll answer this: Are you sticking here or are you for moving on? If you want to go, and go fast, I'll catch up a horse for you and see you on your way."

"I am staying right here," she said.

"Fine. That means you're going to play the cards you've called for and drawn. Now listen to me. If you'll kick in, I think I see the first move against Mike Bundy. Whether you're Lorna Kent or not—"

"I think Mr. Bundy is a fairer, squarer man than you'll ever be, Bill Dorn," she said hotly. "And I won't listen to you. Is that clear?"

"It sure is. I'm through here."

"That's lovely! And I'm so grateful to you for being through and going away that I'll give you a witch's warning: You just look out for that Diana creature, Mr. Blind Bull Bill Dorn! I think she carries a dagger in her stocking!"

"What are you driving at?" Dorn asked sharply.

"I saw the look she gave you! Oh, you great big fools, you men, always thinking every pretty girl is in love with you! Why that stagey little Spanish señorita hates you like poison. If some day she sticks a knife in your back, don't blame me!"

Dorn clapped on his hat and went out. A third time that night a door closed emphatically. From the porch he heard Cap'n Jinks say expostulatingly, "Now you looky here, Miss Lorny." That was all he heard, not her exclamation which broke off into a sob as, letting the old fellow pat her on the back, she buried her hot face in his dusty shirt front.

Storm-Along Bill Dorn stormed along to the stable. He remembered Hank Smith and Mex Fontana but did not slow his step; if they were still hanging around and cared to speak their little piece, he'd like nothing better. He wore a gun again, and never had he felt more in the mood to use it.

But all was quiet out there about the corrals. He went out into the field vaguely bright with the newly risen moon, and roped one of the Palm

Ranch horses. He led it back, changed his saddle, and struck out for the Blue Smokes. As he started he muttered: "Damn a girl anyhow. Here I'm stacking into my fourth thirty-mile ride for the day. A good hundred and twenty miles, and you can thank for anyhow half of it a come-hither-eyed dance hall girl from Nacional who says she's a witch's daughter and sometimes acts the part. Oh hell!"

IX

THE Blue Smokes Mountains were in labor and were about to give birth to no mere mousy thing but to a lusty squalling brat of a town which, like any newborn human, would turn red in the face and make a tremendous uproar to celebrate the occasion. In all essentials it was destined to be twinlike with many a Western mining town before its day and not a few afterward, the sort of town which the West bore and which made their mother over into what she grew to be. Beat back and forth, up and down through Arizona, California, Nevada, Colorado and New Mexico, and you'd find, as the old-timers had a way of saying, "Lots o' towns like County Line, but damn few more so."

County Line was destined to be the youngling's name, a name never officially given it, haphazardly flung at it and sticking as Bill Dorn's nicknames stuck to him. But before County Line was really delivered and had emitted its first yell, several things happened.

Bill Dorn, leaving only Cap'n Jinks to safeguard that confounded girl—well, Jinks and his sawed-off shotgun were not to be sneezed at—had returned promptly to the camp on Silver Creek. Dog-tired, with his saddle for a pillow and his feet to a smoldering fire, he had slept like a log. With the rest of the swarming camp he was up early.

He looked up his old friends, and they were many, and some few of them were no longer friendly because of their losses to Bundy, playing Bundy's game on Bill Dorn's say-so. This morning Dorn had a stub of a pencil and a scrap of paper; to man after man he said, "Look here, Bill,"—or Jim—or Tom—"how much did you lose to Bundy? I want to know, and when I can I'm going to pay you back. Every damned cent."

Some said, "Aw, shucks, Bill, forget it; it's all in a lifetime"; and some were over eager to give him the information; and in nearly all cases he set down figures on his scrap of paper. That chore done he went and sat on a mountainside in a clump of cedars where none would see him, and held his head in his hands,

"Somehow," he muttered, "it's got to be done. Somehow it's got to be done. It was me they trusted, not Bundy. If it hadn't been for me they wouldn't have lost a tenth as much. Take that Antelope Valley crowd; they are cleaned down to their boot heels."

He alone of the whole crowd, and there must have been five hundred men and boys and a sprinkling of women there on Silver Creek the second day, did not drive a stake. What was the use? Bundy and the fifty or sixty men acting for him had without a doubt nailed the treasure chest tight shut. What he did was ride once more, carrying his penciled scrap of paper with him down to Liberty, the little desert town about equidistant with Nacional from the Blue Smokes, but well up on the American side of the border. He went to a bank there where at times he had deposited various sums; he went to the banker, Roger Rutherford, whom Dorn liked and in whose opinions he put considerable trust.

"Mike Bundy has played me for a sucker," said Dorn.

"Sure," said Rutherford. "I tried to tell you that a year ago, but you wouldn't listen. Mike Bundy is the biggest crook in the West, and he is also the shrewdest. The law can't touch him anywhere. If he has nailed your hide to his barn door—well, your hide stays where it's nailed."

"I'm damned if it does," said Dorn.

"I'd like to listen," said the banker. He closed his roll-topped desk and reached for his hat.

"Let's go somewhere we can get a drink and get away from interruptions."

In a private (poker) room at the old Liberty Parker House the whole story was told by Bill Dorn. His friend listened attentively but not in the least excited. "I've known all this for a long time," was what the look in his eye said.

"I've been trying to figure," said Dorn at the end. "I'm not entirely bankrupt, though I guess I would have been pretty pronto if MacArthur hadn't jolted me wide awake with some cold-steel facts there was no dodging. My ranch is on the skids, lock, stock and barrel; Bundy gets it and there's no stopping him. But there'll be a few thousands salvage even there. What I want you to do for me, Roger, is take a power of attorney, do whatever you judge best under the circumstances, and rake me up all the money you can. Let me know in a week how much your bank will advance me on my prospects and assets."

"Fair enough. Need any change right away?"

"About twenty-five thousand."

"There ought to be that much in your account with us. If not, your note is always good enough for us, Bill."

"Thanks," said Dorn.

"There's just one thing: Are you set on locking horns with Mike Bundy?"

"Yes."

"Then you're riding for a fall, Bill. Six months

from now, even a month from now, I don't know about your note being worth a dollar to our board of directors. Mike Bundy is a big man; he's a crook, yes, but he's always inside the law, and I don't know but that he's a good thing for this part of the country. Better pull out with what you've got left and your lesson, Bill. Bundy'll smash you sure as little apples make cider."

"Thanks," said Dorn again, signed a lot of papers and went on his way. That way led him straight back to Palm Ranch.

It was late afternoon, sunset time not far off. Lorna was out in the yard feeding the chickens; he heard her calling, "Coo-coo-coo," and saw her scattering the wheat. The string of white ducks came waddling up from the creek, and he heard the guinea hens' lively din of "pa-track, pa-track!" From the barn a fat, smiling Indian woman was coming with two slopping buckets of milk.

Lorna saw him and pushed back the big floppy straw hat she was wearing, getting the brim out of her eyes to make out who he was.

"Oh, it's you," she said.

Darn the girl, why did she have to be so distractingly pretty? His mind was all set for other matters, not for gray eyes and provocative red mouth and arrant flirts of bronze curls and assorted dimples. She was wearing a little blue dress that caught a man's eye; he wondered where she had got it. She was twice as lovely in it as in her riding things.

"I'm here to talk business," said Dorn tersely. "Or are you set on letting Mike Bundy make a fool of you?"

"No man is going to make a fool of me," she retorted. "And I'll tell you a double-barreled reason why: In the first place I must have been born that way, and in the second, it's a girl's job to make a fool of a man. I read it in a book. And I'll thank you and your horse, Mr. Blind Bull Bill Dorn, not to scare my chickens to death next time I'm feeding them. Come, chicks; come, chicks!"

"I'm here to make you a clean-cut business proposition. Do you care to listen to it or not?"

"Why not? Yet why should I?" He looked after Josefa, disappearing around the corner of the house.

"How much are you paying her?" he demanded.

The strangest imaginable look swept over the girl's face; she came dangerously close to staring at him open-mouthed as well as with eyes grown round.

"Why—Cap'n Jinks brought her over. I—I never thought of her pay!"

"How about food when your present stock runs out? How about a man to look after the stock? How about paying Jinks for sticking around—or does he take out his reward in smiles? You said

129

that you had come out here without a red cent; is that true?"

She nodded miserably. He thought that she was about to cry.

"Mike Bundy offered me five thousand dollars to clear out, whether I'm Lorna Kent or the devil's grandmother," she said crisply, and he had never in his life seen a girl farther from tears. "I'm going to take it and get out of a country that I hate!"

"You're going to do nothing of the kind," said Dorn, and came down out of the saddle as though he meant to stay.

"Hi, Bill!" yipped old Cap'n Jinks, coming out of the barn. "You're just in time for supper. Me an' Lorny was talkin' about you, wonderin' how long before you'd show up." Bill looked sharply at Lorna. She jerked up her chin, pulled down her floppy hat brim, hurled a last handful of wheat at an old Plymouth Rock hen and went running up the steps and into the house. She didn't, however, slam the door behind her. Bill Dorn noted that.

Josefa served a bountiful, piping hot supper, and she and Jinks ate most of it.

Bill Dorn began sketching on the red and white checkered tablecloth with the handle of his fork.

"It's like this," he said. Josefa was clearing away the dishes; the eyes of Lorna and Cap'n Jinks followed the fork as though fascinated by it. "I've been doing considerable riding the last few days; I've picked up a few facts and I've had time to do a bit of thinking."

The fork handle was describing a square a dozen inches or so on each side, and as Dorn went on speaking it moved along the sides over and over again, until they could almost see a three dimensioned wall built up fencing off Dorn's square.

"Down here is the border," he explained. "Way up here is the Villaga Rancho. Here's Palm Ranch. Here's the new camp on Silver Creek. Over here's Antelope Valley, and down in this corner is what used to be known as the Dorn Ranch. Roughly this territory is fifty miles square; that means it contains twenty-five hundred square miles, and that's one million six hundred thousand acres. A lot of this land is worthless; a lot of it, including the ranches I've mentioned and several smaller properties, is valuable; a lot of the worthless land could be made valuable with water put on it. Mike Bundy is by way of controlling this entire tract."

"Bundy said so himse'f t'other night," said Jinks.

"He's going to rake in the Villaga Ranch one of these days and make it one of the finest properties in the state. He'll want a good road from there for a long haul, down to Liberty or Nacional. Which way will his road go?"

"Through here, o' course," said Cap.

131

"Next, there's going to be a boom up in the Blue Smokes. There'll be a town there before we know it. They'll have to go outside for their supplies. That means another road. What'll they do? Make a dry haul of sixty miles, or come this way? Don't you think Bundy has figured all that out? There's bound to be an important—even an essential—crossroads right here on Palm Ranch. And there's going to be a lot of travel on this trail. Already there are five hundred men on Silver Creek. There are apt to be five thousand. They'll be going back and forth; they'll have to have supplies, building materials, mining equipment—everything. And if Miss Kent closed her gates against this stream flowing both ways, whether she is Miss Kent or isn't Miss Kent— well, it would be the first blow square in Mike Bundy's eye!"

"Could she do such, Bill?" demanded Jinks. "Folks has always come through this way."

"Certainly she can. The ranch has been fenced for years, with gates to open and close, with passers-through allowed to take the short cut and to water their stock just as a courtesy from Mrs. Kent. There weren't forty men going through in a year. Now with thousands pouring along she'd be well within her rights to ask them to make a wide swing around her property. That would lengthen the road by a good ten miles, since the only decent road would be through Pocket Flats; it would give the freighters a seventy mile pull instead of sixty, and a dry haul besides."

"That sounds to me," said Lorna, and screwed up her face distastefully, "like a pretty low-down, mean trick, Bill Dorn."

"You don't fight the devil by throwing flowers in his face," said Dorn.

"It's taking unfair advantage. It's mere spite work. It would harm many people, not Bundy alone, and would not improve my situation in the least."

"You harm no one, except Bundy," he said without looking up at her, his eyes intent on the fork still tracing boundaries, marking out strategic sites, describing roadways. "You improve your position immeasurably. You are the one who builds the first sixty mile road from Liberty to Silver Creek. You are the one who furnishes what supplies the new camp will want. You are the one who starts a string of freight wagons, hauling both ways. Don't you see that's what Bundy has in mind? Don't you see why he wanted to grab this place? Twenty-five thousand dollars?" He snorted. "You can make it worth ten times that; maybe ten times ten before you're through with it."

Perhaps her logical question would have been: "I? How on earth am I to finance a thing like that?" Instead, regarding him probingly, she demanded:

"And you want to see this done—just because you so hate Mike Bundy?"

"I am out to pull Bundy down. You know that. You know why. And it was you who put the idea into my head to keep the man alive and wring restitution out of him instead of putting a bullet through him. I saw the sense and the value of your suggestion. Now I am putting an idea into your head. Will you see its value or not?"

Then she did ask the obvious and logical question. "Having carelessly mislaid my purse somewhere," she said sarcastically, "just where am I to find the few cents to do this simple little thing? Oh, you're talking nonsense and you know it!"

"My own affairs are pretty badly messed up," Dorn conceded frankly, "but I can raise enough money to start operations."

"You'd loan it to me? And even yet you don't know whether I'm Lorna Kent—"

"Or the devil's grandmother. I'll bet any reasonable amount that you are Mrs. Kent's heiress. I'll make sure before we get in too deep, though—"

"Nice of you," she said sweetly.

"But I wouldn't lend you a cent. I'll buy you out, offering as much as Bundy has offered, and a shade better than that. Say, seventy-five hundred cash to you, and I take over the mortgage. Or—"

"Yet you say this property ought to be worth ten times twenty-five thousand. Why, that's two hundred and fifty thousand dollars!"

"And I said further that in time the thing might grow into a proposition worth ten times ten times its present figure, and that's a fat two million. Naturally I've other plans and naturally I'm not speaking of them if you're on Bundy's side instead of mine."

"You said you'd buy me out—or! Or what, Mr. Dorn?"

"We draw up an agreement and go into it together."

"Partners!" she gasped. "You and I?"

"A close corporation; you throw in the ranch, I dig up the cash." A sudden sharp, dry, cracking sound startled both of them. It was only Cap Jinks cracking the boniest fingers in the Southwest.

"It's a deal," he said as one speaking with authority. "An' me, Bill, I'm your head man down to Liberty, doin' the buyin', startin' the freighters, pickin' up your teams, an' all that!"

Sudden Bill Dorn grinned at him; for the first time since arriving the rigidity of his face softened and Lorna saw again that highly interesting phenomenon, rare good-humor breaking like sunshine across a visage that had been as bleak and harsh as a desert stretch.

"Do you suppose I'd think for a minute of anybody else for that job, Cap?" he said heartily, and clapped a hard hand down on the lean old shoulder. To Lorna he said, explaining: "Cap ran the first line of freighters between Capon City and

135

the border, and that must have been thirty, forty years ago. He made history, he made money—and he's the man for the job."

The old fellow's eyes were shining.

"An' I got a mite o' that same money lef', Bill," said he. "I ain't askin' for any share in the partnership, I'll take mine out in wages. But I c'n len' you a few dollars an' glad to, takin' a lien on your rollin' stock."

Bill Dorn nodded. Without looking at the girl across the table he went back to work with his fork, retracing lines, a frown of deep concentration returning to his brows. Lorna once more watched the slowly traveling fork; more than ever it fascinated her.

She jerked her head up and found that at last Bill Dorn's fork was still and that he was staring curiously at her. She exclaimed: "But—can't you see?—there'll grow up a town here, too! There'll *have* to be one, half way—"

"Of course."

Lorna looked again at the red and white tablecloth. Later on she thought of it as the swaddling cloth of the new desert town of Half Way.

"Bill!" said old Jinks, all eagerness like a boy of ten, teetering on his toes. "You c'n stay here tonight, cain't you, to guard, protec' an' look after Miss Lorny. Me, I'm on my way an' in a hurry!"

"Of course not, you darned old fool," said Bill emphatically.

"Hell, why cain't you? Oh, you mean account folks talkin'? Shucks, that ain't nothin'. Let 'em talk. Besides," he added brightly, inspired, "here's Josefa! Chappyrone, ain't she? Now you let me go!"

"Nothing doing, Cap. What's on your mind anyhow?"

"This freightin' scheme of your'n, it's soun', sure an' sensible, Bill. Likewise it's so durned nat'ral that a man would see it a mile off without spectacles; it don't take no genius to figger that sort of a play. So Bundy's got it already in his eye, ain't he? The likely place to freight from is Liberty, ain't it? There'll be just so much supplies, jus' so many wagons an' decent horses to be had. Who'll grab 'em, me or Mike Bundy?"

"You're right, Cap." Dorn nodded at him approvingly. He turned to Lorna. "Is it a go?"

"Yes!" she cried excitedly.

"You sell out to me? Or we go in partnership?"

"I won't sell! Partners!" Then she remembered, and eyed him as from a vast distance. She said, as cool about it as a winter wind off the ice fields, "A business partnership, Mr. Dorn."

"That's what I meant," said Dorn, and went for his hat. "I'm off to Liberty again. You stay here tonight, Jinks. Tomorrow you can streak down to Liberty and run things."

"So long, Bill," said Jinks sourly. "I hope you split yourse'f from crotch to chin with all your ridin'."

"I hope so too," said Lorna, and made a face at Bill Dorn's departing back.

X

A SMALL band of horsemen, seven in number, pulled up short at a big sign on the northeast gate of Palm Ranch. The notice was printed, all in capitals, on a sheet of butcher paper nailed to a plank. It read:

GENTS!
KEEP OUT!
THIS HERE IS PRIVVITT PROPPITTY. THINK IT OVER BEFORE YOU ALL GET MAD. THEYS A GOOD ENUF ROAD AROUND THE RANCH OUTSIDE THE FENCE. WITH HUNDERDS OF FELLERS AND MABEY THOUSANDS RIDING BACK & FOURTH ALL DAY AND ALL NIGHT ITS AGIN THE BEST INTERRUSTS OF PALM RANCH INC TO HAVE A PUBLIC RODE GOUGED RIGHT SPANG THREW ITS MIDDEL. SUCH A GANG COME WHOOPIN THREW HERE YESTIDDY THAT OLD BOSSY THE COW GOT SO SCAIRT SHE WOULD NOT LET HER MILK DOWN & OUR HIGH BRED BANTUM

ROOSTER (NAME OF M. BUNDY) HAD A FIT & CHOAKED CLEAN TO DEATH. SO YOU RIDE AROUND. IF YOU WANT WATER TO DRINK YOU CAN FIND IT NICE & COLD & FREE FOR MAN & SADDLE HORSE DOWN BY THE TURN AT THE CORNER. FOR FREIGHT TEAMS THEYS A SMALL NORMAL CHARGE OF TEN DOLLERS PER HEAD FOR STOCK & THEY CAN DRINK TIL THEY BUST.

SINGED: CAPT. ASHBURRY JINKS, GENERAL MANAGER, PALM RANCH FREIGHT CO. INC.

"I'll be damned," commented Stock Morgan mildly.

"Me, too," agreed Bud Williams. The others—John Sharp, Ken Fairchild, old man Middleton, Duke Jones and Curly O'Connor—concurred silently. Stock Morgan leaned down from the saddle and opened the forbidden gate. The seven of them swooped through, the gate was closed behind them, and they clattered to Palm Ranch headquarters.

In the late afternoon Palm Ranch was steeped in peace and golden sunshine under skies as serene and fathomlessly blue as the eyes of Andalusia's fairest La Güera. A hen cackled from a haystack; on the back porch of the ranch house a buxom Indian woman churned languidly and sang La Paloma; squatting on his high heels beside the barn door a ranch hand mended a tug chain with wire; out in the upper field a young fellow, all tall boots and big gray Stetson and checked shirt, was sweating and swearing over post-hole digging.

Stock Morgan yelled at the man by the barn, "Hey! Is Bill Dorn here?" and got for answer a curt, "Nope he ain't."

"Where'n hell is he?" demanded Morgan.

"Dunno."

"When'll he be back?"

"Dunno."

Ken Fairchild at his elbow said in an undertone, "There's the girl, Morg."

She was coming toward them through the palms down by the creek, wearing her riding rig and big floppy hat, a pencil and pad of paper in her hand. Seven soiled and battered hats came off as she raised a pair of pretty gray eyes to the hats' owners.

"We're lookin' for Bill Dorn, Miss," said Morgan. And he added, as her eyes grew speculative: "We're friends of his. Me, I'm Morgan. These boys are Ken Fairchild an' Johnnie Sharp an'—an' the rest."

"Oh," said Lorna, and smiled at them. "Won't you light down? Mr. Dorn ought to be along any minute now."

Duke Jones got a good look at the Indian

140

woman and called: "Hello, Josefa. Love me like you used to? You used to give me all the buttermilk a man could drink."

"Come along, *muchachos*," grinned Josefa. "Plenty butt' milk, col' like Chreesmus."

They drank buttermilk and lounged about waiting for Dorn. Lorna, with so many eyes upon her, went into the house. From a shaded window she saw Bill Dorn come riding up. Thereafter she watched eight men out in the yard squat on their heels and pull out their Durham bags to roll cigarettes, or extract big-bladed pocket knives from capacious pockets and set to work whittling sticks which they threw away only to grope around for other sticks to whittle and discard. Some chewed tobacco and spat at marks with varying degrees of accuracy.

Bill Dorn talked to them steadily, soberly, without once raising his voice. They were like stolid old Indians—or like little boys playing Indian, just as you pleased. At the end Dorn snapped his knife shut and pushed his hat brim back and stood up and said: "And there you are, gents. You can come in on the play any way you want, or you can stay out. I'd like to see you chip in with some mazuma, because I know I'm going to run short of the stuff it takes to buy things with. If you're busted, or if you want to hold on to what you've got, do so. In that case, throw in with me, grab a job on my payroll, and if the time comes that we've got to fight it out with Mike Bundy, then throw lead on my side."

"When are you startin' your freight teams, Bill?" asked Bud Williams who had been a Dorn Ranch cowboy almost since he could remember.

"The first pulls out of Liberty at daybreak. I'm still short a couple of teamsters."

Bud Williams stood up and threw his cigarette away. That was careless of him; he stepped over to it and swiped it out with his boot.

"You're short only one," said Bud. "I'm on my way to Liberty now. I'm used mos'ly to steerin' only one cayuse at the time, but I reckon I can han'le the leathers on six of 'em." He grew hesitant; then he blurted out, "Hell, Bill, it's like ol' times, huh, workin' for you ag'in?"

"Hol' on a shake," called Curly O'Connor. "Bill ain't short nary a teamster. I'm ridin' with you, Bud."

The two lounged back for a farewell drink of buttermilk. Rounding the house, like one man, they hitched up their belts, cocked their over-sized sombreros and did their damnedest to catch a glimpse through an open window of the girl about whom already the whole countryside was talking.

"She's a peacherino," proclaimed Bud Williams as they rode away, Liberty-bound.

"I'd even marry her, if that's the only way to make her happy," said Curly O'Connor.

Out in the yard Bill Dorn settled down on his

heels again and with the other heel-squatters talked for a solid hour; Lorna began to wonder if all their legs hadn't gone to sleep. Then Dorn brought his friends into the house, to introduce them to her. Again she was wearing that crisp, cool little blue frock; again he wondered where in thunder she had found it. Cap'n Jinks could have told him what a resourceful girl could do with needle and thread, a big pair of scissors and an old blue dress of Mrs. Kent's.

"These boys," he explained, "are throwing in with us. They're friends of mine and have been for years; they're friends of yours from now on. Stock Morgan and Johnnie Sharp and Clem Middleton are chipping in with some money, and money is what we're going to need a lot of! Duke Jones and Ken Fairchild are short of cash because what they used to have is jingling in Mike Bundy's pockets now, along with their acres and cows. Just the same, one way or another, they're our crowd. Do you think Josefa can feed the hungry bunch of us?"

"I'll see!" said Lorna and fled the room.

In the kitchen Lorna said: "Josefa! There are a million men in there and they're as hungry as a pack of wolves! What can we feed them?"

A complacent Indian smile spread itself across Josefa's face like melted butter over a baked potato. *"Vamos a ver, Señorita,"* she said and went her slowly moving, competent way.

The men ate and looked at Lorna when they safely could; a good long look at her was better than dessert. Then they said good night and went away. Bill Dorn remained.

"They're aces," he told her, "every damn one of them, and you can bank on them until the cows come home. That's our nucleus; that's our hard, tight little wedge that's going to split Mike Bundy wide open. Believe it if you can or don't believe it, now that they're your pardners every man of them would go to hell roaring for you."

"What are we going to do now?" she asked, meaning to keep both her tingling impatient little feet on the solid earth. It was so easy to swing heavenward on daydreams! But what were they going to do to keep something in the pot for Josefa to cook?

"First," said Dorn, "we're going to guard you as though you were a jewel of great price." And Lorna thought, "He might have used the same idea and made it quite nice!" Her thoughts, however, and his were far apart. He continued soberly: "You happen to be the one joker in Bundy's deck. If he could wipe you out, if he could snatch you out of here and throw you back across the border to stand trial down there for killing One Eye, he'd laugh up his sleeve. As long as you keep on being Lorna Kent and Nellie Kent's heiress he is hogtied. So I've got those two boys working out here, Hopper and Kenyon; they're washouts doing ranch work but they could shoot the eye out of a needle a mile away in the dark, and they're your watch dogs."

She shivered. She couldn't help it. But then she asked, quite matter of fact, "And next?"

"The ball opens at daylight. Our teams start hauling from Liberty to Blue Smokes. Good old Cap Jinks will have them off at the crack of the whip. You'll see that they're taken care of here; Josefa and the two new hands will be on the job. I'm off to gather in an extra string of horses; we're going to need 'em."

"The teamsters will need a place to eat and rest and maybe sleep," said Lorna. "There's no room for all our men in the house here. We'll have to arrange for that."

"You do it, won't you?" he demanded, thinking of other things. "Suppose you figure that out; it will keep you from getting bored!"

She stretched out her hand, palm up.

"I'm going to require funds, Mr. Blind Bull Bill!"

Out of his pocket, exactly like a stage magician extracting a white rabbit from a silk hat, he pulled a fat roll of bank notes. He began peeling them off; he handed her an amazing sum.

"Also you've got to keep books for us," he said. "I'm no hand at that. For both our sakes I hope you are."

He got up and went away. Lorna looked at what

she held, then apprehensively at the unshuttered window. Five hundred dollars! She had never had five hundred dollars in her possession at one time in all her life. She jumped up and ran to the kitchen; it was there that she had left her pencil and paper. She came back to make her plans—on the red and white squared tablecloth! Visions grew up from it like mushrooms in a fatly fertile soil.

These were times in which Bill Dorn counted himself living luxuriously if he slept six hours a night. Next door to cradled in the saddle, he was in luck for the hard-riding endurance it gave him. He changed horses when he could, but kept the same old faithful saddle, the same legs. How many miles he had covered in the last ten days he didn't know.

He rode that night to Rancho Villaga; that, he thought, was his one best bet when horse-buying bent, and the Villagas were only fifteen miles away. Also they would put him up over night, and a man needed a good bed once in a while. And then there was Diana.

White moonlight was flooding the whitewashed walls of the old home. Don Francisco was sitting still and meditative over a glowing cigar in the patio—the *placita*, they called it. He was a little man no bigger than your thumb, or anyhow he gave you that impression. But all there was of him, some five feet six inches perhaps, counting his tall-heeled boots, was fine courtesy and hospitality. He jumped up and embraced Don Bill and patted him on the back.

Then the two sat in the moonlit stillness of the placita, a place of enchantment, and talked.

The Hacienda Villaga, along with Don Francisco in his hand-carved boots and snowy hair and imperial and stiff starched white shirt, looked like a million dollars. Yet it remained that Don Francisco's pockets were empty, and so was Don Francisco's patrician stomach. Just now he had been brooding miserably. During the late afternoon his eyes had fixed themselves on a butter-fat young steer wearing the Villaga brand—and he dared not call out to one of his many vaqueros to have the thing butchered! For it, along with the last Villaga pig and crowing rooster, was mortgaged to Michael Bundy.

Bill Dorn had to laugh, but smothered his laughter. It was funny; man, it was funny! Yet pathetic, too. And it was far worse than just pathetic. For Don Francisco was saying complainingly, though he patted his *compadre's* arm while he said it: "And it was you, *amigo mio*, who told me to go ahead. You who said to me that with Señor Bundy I could not lose anything, that instead I would refill the Villaga empty pockets! And now, what shall I do? Must I go out and eat the grasshopper like an Indian?"

"I want to buy a string of horses," said Dorn.

Old Villaga waved his white hands.

"I would sell you my soul for fifty centavos, *pero, Señor*, it and everything else is under chattel mortgage to Don Michael! I cannot even eat chicken for dinner without peeping out of my eyes to see if he is looking at me eat his chicken!"

Diana came in like something out of a dream. She had dressed as though she knew someone was coming—and how rarely did visitors come here to the far away rancho! *Ay, que lastima!* All in black, lacy, low cut over her lovely bosom, a Spanish shawl over her smooth white shoulders with the satiny gleam of pearls through it, a high Spanish comb in that jet black yet Burgundy-tinted hair of hers, the amazingly luxuriant hair of New Mexico, she came sweeping in, startling in her beauty like the night. And she was all smiles, all melting graciousness. As was habit with her she put out both hands, not gauntleted this time, bare white hands heavy with rings—heirlooms, these, too sacred to sell though one starved—and squeezed them into Dorn's.

"Don Beel! You are welcome, like a nice cool rain on a sultry hot summer day." She whirled, polished high red heels flashing, full skirt billowing, to face her father. "*Papacito!* You may now have your cigar in perfect peace. I am going to take Don Beel away with me under the fig trees and flirt ever so madly with him."

"Bless you, my children," sighed Don Francisco, and returned his fuzzy thoughts to his own particular olla podrida of scrambled finances and gastronomical problems.

"Look here, Diana," said Don Bill on the green bench under the figs. "I want to know the truth. What's come over you lately? You're different; you're always acting a part. What you said the other night down at Palm Ranch—was that the truth? When you said that the girl there was not Lorna Kent but a fake?"

"You think she is very, very nice, *no?*" demanded Señorita Villaga.

"Never mind what I think. You answer me."

While he sat she pirouetted before him. She seemed to enjoy making her full skirts billow. She stooped forward suddenly, pretending that she was going to bite him. She laughed gaily at him, and he saw that her big midnight eyes were terribly serious.

"You tell me about Don Michael!" She was in dead earnest and no longer made pretenses. "He is a conqueror; among men he is a king; he is a rajah among women, that I know. But—shall I trust him, Don Beel?"

"You poor little devil," grunted Don Bill. "You are in love with him."

Her eyes blazed at him; then they melted into tears. She dabbed furiously with her lacy handkerchief. Then she laughed and snapped her fingers and again twirled in front of him like a ballerina as she became very gay. Too gay in fact. She was very young, not much over nineteen, and very emotional and of course very foolish.

"You won't tell me?" he asked. "The truth? About Lorna Kent."

"*Uf!* You are a man, and a man does not understand what a girl is, a girl like me. You men are the toads and we girls, the fine ones, are the butterflies. Yet we drop down to the earth, and we flutter our pretty wings and we walk in the dust in front of you. And you, with your eyes of a toad—Oh, I would like to be nice and dead!"

That was an answer for any man, toad or not. It made Bill Dorn tremendously uncomfortable because he didn't know what to do about it, what to say. Her lashes, longer than they had any right to be, had tears on them like dewdrops. Of course she was in love with Mike Bundy. Equally of course Bundy was using her as he used everything else that came his way, treading her down in his forward march.

"Diana," said Dorn soberly, "we all know now, since Bundy has had to come out in the open a bit, that he has been too slick for the lot of us. You ought to know best whether he'd in the least help you making a mess of your life. If somehow he has persuaded you to tell a string of tall stories about that girl down at the Kent Ranch, saying she isn't Lorna Kent when maybe you don't know a thing about it one way or the other—"

Both heard crunching footsteps and made out someone coming through the garden toward them.

"It's that old sheriff always nosing around," exclaimed Diana petulantly. 'Before he gets here I'll tell you just one little thing, Don Beel. That girl down there! *Puf!* You go back to her and you say this: 'Me, I know who you are! You are not a Kent at all; you are Lorna Brown, that's what!' And *then* you see what color her face gets, Señor!"

Diana with one of her Spanish shrugs turned to greet the oncoming figure.

"Buenas tardes, Señor," she called out. "Here we are. Don Beel and I looking at the moon. It's a nice moon tonight and Don Beel wants to make love to me."

"Hello, Diana," said the sheriff. "Hello, Bill. What are you doing up this way?"

"Thought I might buy a few horses from Don Francisco. What have you lost around here?"

"Lost? Lots of time; a good bit of sleep, too." MacArthur eased himself down to the green bench, sitting beside Dorn while Diana elected to remain standing before them in the moonlight. "Things moving along all right, Bill?"

"As far as I know. What's on your mind."

"Nothing. Same as usual." He started rolling one of his cigarettes which took so long in the making. "So you're out to break Bundy, are you, Bill? He's got a lot of money, so they say. Where's yours?"

"I'm out to get back a little if I can and to see if things maybe won't work out so that my friends get back some of theirs."

"Never can tell till you try," agreed MacArthur. He seemed to meditate. Suddenly he observed, "You're looking fine tonight, Diana."

She laughed at him. "How can you tell? In the night you can't see me."

"There's a moon. Anyhow a man would see you in the dark like a candle. Say, Bill!"

"I knew there was something on your mind," grunted Dorn.

"Thrown your luck in, horns, hoof and hide, with the Palm Ranch outfit, haven't you? Things are kind of funny down around there, ain't they?"

"Fire ahead, *amigo!* You didn't use to be so tongue-tied."

"I got to wondering what old lady Kent died of so sudden like. There were only two people on the ranch with her at the time, the half breed that did the chores and a ranch hand. They said that she fell off the porch head first when she was leaning far out to water a pet flower and the railing broke; that they didn't see her fall but found her there dead. They buried her. Then they went away."

"Well? I guess they didn't go too far to tell you about it, did they?"

"No," said MacArthur, "not too far. Only they couldn't tell me much. She generally had an Indian woman to do the housework, but she was always hiring and firing the inside help. So there were only the two outside boys and both were off hauling wood when it happened. So they didn't know anything except what they found when they came back to the ranch late that afternoon. But somehow—"

Dorn looked at him sharply. The sheriff's hat was pulled forward; a black shadow hid most of his face.

"This here is between you and me and Diana," MacArthur continued slowly. "Last night late I did a mite of grave opening, lawful about it of course. I wanted a look at the body and, after I talked to him, so did the coroner. Seems like we didn't get around to it fast enough. There didn't happen to be a body there to look at."

"Good Lord!" gasped Bill Dorn, and Diana Villaga murmured a shocked, *"Virgin Santisima!"*

"It's murder then?" demanded Dorn.

"How should I know? I only tell you things are sort of funny at that ranch. Am I right? Here's something else. There's that girl that says she's Lorna Kent. Well, down at the Parker House Hotel in Liberty, looking scared to death and saying she's scared to come out to the ranch because of things she has heard, is another girl, and she says *she's* Lorna Kent. Makes a man take notice, don't it?"

Bill Dorn, sadly perplexed, didn't have a word to say. Diana exclaimed triumphantly: "You see! I told you! This one is Lorna Brown, a nasty little impostor!" As for the sheriff he smoked reflectively, but watched both Dorn and Diana like a cat trying to keep an eye on two mice at the same time.

XI

So SUDDEN BILL DORN did not stay under the Villaga roof that night after all. He grew restless; he wanted to get off by himself and think things over; he felt also an urge to move along to the new camp on Silver Creek. Despite the warm invitation from Don Francisco and the romantic supplications of Diana, who whispered, "Ooh, but I am so lonely!" he got promptly away. But not alone, since the sheriff decided to ride with him.

The first things Dorn and the Sheriff saw when they rode quietly into the sleeping ravine—too small and narrow a place to be termed properly a valley—were the four high-piled freight wagons which Dorn knew were his own. His, and that girl's, the one back there at Palm Ranch. They must have arrived here long after dark; two of them were canvas-covered, the other two stood out stark with their raw lumber, material for sheds, shacks, houses even.

But the human eye, hungry and predatory always and never satisfied with its first feeding, keeps on prowling in search of what it may pounce upon. Thus both men were quick to see what looked like a little white ghostly mist. Now there was no sense in a mist along Silver Creek tonight, a warm, balmy evening as dry as you please. It curled upward from the rear wagon. And just then they saw a bright, hot flare sprouting up under the front wagon.

"Fire, dammit!" yelled Dorn. "They're firing the wagons!"

Two or three or four dark forms broke away from the wagon train and started running. One couldn't be sure how many they were, couldn't quite be sure of anything about them except that, surprised at their incendiarism, they ran headlong toward the camp of sleeping men.

The sheriff lifted his voice, roaring out at the top of his lungs a command to stop running or he'd shoot. For answer the runners ran all the livelier, dodging through the small pines, and both Dorn and the sheriff unlimbered after them, emptying their guns. A few wild shots came back in answer, venomous enough but doing no damage whatever.

There followed an instant of silence, then the entire camp came alive like a swarm of bees into whose hive a rock has been hurled. Men in various degrees of undress and stupefaction began yelling questions. When they saw the flames spurting up from all four wagons, they came running. A hundred willing hands were lent before any questions got answered; what with all this assistance, Dorn and MacArthur had no very great trouble extinguishing the fires before any real harm was done. While they were still hard at their task the two canvas covers were thrown back and two blinking-eyed, sleep-groggy teamsters came tumbling out of their cozy beds. They were Curly O'Connor and Bud Williams, freight line teamsters since yesterday. When they came thoroughly awake, as they did when their bootless feet struck ground, a more irate pair of mule skinners couldn't have been found in a good long walk up and down the world.

Mad enough to bite a tenpenny nail in two, raring to get their fists in somebody's face, their thumbs in someone's eyes and their claws in someone's hair, they found no one to fight. Baffled fury was the name of the explosive in the breasts of Curly and Bud. As for Bill Dorn, he had gone white with rage. He knew beyond argument that this was Mike Bundy's work, yet there was no Mike Bundy at hand to charge with it.

And then, all of a sudden, there was Mike Bundy, looming large among the rest, rubbing his eyes, demanding, "What the hell?"

Bill Dorn charged at him like a young bull down a green springtime pasture. All the ideas that Lorna Kent—if that was her name—had put into his hot head, all the things that had sprouted and grown from her planting, were swept clean away by his gusty young wrath.

"So there's nothing too small for you to do," he roared at Bundy before he was within striking distance. "I know damn well that this is your work, and don't try to lie out of it!"

Mike Bundy had no time to lie out of anything. Bill Dorn's clubbed fist took him under the square jaw, and Bundy went down like a tree falling. But he came up fast enough and a gun was in his hand. He said, in a deadly, cold voice: "I'm tired playing with you, Dorn. Every man here knows you're out to kill me, despite the things you've said by way of a smoke screen. Fill your hand, you yellow dog."

That was the second time Bundy had called him that. Dorn yanked out the gun sagging heavy at his belt. Thus the thing started like a play of spontaneous combustion. It ended just as fast. For all of a sudden, out of a mob of wide-eyed, slack-jawed standers-by a small nucleus of purposeful men emerged in full action, taking destiny into their own hands. They were that small, tight, hard-bitten lot who had understood Dorn's point-of-view of yesterday and who meant to keep Mike Bundy alive and in circulation, blow high, blow

low—Stock Morgan and Ken Fairchild, Middleton and John Sharp and Duke Jones, all of Dorn's compact little band of anti-Bundy henchmen excepting the irate Curly and Bud, just now forgetful of everything except that their wagons had been fired and that someone ought to be beat to a jelly for the offense. The five, however, were sufficient for the occasion. Again a fight between Dorn and Bundy came to an abrupt end with nothing decided. Morgan and Duke Jones dragged Bundy's gun arm down; Fairchild and Sharp and Middleton hung like leeches on Bill Dorn. And Dorn, his head clearing instantly, said, though sounding surly: "All right boys. You're right, of course."

The next, day Bill Dorn witnessed the birth of the bawling, squalling brat of a town that came inevitably to be called County Line. For a short time, under Bundy's shadow, it was known as Bundy's Town, but it, like Bill Dorn and others, drew its nicknames rapidly, and the one that stuck was County Line.

For Bill Dorn a first triumph lay in the disposal of the contents of his string of freight wagons. Down in Liberty old Cap Jinks had bought shrewdly out of an ancient knowledge; more than just that, he had marked the various and rather breath-taking selling prices of his goods in the same flourishing way he had created the sign against trespass that he had nailed to a Palm Ranch gate post. His letters and figures were big and black and arresting. There was raw lumber for shacks or their frames, and rawer liquor for dusty throats; there were picks and shovels and boots and sides of bacon and red beans by the hefty bag. You could step up and take away what you liked, but at a price. And what a price! Still one had to admit that the supply was limited, the demand urgent, and that the goods had been hauled many a weary mile across desert and rocky hill. The way that Cap Jenks had things figured out, "When you need it bad, a ten penny nail's worth jest as much as if it was made out'n gold."

Men who had money bought freely and never raised a voice against the cost. Those who had no money shrugged their shoulders and did without, yet it was noticeable that they soon vanished from camp. Some of them were scratching the surfaces of their claims, hoping to turn up a spot of color, a vein in the rock or a nugget they could knock free, that would buy them what they wanted.

There is an old Scotch story which in this connection will bear repeating. Twenty Scotch sailors, arrived in port, sent one of their number ashore to buy provisions. Each man gave him a dollar. He returned with twenty bottles of whisky and one loaf of bread. They upbraided him, yelling at him, "Why the hell, mon, did ye get a' that bread?"

Cap Jinks, knowing his way up and down the thirsty country, sent an abundance of fiery liquor. It was sold by the gallon, nothing less. The liquor sales alone paid the whole expense of the freighting and costs, and set aside a neat profit of seven hundred dollars.

The camp fell apart as neatly as a ripe peach. The place split on Mike Bundy. His camp it was, to be sure; he had his followers, most of them hirelings, and he had as bitter enemies as any man who ever walked as a pirate captain on his own deck in the sun and felt a cold shadow over him. There was Silver Creek, amiably at hand; on the north for the most part were the Bundy men, making their shacks, raising frames for canvas, throwing down their bed rolls, while across that slight silvery liquid barrier other men, not of Bundy's persuasion, were swift in establishing themselves. And both sheriffs, MacArthur and Slobby Martinez, scratched their heads and hoped for the best. Sooner or later they'd have to have a surveyor or two up here. Between themselves, pacing along divergent lines, they strove to establish the county boundary, yet both in the end admitted they didn't know right exac'ly where'n hell it was.

Before nightfall Mike Bundy shot up a big pavilion of sorts, a place where a plank bar stood ready to dispense drinks—whisky only, but who wanted anything else?—and to offer under coal oil lamps a varied assortment of games of chance—poker, faro, seven up, even a warped roulette table which the knowing ones gave a wide berth. The damned thing looked as crooked as it really was. Then came the dance hall girls he had brought up from the border. As Dorn had already said, Bundy wasn't overlooking a bet anywhere along the line. By dusk the camp was giddy. By full dark it was roistering. Before midnight a young fellow named Sandy Bucknaw had killed a man named Pete Manton, and the fairly young woman who had been in her irresponsible way responsible sickened and fainted, and a squad of Pete Manton's friends hung poor bedeviled Sandy from a handy pine—and in unsober fact County Line was an entity. The town was born. Alive and kicking, as they said in that day of the newly arrived here on earth.

"It's going to be one of the big gold towns of the West," men said early in the history of County Line. And all day and for many a day men kept pouring in, as they do always when gold is found. They came along in a swelling tide, on foot, on horse and muleback, in wagons and top buggies; and one lithe, blithe, sunny chap came swinging in on crutches. All of them, under their sweaty shirts, seemed to wear wings.

"Let's you and me go jump in the crick and drown ourselves," Sheriff MacArthur suggested to Sheriff Martinez. Martinez only sighed.

Bill Dorn, one thought only in his mind, sought out Stock Morgan, found him and John Sharp with their heads together, and presently had all his small group about him. He said: "Look here. This thing is apt to be big. Gold comes up out of the ground, then goes into men's pockets, then streaks on through. The town is here already. You've got your claims already. Next, grab some spots that look like street corners—places for stores, for a hotel, for a stable and blacksmith shop. All that sort of thing. If you'll throw in with me we'll form some sort of a company; we'll drive a wedge into Bundy's plans, a fist into his belly. And all you fellows from Antelope to the Villaga ranch will get back some and maybe all that you have lost through my damfool advice. It's the town that's going to pay, not the gold mining; that's the way it always goes. I can see it as plain as a new tin can shining in the sunlight."

Bundy came over to them; he looked steadily at Dorn a moment, then demanded:

"Do you think there's going to be room here in this town for the two of us?"

Dorn answered him coolly: "Yes. It's going to be big enough, spread-eagle all you please."

"I know what you're up to," said Bundy, looking stormy yet speaking smoothly enough. "Name your price, get out and I'll pay you."

Dorn meditated. "I can take my losses," he said after a while. "In the first place, I'm used to it;

then it serves me right. But there are a lot of folks I dragged along down with me. I'd say offhand that about a quarter of a million dollars in cash would square the count."

Bundy pretended to search through his pockets. "Must have flipped it over the table to one of the new dance hall girls," he said, and stalked away. But before he had gone ten steps he spun about and came back. This time he spoke over Dorn's head, at Stock Morgan.

"You, Morgan," he said, "used to carry a pretty level head on those chunky shoulders of yours. Most of these boys, I think, would listen to you if you had anything to say to them. You can chip in with me right now and ride high; or you can stick with Here-We-Go Dorn, and crack up."

"You c'n go to hell, Mike Bundy," said Morgan.

Bundy shrugged.

"Have it your way. Only the gate's open if you change your mind. And to stick a flea in your ear, here's this: Palm Ranch is as good as mine right now. The girl down there is a fake. The real heiress to all old lady Kent's holdings—and that's mostly mortgages to me—is down at the hotel in Liberty. I've had a talk with her already; she's got proof with her that she's Lorna Kent; she's scared half to death, and I can buy her out for a hundred dollars. Roost on that egg over night, Morgan; see what you hatch out, and come to me when you're ready. I'm in no hurry."

With that he sauntered off. Morgan turned somber, questioning eyes on Bill Dorn. And all that Dorn could do was shake his head and get up and go about his business. His affair was, first of all, the purchase of some more horses, and he learned from his friends that they might be had, such as he required, down in Antelope Valley. Ken Fairchild rode away to buy them and convoy them to Palm Ranch. Then Dorn went on his next errand.

It was to Liberty. If there was a girl down there who said she was Lorna Kent, if she had proof of her contention as Bundy averred, Bill Dorn wanted a word with her. On his way, he stopped briefly at Palm Ranch, arriving after lamplight time. The little house where the girl was, who "sang and she danced too" in Nacional, was quite gay in the moonlight, with palm shadows over it, with its windows lit up like the small square windows in Christmas cards.

Dorn did not go to the house at all. At the stable he left his horse, changing to another and having a few words with the stable hand whom he himself had hired.

"You needn't say I dropped in," he said as he mounted again to ride on. "I'll be back late tonight or early tomorrow morning."

Late as was the hour when he rode into little dried-up, dusty Liberty, there on the hotel porch sat Cap'n Jinks in an ancient rocking chair that might have been of equal vintage with himself.

"Hello, Willie," he said, removing a short-stemmed black, ill-starred pipe from the corner of his mouth, then promptly sticking it back. Around the pipe stem he added, "I kind of suspected you might be droppin' in."

"Hello, Cap," said Dorn, stretching his long gaunt frame to get the kinks of fatigue out of it. He looked down curiously into the screwed-up, shrewd old face turned up to his. "What made you look for me?" he asked.

"Come to see Lorny Kent Number Two, ain't you?" demanded Jinks. "Or happens she's Number One?"

"I heard about her—"

"So I reckoned you would. An' nex' I figgered when once you'd heard, you'd ride along in. Well, well, it's kind of late, ain't it? To call on a young, innercent gal like her, I mean. An' even so, mebbe you're on time. It's my bet she ain't gone to bed yet. Fu'thermore, as the feller says, mebbe she's got her some comp'ny!"

Dorn was quick to realize that Jinks wasn't idly gossiping. Nor had he sat up in his creaking old rocker all this while just to look out into the moonlit road. Dorn glanced at the hotel itself; all was dark save for a weak glimmer in the hall where a lamp, wick turned low, would burn all night. "Who's her company, Cap?" he asked.

"Two gents sashayed in here only ten-twenty

minutes ago," said Jinks. "Their spurs was on their heels an' their guns was hangin' low, an' by name they're Hank Smith an' Mex Fontana, while by natur' they're a couple o' sheepkillin' yeller dawgs that goes where their master sends 'em. An' if I ain't mistook, they're visitin' the new Lorny. Anyhow, I been settin' here an' they ain't come out yet."

"Where's her room?" asked Dorn.

"Last one down the hall, on your lef'. Better sort of watch how you walk, Will."

Dorn strode down the dim, narrow hallway, came to the last door, saw a faint line of light under it, listened for voices, heard nothing and rapped with his left hand. His right was on his gun.

There was no answer, no sound save that of old Cap'n Jinks' slow, cautious footfalls following him. Dorn put his hand to the door knob, found no bolt had been shot against entrance, threw the door open and looked in. There was no one there. The room was in the wildest disorder. Bed clothes trailed to the floor, an old wardrobe stood gapingly open and empty; of any sort of girl or her visitors there was no trace save in such haphazard scraps, like leaves blown in a gale from a tree, as remained after hasty departure.

The window into the stable yard stood wide open; the mosquito-net screening had been torn to listless, drooping shreds. On the floor was one shoe, a slim, frail thing a girl had worn; near it a crumpled scrap of a tiny handkerchief. Dorn noted in an abstracted subconscious sort of way the corner of a sheet of paper thrusting itself into notice from under the warped pine dresser. A chair lay overturned; there was the big dusty imprint of a man's boot on a corner of the bed counterpane on the floor.

"Dammit they got her, an' me I never heard a sound!" Cap'n Jinks was saying, and sounded close to tears. "Out the winder they went with her while I'm squattin' at the front door." He came in and began peering and poking around. "What-in-'ell, do you reckon, Will? Who was she an' why did Mike Bundy want her carted off?"

Dorn slipped out through the open window and went up and down, around the building, into the stable, to learn what he could. When he returned, having learned nothing except that the horses which Smith and Fontana had ridden were gone, he found Cap'n Jinks staring down at an assortment of trifles he had spread out on the dresser. They were the shoe, the handkerchief, the sheet of paper and something he had raked out from under the bed—a well worn black leather belt with a big shining silver buckle. He had never a question to ask; he knew that the girl was gone, he knew who had escorted her, through the window and away. But Dorn, already frowning, looked into the puckered old face and demanded sharply:

"Well, Cap? What's up?"

"That there's a shoe, an' yon's a belt with a silver buckle, and yon's a letter. That's all that's lef' us, Will; the gal an' all her other belongin's has went, an' went clean."

He didn't lift his shrewd old eyes from the articles on the dresser; he seemed at the moment to have no interest in anything else.

"Who the devil is this girl?" demanded Dorn.

"Might be she's Lorny Kent," sighed old Jinks. "Anyhow this here buckle says L. K., as big as life; an' this here letter, one that was wrote a year ago, is to 'My Darling Lorna' an' is signed 'Your Aff. Aunt, Nellie Kent,' an' the shoe don't say nothin', bein' like mos' shoes." Then he did lift his puzzled eyes to Dorn's. "Me, I'm keepin' these trophies o' the chase, as the sayin' goes, Will. When young I figgered I'd be a great Nick Carter detective some day. I ain't never had the chance before. Mebbe it ain't too late yet."

Dorn said impatiently: "Good God, man! If those two devils have got this girl—I don't know what kind of a girl she is, either, but if they've got her—"

"Well, they have, an' you can tie to that, Willie. What kind is she? Nice gal, I thought her. Yep, they got her, an' they got a good safe head start on us. Now jus' what'n hell you'n me is goin' to do about it, I dunno. Happens you know?"

Dorn had to shake his head. No, he didn't know. And there were a lot of things he didn't know— but meant to find out.

XII

THEN came the Boom. For those were the Boom Days. All the great American Southwest swaggered like the youth it was, brave in its first pair of long pants; nothing was too crass for it, nothing too sudden, nothing too big. Black powder was to be packed in everything, was to explode at the hot glance of an eye, was to send up skyrockets and blossom in festoons of fire down the purple skies. Like an explosion Bundy's Town came into being. Thereafter it grew up like a giant mushroom—toadstool rather, for it was a poisonous sort of monstrous thing. County Line, you were conceived in greed, you were cradled in lust of gold and many other sordid things; what is left of you is now one of the monuments of the West, standing over dead things. And right next door to you, "as the feller says," as Cap'n Jinks would say, is Halfway!

The girl at Palm Ranch remained there; she showed a firmness of chin and a steadiness of eye and a capability for taciturnity which were downright amazing for so young and pretty a girl; and it was she who really created Halfway. As it had shown itself to her in visions, it came up out of the checkered squares on the tablecloth and took solid form at the head of a tiny meadow, just out

169

of sight from the ranch house over a hill. She was something of an artist, she had imagination and along with it the ability to create her dream in abiding form.

That first five hundred dollars which Dorn gave her as they sealed their "purely business partnership" vanished much after the fashion of a stack of hot cakes set before a hungry ranch hand. From the first, men and horses convoying the freighters must be fed and bedded down; there was hay in the barn on which stock could dine, on which men could sleep. But she looked ahead and saw that the hay would not last, nor would the barn suffice as a wayside inn.

When she selected the spot where a lunch room and some sort of sleeping quarters should be erected, she sent word down to Cap Jinks in Liberty for materials and for workmen. The next freight team brought her a carpenter, a carpenter's helper, and three strong-arm men, all of whom went immediately on her pay roll. Along with them came a handful of lumber, their tools and, as she had ordered, a thousand feet of pipe. The pipe was to bring water down to the new camp from a place higher up Palm Creek.

She got into the way of writing brief scraps of notes to Jinks by nearly every team that went through, Liberty-bound. At first Josefa cooked for the teamsters and laborers; then a man cook was demanded and came up, endorsed by Ashbury

Jinks, a clean, happy Chinaman with multitudinous knives and cleavers, who became one of Halfway's chief assets.

The lower end of Palm Valley was in alfalfa; it needed to be cut, the hay hauled to the barns, ready for the horses. More men were required. Then the girl demanded, "Why shouldn't we be selling hay to County Line, too?" So the cultivated area was broadened, virgin acres were taken in, the irrigation ditches carried the needed water to the lands which were dry and brown one month, lush and green the next. And then Jinks got a letter which read: "Dear Captain: We're running mighty short lately on milk and eggs, so please send me up by the next wagon some cows and chickens." And by the time he had had his laugh over it and then had got busy in obedience, she wrote him: "It's a shame the prices we have to pay in Liberty for fresh vegetables, because you told me so; and what is worse, they're never fresh. So I am having some vegetable gardens made; I'll need a good gardener and some seeds and things. You know: onions and cabbages and potatoes mostly, but greens and cucumbers and tomatoes too. And one of the men told me that we could have the finest melons in the world up here. So send me some to plant, that's a darling. And we might plant some more fruit trees too while we're doing it. And send me some men who can make a good dam. We have to raise the water level to cover all our fields, and besides a man told me it would be a good idea to have a dam big enough for storage. And we need a new broom, and Wong says for you to send him a nice new big restaurant range or he heap quit plitty damn quick. The men are eating themselves fat on Wong's cooking; they'll be sure to mutiny if he goes. So better send the stove. And don't forget the broom."

He sent both. The broom had a pink ribbon tied around the handle.

"You'll see," muttered Cap Jinks to the first man he ran into—it happened to be Bill Dorn, just arrived in Liberty—"nex' thing, she'll be askin' for a typewriter an' a private seekertary."

"And some more money," said Dorn.

"Shore. An' likely she'll git 'em all. But you jus' listen to this, Will." He read a note as yet unanswered; in it she asked for flower seeds. She listed the various flowers, a score of varieties the very names of most of which were unfamiliar in Jinks' ears. But what he did know was a rose when he saw it, and when she mentioned roses— "all kinds, lots of the climbing ones"—he realized that she was a mere human after all. "Seeds for roses?" he snorted. "Hell, Will, they don't come from seed." He was sure of that. Then he scratched his head. "What'n hell do they come from? It ain't bulbs, is it?"

Offhand Bill Dorn couldn't think up the answer. He said: "Better send what she wants, Cap. She's doing a great job up there—even if she is putting fancy trims around the edges. Unless Bundy busts us before we can bust him, Palm Ranch is going to be a big money making proposition one of these days."

"Got her figgered out yet, Will?"

"No," said Dorn, and was very short about it.

"There was a lot of things you was goin' to find out—"

"So long, Cap," said Dorn, and went away.

He did know that she was creating something fine and fertile and beautiful. He realized that not another person in ten thousand, man or woman, would have grasped this sudden opportunity in quite the same sympathetically skillful hands. Look at Bundy's town, County Line; it was raw, uncouth, ugly; a blister spot ready at any time to fester. Then look at Halfway! The establishment in which Wong presided was low and somehow cozy with wide overhanging eaves, and was built about three sides of a square, and in the square were green benches, green tables, a tree and running water piped down from the hills. It wouldn't be long before vines crawled all over the place and flower beds set it off in the gayest colors flowers knew. While at County Line they were gouging into the entrails of the earth, making gaping wounds preparatory to dragging gold out, always they were marring beauty and leaving scars that would not entirely disappear in a thousand years. And there at Halfway, as though to make amends, fields were being clothed in tender green, trimmed in colors like a lady's gown with soft bright laces, and even the bright little houses were like pictures.

Then there was the dam. Instead of coming into being as the small, unambitious thing Lorna had at first requested to raise the water level a necessary few inches, it became, after several prolonged discussions and much labor and expense, one of the major features in the Palm Valley Ranch development project. Men who understood this sort of construction were imported, materials hauled from Liberty; a sturdy concrete wall was erected at an ideal spot where the jaws of the ravine narrowed between steep rocky banks; water was impounded in sufficient quantity to assure many and many a now dry acre of teeming fertility in the months and the years to come. Here, too, Lorna insisted on the planting of trees, cottonwoods and slim young aspens for the most part; thus here, as everywhere, she contrived her lacy edging of beauty to that which was sturdily utilitarian.

Altogether these were the fullest, busiest of days, and all the while the strings of freight teams pulled back and forth, gray under desert dust, the groaning wagons high-piled with everything in the world from mining machinery to flower seeds. Here at Halfway the hours ran by swiftly, crowded with fresh creative endeavor, while up at County Line activity was hectic day and night, and in Mike Bundy's great barn of a place, given over to drinking, gaming and dancing, there was scarcely a night without a fight, hardly a week without a killing. Yet in all this purposeful activity there was one man who began to grumble that he guessed he'd lost step with the world. It was Sheriff MacArthur. He said to Bill Dorn:

"Dammit, Bill, you're having a lot more fun than what I am. I started proving to myself who killed Jake Fanning, and even who rubbed out One Eye Perez; and it did make me a mite curious what happened to old lady Kent and where, if anywhere, she's buried now—and I even wondered if this girl here is really her niece—and I came pretty close to wondering who that other girl was down at Liberty, and what happened to her—and seems like I'd go on wondering about all these things for quite a spell yet."

Dorn regarded him narrowly. You never could tell when the sheriff was coming clean with all that was in his heart, when he was just beating around the bush and poking into it to see what he could scare out. Now, when his listener did not answer, he added:

"You don't know any more about this girl than you did, do you, Bill?"

"No," said Dorn.

"Haven't even been asking her about herself,

I'll bet a man," said MacArthur. Then he rode away without saying where, and that same day Bill Dorn did at last ask the girl a question.

He met her down in the cañon under the palms as she was returning to the ranch house from a busy, happy afternoon at Halfway. It was growing dusk, and there was a lemon sky with the palms looking very black against it, when he saw her coming toward the narrow footbridge across the creek. He met her there and stopped at his end of the bridge, so she had nothing to do but stop where she was, half way across. He said, "Howdy," and after she had looked at him curiously she said, matching his tone the best she could, "Howdy."

He started rolling a cigarette, and her lips twitched into a smile which she banished hurriedly before he could see it; she knew that he was making an excuse of cigarette-rolling in order to take time to get his next words lined up.

"We can't go on like this forever, you know," said Dorn.

She appeared puzzled. "Like what, Mr. Dorn? Isn't everything going splendidly?"

Having completed his cigarette he tossed it into the stream and for a moment watched it whirl away. When he looked up it was to catch her eyes bent steadily and very soberly on him.

"You heard all about that other girl down at Liberty," he said slowly. "I've never mentioned her to you, but I know MacArthur has and of course Jinks has."

"Of course I've heard about her."

"Do you happen to know who or what she was?"

"I know absolutely nothing about her."

"She said that she was Lorna Kent. I believe a good many people are persuaded that she was. I've never asked you a thing—"

"Why haven't you?" she flashed back at him challengingly; he fancied he saw a faint flush in her shadowed cheeks and a quick hard brightness in her eyes.

"That time when Diana Villaga said that you were a—that you were not what you pretended—"

"Impostor is the word, if you've forgotten it, Mr. Dorn."

"Well, dammit," said Dorn, suddenly heating up, "I ask you now and you've got to answer: Are you Lorna Kent or not?"

She looked at him defiantly, then answered with a curt, unexpected, "No."

"Then who in the devil's name are you? What do you mean by this sort of thing? Somehow I've banked on you; I've gone to all sorts of fool lengths and—I say, who are you?"

"Will you let me pass, Mr. Dorn?" she said, as cool as ice. "So far, having answered your first question, I fail to see why you should be interested further. But out of the over-flowing goodness of my heart, I'll warn you of one thing: I'm here to stay, and this place is going to belong to me before I'm through, and you—you can go right to thunder!"

She tried to thrust by. He caught her by the arm, turning her around so that she faced him.

"I know who you are," he said, remembering Diana. "You are a girl named Lorna all right; maybe that's what put the Lorna Kent idea into your head in the first place. But you're Lorna Brown! And now am I right?"

Her eyes opened up, big and round with astonishment. "Lorna Brown? Why, yes I am. But how on earth you know—"

She broke free and fled through the grove and up to the house. He did not attempt to hold her, did not at the moment wish to follow her. He didn't even watch her go, and she didn't look back but ran as though she felt he were close behind her. He heard the quick light patter of her feet going up the steps, then the slam of a door. And still he stood where he was, staring down into the darkening creek, thinking. There was, he judged, much to think about.

"I was always a fool anyhow," he muttered once. "Just after Bundy gets through making a monkey out of me I take this wild chance on her!" In profound disgust he reminded himself of one of his many nicknames, one which now appeared to fit him. "Born-a-Dorn," he grunted.

For one thing, a devil of a lot of money had been spent here on Palm Ranch, Bill Dorn's money, spent freely because he believed in her. True, she hadn't taken a cent of it for her own use; it had gone into the ranch itself. Just the same—if Mike Bundy did succeed in gathering the place in—all this would go to Mike Bundy.

For another thing, he had allowed himself to grow to think a lot of this Lorna Brown. "Always taking fool chances, that's me, Born-a-Dorn. Why haven't we got a good mule on this job? I'd go and poke a stick at him until he kicked me to death."

It was dark before he left the creek. He went, walking slowly, to a spot from which he could get a good look at Halfway, all gay and bright with a score of lamplit windows. Anyhow she had made the prettiest little bit of a town he had ever seen. He'd have to give her credit for that.

He turned back slowly toward the ranch house. It was not too dark for him to make out the string of freight wagons which, heavily laden, had arrived from Liberty in the late afternoon, which had stopped here for the night as usual, breaking the trip to County Line. Well, they represented a venture that was paying; its profits were steady and about twice as big as he had hoped in the beginning. He shook his head and his sigh came pretty close to being a groan. If this Lorna girl was no longer to have a hand in all this, a good part of his interest was going to go with her. Funny, what a girl could do to a man.

He had almost reached the house when he came to a sudden involuntary stop, arrested by the sound of voices within—Lorna's voice and Cap Jinks'—pulled up short by Lorna's laughter. She was laughing as though this were the happiest, most carefree evening of her lifetime. And that, altogether inexplicable to Bill Dorn, was what stopped him dead in his tracks and pulled the heavy scowl back upon his brows.

"There's no understanding a girl like that!"

It might have been two minutes that he stood there, three minutes even. Then the door opened and he saw old Cap framed in it, his disgraceful old Stetson crumpled in one hand while his other held Lorna's in a lingering good night. Then Jinks came out and down the steps, walking like a boy, and the door closed after him, and he blundered full tilt into Bill Dorn.

"What in the devil can she find to laugh at like that?" demanded Dorn.

"Oh, hello, Will. I jus' got here an' am pokin' over to Halfway to wrastle a late supper out'n Wong. Didn't see you, Will. What are you hangin' aroun' out here for? Let's see, you asked me something. Lorny's real cute, Will. An' she's a humdinger, too. An' she darn near made even me laugh that ain't et supper yet. An' still an' ever I'm dinged if I could see anything funny in what she said!"

"What *did* she say?"

"We was talkin' about this puzzle of who was the real Lorny Kent an' who wasn't. She ups an' tells me. 'I ain't Lorny Kent an' never was,' she tells me. Then I says, gogglin' sort of, 'Hell's bells! Then that girl down to Liberty was!' An' she says, sharp an' sudden, 'No, she wasn't nothin' of the sort!' Then I says, 'Then who in blazes was she?' An' she says, 'I dunno.' An' I asks, 'Then how in thunder do you know she *wasn't* the real Lorny Kent?' An' you couldn't guess what she says to that, Will! Not in a thousand years you couldn't guess!"

"All right, tell me then."

Old Cap snagged him by the arm with fingers which nipped him like a crab's pinchers.

"She says to me—an' then she starts laughin'!—she says, 'She wasn't Lorny Kent because there isn't any Lorny Kent and never was!' An' what do you say to that?"

Dorn's frown didn't come off. He removed Jinks' hand and said only: "You better toddle along to your supper, old-timer. When I know what else to say I'll tell you."

So Jinks went his way, and for a time Bill Dorn stood where he was, staring at the house with its closed door and lighted windows.

Then he went up purposefully to the door, and knocked just as purposefully.

"It's time you and I had a good talk, with no monkey business," he said when she let him in.

"I'd love it!" cried Lorna, very gay. "What shall we talk about? There are so many interesting topics of conversation. Suppose I suggest that we discuss the problem, How old is a rooster? And *may* I take your hat, Mr. Dorn?"

He said quite soberly, "Do you mind if we skip the nonsense this time?"

Lorna opened up her eyes big at him. "But surely, Mr. Dorn, you don't call it nonsense about a rooster? Josefa was asking me. She said, 'When it's first born you call it a chick, and when it's grown up enough to run all over the place with the rest of them, you call it a chicken, and after a while you call it a rooster. Just when—'"

"What did you mean by telling Jinks just now there never was any Lorna Kent?"

"So he told you?" She made lovely arches of her brows, round limpid mystery-pools of her eyes, a sort of rosebud of her mouth. "The gabby old thing! He promised not to tell."

"I could shake you until your teeth chattered," said Bill Dorn, and meant every word.

It had not yet come to be fashionable to say, "Oh, yeah?" so Lorna said, "Is *that* so?" Never was a girl more in the mood to tease and tantalize a man, never a man more prone to an irritated response. Perhaps he would have caught her by the shoulders and shaken her, but it was just then that the explosion occurred which shook this upper end of Palm Ranch like an earthquake. There was a booming roar which shocked the eardrums, and the floor trembled.

They could only stare at each other, speechless. And before either found a word to say the second explosion came. By that time both were running to the door, and Josefa came scurrying in from her room, screeching in terror.

From the porch they heard men's voices shouting, some from the stable yard, some heard faintly even from Halfway; and they saw a great angry yet beautiful flame shoot up from the barn. Next came a cracking of rifle and pistol shots, mostly from Halfway, though there were other shots being fired somewhere beyond the blazing barn. And on top of all this, as though Palm Ranch were a victim of spontaneous combustion, bright lights of fire flared up in several other places.

Lorna didn't in the least realize that she was clinging to Bill Dorn's rigid arm with both hands. She said in an awed, frightened voice: "What is it? What is happening?"

It dawned on him first, and he shook her off and ran down the steps, racing toward the barn. He was yanking his gun out of its holster as he ran, but bethought himself to yell back at her without stopping or turning:

"Go back into the house! It's a raid—it's that damned Mike Bundy burning us down."

She called something to him. He didn't even hear. He heard the snarling of guns and only prayed to be in time to take a hand.

XIII

A<small>S</small> D<small>ORN</small> ran he made out that fires were blazing in several places, and he saw the vague figures of running men. Two or three sped around the corral to vanish behind the barn. They were yelling and shooting as they ran; he shouted to them but held his own fire, since it was impossible to know whether these were the raiders or some of his own men pursuing them.

Never checking his speed he saw that three of his freight wagons, cargo-full, were blazing; that the big hay-filled barn was afire; that a red glow stood up against the sky above Halfway. Then, coming into the area lighted by the burning wagons he saw a man half lying, half crouching on the ground. The man heard and saw him and called weakly yet in desperate earnestness: "Go get 'em, Bill! Give 'em hell."

Dorn recognized the voice, knew that the man was Curly O'Connor, badly hurt, saw Curly sag and melt down into the ground, but kept on running. But he shouted back: "Take it easy, Curly. We'll be with you right away."

Before he saw the raiders, in full flight now, he heard beyond the barn the hammering of horses' hoofs and shouts of challenge and defiance and a continued rattle of shots and then one long thin scream of agony—and on top of the scream a shout of victorious laughter. Already another man than Curly O'Connor had got in the way of a bullet, but as yet Dorn could not guess to which party he belonged.

Then he saw the two or three of his own men, Duke Jones and Bud Williams and a new hand or two, running out into the north pasture, firing as they ran after a small knot of rapidly vanishing riders. At first Dorn thought there were a hundred of them; then he made out that there were only a dozen riders at most. The rest were the Palm Ranch horses being stampeded. Already the fugitives were as good as out of range, yet he emptied his six shooter along with the vials of his wrath after them.

"They got Curly, damn 'em," said Bud Williams, his empty rifle hot in his hands.

"I know," said Dorn hurriedly. "One of you boys hurry back and see what you can do for him—"

"They're still fightin' over to Halfway," said Duke Jones, and started off in the direction of the fire and uproar over there, just out of sight under the brow of the hill though flame and smoke smudged the sky above. "Who was it yelled just now, like he'd been hit?" demanded Dorn.

Duke Jones laughed. "One of them damn nightriders. Me, I knocked him out'n his saddle an' he's still layin' where I set him down."

They all ran, the four of them, to see what was

happening at Halfway. Curly would have to wait; so would the man whom Duke Jones had shot. Sudden Bill Dorn led the way and kept the lead and increased it, such terrible anger burning into his vitals as he had never yet experienced in his life—not even when he had first gone to fight it out with Mike Bundy that day down in Nacional. Those explosions still rang in his ears as did the choking voice of Curly O'Connor; and now with his back to the blazing barn, its flames still lived where they had seared themselves on his eyeballs. As he raced along toward Halfway the glow in the sky became ruby-red and stood up higher and spread out wider, and he knew that before dawn Lorna's pretty little town would be only a memory recorded in ash heaps. Again he could only pray to arrive in time; again, having filled his empty gun as he ran, he arrived only to unload it and the last dregs of his wrath upon a scattering, fleeing half dozen riders, vanishing like their fellows into the darkness of the north.

Altogether there were now about twenty men having their headquarters at Halfway, and to a man—some having leaped startled from their beds—they were standing out in the yard, black wavering shapes against the background of the small raging hell of burning buildings. The first man he made out distinctly was old Cap'n Jinks dancing up and down like a maniac, as indeed he was for the moment, following up, with curses as

186

hot as the flying lead, the shots he had just fired from his old sawed-off shotgun.

"Anyone hurt here?" asked Dorn anxiously.

Wong, the Chinaman, began giggling.

"One man, he gettee plitty bad hurt, Missee Dorn. You come look-see. Me, I see um throw fire inside window; me ketch um heap quick."

Then Dorn saw the weapon the cook still held in his hand, a broad cleaver which he kept always as bright as new tin; its edge right now, though it gleamed in the conflagration, gleamed dully, and drops like ink gathered and dripped from it. One of the new hands, a young fellow named Martin, saw it and shuddered and said, "Oh, my God!"

"I show you," grinned the Chinaman.

Already men were doing all they could to fight the fire, not to put it out in the main building where it was already in full blossom, but to save if they could the smaller adjacent building. There was but little breeze blowing to fan the flames; they got buckets, found axes, used shovels to throw sand, and yet saw that what little would be left of Halfway was going to be as good as nothing.

"Let's see the man you mowed down, Wong," said Dorn.

At first, even when they stretched him out in the full light, no one knew him. Wong, still chuckling, told them: "You see? I fix um good! He no suck eggs in no more hens' nests!" The man's head had very nearly been split open by that

187

fearful kitchen weapon so dear to Wong's heart.

It wasn't a pretty sight. Martin, for one, turned away and was sick. Dorn forced himself to look closer. When he stood up there was a deadly note in his voice.

"It's like you'd lopped off one of Bundy's hands, Wong. It's Hank Smith. Dead as he is, it's the same as though he'd opened his mouth and said, 'This is Mike Bundy's job of work.' Well, we knew that already."

Wong, too delighted to miss the opportunity, said: "Mebbeso Mike Bundy tell 'em not to open his head about it all—but look at um!"

"What're we all standin' here for like hobbled jackasses?" shrilled old Jinks. "Let this damn place burn; it will anyhow. We c'n still ride a horse, can't we? We c'n ketch them devils up and blast 'em off the face of the earth."

Dorn turned away, walking back toward the barn thinking of Curly O'Connor.

"Come along with me, Cap," he said. "Curly's bad hurt, and you can do more for a man in his shape than any of the rest of us. You boys go out after the horses; likely it will take you an hour to get a rope on the first of them but hop to it. I'm riding over to see Mike Bundy, and any of you that feel like coming along are invited."

"We can't save any part of the barn," said Bud Williams, "but maybe we can pull one or two of the wagons out of the fire if we hurry."

"Hell take the wagons," said Dorn, curt with anger. "They're burning like shavings soaked in oil. Bundy as usual has done a thorough job."

"What was them big explosions?" asked the new man, Martin.

"That's so," muttered Duke Jones. It was to Dorn that he explained: "Our new dam's all blown up sky-high, Bill."

"Hell take the dam," said Dorn. "Our job's to get Curly to the house. Say, a couple of you boys poke out into the pasture and find out who it was that Duke shot out of the saddle. It might be—"

Cap Jinks said prayerfully, "Might even be Bundy himse'f! An' still alive!"

No such luck. It wasn't Bundy, but it was a man whom all of them knew well, and when they saw who he was they stood staring with incredulous eyes. But that was only after they had carried a dying Curly O'Connor in arms as gentle as cradles to the house, only after Curly was dead and covered with that final sheet which is like a fresh fall of snow on a new grave.

Lorna and Josefa heard them coming and came out on the porch clutching each other. Both were terribly frightened, and as for Lorna, she was immoderately distressed, almost hysterically grieved and angered. Before she knew that anyone was hurt the tragic realization was stamped upon her that her pretty little town, the thing into which she had put all her heart and soul and which she loved as a young mother loves her first baby, lay in ruins.

Cap'n Jinks hurried ahead of the slowly moving procession and put an arm about her shoulders, hushing her.

"Sh, Lorny," he said very gently. "Don't take on so. They're bringin' Curly in. He's been shot. Looks like he was dyin'."

Lorna clapped her hands to her mouth; she began to shiver and crouch closer into the old man's embrace as a new horror came into her eyes.

Curly had lost consciousness when they put him down, but before the end came he roused a little and looked about him and understood. He even tried to grin, figuring that a man ought to take whatever came as though he didn't mind. Then the tears burst from Lorna's eyes and streamed down her hot cheeks, and she came to his bedside and knelt and put her arms about him, trying so desperately to hold him back. He was dead, swiftly and without pain, before she knew. Of the men standing by, their hats in their hands, their faces blank and dead-looking except for their glowing eyes, it was Bill Dorn who stepped forward softly and drew her away.

Then from the pasture beyond the barn arrived three men, two of them Palm Ranch hands half supporting, half dragging the third man who was badly wounded yet who received small consideration from his captors. For he was that one of the fleeing raiders whom Duke Jones had so joyfully shot out of the saddle.

Every man in the room, Duke Jones included, looked at him in slack jawed wonder. It was one of Diana Villaga's brothers, young Juan.

There was blood on his dead-white face, but that was nothing. There was blood on his white shirt, making it sopping wet, and there could be no doubting that Duke Jones' bullet had come close to being the death of him. His hat was lost, hair and brow were grimy and damp.

The men holding him let him slump down into a chair. He sat with his spurred boots shoved out in front of him, his arms dangling at his sides, his chin on his breast.

"Juan!" exclaimed Dorn, to whom the boy's presence here in such a rôle was like a fist in the face. "You? One of the Villagas burning us out?"

Juan Villaga didn't answer, didn't so much as stir. Old Jinks stooped to peer into the white, blood-and-dirt-smeared face.

"The kid's been shot up pretty bad an' he's fell off'n his horse on his head," he said, straightening up. "Maybe he's faintin' an' maybe he's dyin', an' anyhow who's got a slug o' whisky to pour down him?"

Half a dozen willing hands reached toward their owners' hip pockets. But Juan Villaga wanted none of their ministrations. At last he raised his head and glared sullenly into the faces turned upon him, his dark smoldering eyes coming to rest at last on Bill Dorn's.

"It's worth getting shot, just to see everything you've got burned to the ground," he said distinctly enough, though it took will power to force the words out, so weak was he with so much blood drained out of him. Duke Jones' bullet had broken his right shoulder, had torn its bloody way out through the right side of his chest.

Lorna began to sway where she stood. Martin, the new hand, who could sympathize with her vertigo, caught her as she was falling and let her down on the bench against the wall. No one else even noticed the two of them.

Bill Dorn's face grew harder, sterner at every word the boy spoke.

"What made you decide to chip in with Mike Bundy against our crowd?" he asked in a level, utterly expressionless voice.

Already Juan's chin was lowering toward his chest, but again it came up, with an effort and slowly.

"Who told you Bundy was in on this?"

Dorn laughed at him. "If we needed any telling, Hank Smith told us!"

"Hank Smith? He told?"

"He's out there, dead," said Dorn. "And he wouldn't be out there and he wouldn't be dead unless he were Bundy's man."

192

Involuntarily Juan started to shrug, but a shrug now was impossible for him and he winced with pain.

"What do I care about Hank Smith? He was a dog anyhow."

"Yet you rode with him! Never mind that. Tell me, what have you got against me? I thought we were friends! And the rest of the Villagas—"

"All the Villagas hate you!" the young fellow burst out passionately. "They have hated you since you led them all to ruin. And do you think they would not like to see Bundy or any other man ruin you in your turn? Fool!"

"Then they knew about tonight? Your father knew? Your brother Ramon was perhaps with you? Your sister Diana knew?"

"They did not know," muttered Juan, more sullen than ever. "I am the only one of the Villagas who meant to do something. And they will never know I came here tonight until you run and tell them."

Dorn turned away feeling somehow sick at heart.

"I'll never tell them, Juan," he said wearily. "It's nothing to me. If you pull through alive you can go home and tell them what lies you like." But perplexed he swung about to demand sharply: "Still I don't get any sense out of this! If you say I helped ruin your father, how about Mike Bundy? Why should you chip in on his side of the row?"

Juan Villaga, head down again, didn't even make the effort to lift his eyes.

"Don Michael is my friend," he said sullenly. "And now do you want to keep me here? Or shall I go?"

"The nerve of him!" exploded from an irate Bud Williams. "Here's our place torn all to hell's smithereens, here's our freight wagons and thousands of freight gone up in smoke, here's our dam wrecked and—and—" He choked over it, holding it to the last, because he and Curly O'Connor had been close together like Siamese twins for years, and it was hard so early to speak Curly's name; but he shot it out clearly enough: "Here's Curly dead. And this greaser Villaga wants to go home! By God, he'll go home on the end of a rope!"

Dorn didn't have much to say. Of a sudden he felt numb inside and out. If Bud, Curly's best friend, wanted Juan Villaga hanged as high as the moon, why not?

Juan Villaga stood up, though shakily.

"You call me greaser?" he said through bared teeth. It was the final insult to one of his fine strain of blood. He overlooked the threat of hanging.

"Oh, hell, let him go," said old Jinks. "He's only a kid anyhow; likewise he's mos' likely to bleed to death before he gets anywhere. Besides you can't blame him, for a Villaga ain't got any more sense than a little gray seed tick. On top of all which, it ain't much fun killin' a man as sick as he is, an' it's never much fun killin' a skunk. C'm'on, boys. We got us some ridin' to do, like Will says. The other fellers must of rounded up the horses by now."

Juan Villaga took his chance and walked out of the room with none to stay him. He lurched at the door and came up with a grunt of pain against the jamb. Jinks hurried forward to steady him.

"You pesky little bantam rooster," he growled deep down in his thin brown throat, "can't you see you're bleedin' to death? And besides, where'n hell's your horse? Here, wait a shake." He turned and called to Josefa who, chalky white, was talking voicelessly to herself in a corner. "Bring me some rags to tie this kid up, likewise some whisky. He's only a pup anyhow that thinks he's a grown he-dog."

"Damn you!" cried the boy. "Let me go!"

They let him go; they even got him a horse—that was after the stampeded stock was at last hazed back into the corrals—and some man helped him up into the saddle. Bud Williams had nothing further to say.

Then the Palm Ranch hands, pretty nearly to the last man, prepared to ride. Several rode bareback that night, because so many saddles had gone up in the gush of fire. Even Wong, though he hated and feared all horseflesh, elected to join the party; he carried a rifle slung over his shoulders by its strap, but he carried his dependable cleaver too.

Lorna came running after Bill Dorn. She had come close to fainting dead away when they brought Juan Villaga in, but now was tinglingly alive from head to foot; Dorn saw the bright sparkle of her eyes even in the starlight. She began speaking passionately, swept back into the bitter and rebellious mood that had gripped her before Villaga's coming, before Curly's death.

"I told you once not to kill Mike Bundy!"

"Take it easy, Lorna," said Dorn curtly yet not altogether without sympathetic understanding. "You go back to the house. This is our part of the day's work."

"He has ruined in a night all we have worked for so long! Oh, Bill! He has buildings to burn; burn them! He has wagons to destroy, and freight; burn and burn and burn them! He has blood to spill—like poor Curly—"

"Lorna—"

"Oh, Bill! My little town that was so beautiful, that was going to mean so much to so many people—"

He put his hand like a big friendly paw on her shoulder, heard her burst into violent weeping, then broke into a run to join the men who had gone on ahead.

XIV

Exac'ly what you got in mind, Will?" asked Jinks. "Them polecats that burned us out has got anyhow an hour head start on us. Mos' likely, too, they've scattered as many ways as there's men among 'em."

"We're going straight to County Line," said Dorn as he went up to his horse's bare back. Since there were not saddles for all, he was not going to take it any easier than the men he asked to follow him. "We'll find Bundy there, whether he rode with his pack or held back to build himself an alibi."

"An' when you find Bundy?" Jinks demanded.

Bill Dorn only snorted, snuggled his rifle up under his left arm and they were off and away, fourteen men of them headed for the Blue Smokes on as grim an errand as any man of them had ever committed himself to. They rode with anger and hot impatience in their hearts, yet they guarded against undue haste at the jump, looking ahead to the considerable distance to be covered.

And as they rode they now and then looked back, all of them at one time and another, saving two men alone. Those who twisted their heads about to watch the angry red banners of flame standing sky high above the hay-filled barn, and after distance and rolling hills shut out sight of the flames to mark the blood-red glow in the sky,

197

spoke among themselves seldom and always in undertones. Those who never once spoke and never looked back were Sudden Bill Dorn, every thought centered on Mike Bundy, and Bud Williams who had ridden so many a time to a fight or a frolic—they were much alike!—with Curly O'Connor at his elbow.

Straight to Mike Bundy's big barn of a casino Bill Dorn led the way, and he and his following paid not the least attention to the crowd so swiftly gathering or to the storm of questions shouted at them. At the rear of the building Dorn slid from his horse's back and began pounding on the door with the butt of his rifle. It was here that Bundy had his County Line headquarters.

The encamped gold seekers, adventurers and general riffraff that made up the place, continued to swarm out, some dressed with all on save the boots they had kicked off to tumble into their bunks, some in nightshirts or other odds and ends of night regalia, all with confused eyes and tumbled hair, many clutching guns. And though they continued to shout questions and got never a word of answer from the hard-eyed, tight-lipped little knot of mounted men, almost instantly word flew about:

"It's Sudden Bill and he's gunnin' for Mike Bundy!—It's Roll-Along Dorn with blood in his eye an' a gang at his back, an' they're goin' to lynch Bundy!"

Dorn hammered the door off its hinges and stepped inside, taking his chance with the inner dark and with Bundy's swift assault, not stopping an instant for cool thought, caring for but one thing just then. The room was empty. He struck a match; Bundy's bed hadn't even been slept in.

As he stepped outside again, the crowd, indistinct figures in the faint uncertain light of just-before-dawn, their faces mere gray blurs, indistinguishable, he was greeted by a silence so heavy that you knew men had momentarily stopped breathing.

"Where's Bundy?" asked Dorn. "Does anyone know where Bundy is?"

Out of the dark and from a distance a high-pitched voice sounding like an adolescent boy's, spoke up:

"He ain't here! He ain't been in camp for two-three days."

His voice broke like a young rooster's that is learning to crow, and men laughed all about him. But they stopped laughing almost before they had started. Duke Jones muttered, angry and disgusted: "He's hidin' some place, the rat. Much good that'll do him."

He came jingling down from his saddle; Bud Williams struck ground together with him and both came the few steps to where Bill Dorn stood at the rear door of Bundy's gambling place.

"The damn place burns, don't she, Bill?" said Bud, already hunting for matches.

"You're damn right she burns," said Dorn. "Come ahead."

He turned back into Bundy's room, struck another match and lighted the lamp on a small marble topped table. Duke Jones found the door, leading from this room into a sort of hallway between flimsy board partitions that reached half way to the ceiling, slipped a bolt back and led the way on into the big main room. To make their work easier they lighted a couple of other lamps; the yellow light made rather a mystery of the crude empty barnlike place but showed them the long pine bar, the barrels and bottles behind it, card tables, roulette wheels, various gambling layouts, and all the untidy clutter of such a place at such an hour.

Bud Williams stepped behind the bar. He selected with care the finest bottle of whisky he could find; he said in the odd voice of a man who speaks with his teeth hard set, "Here's to Curly O'Connor!" and with the swipe of that one bottle he smashed a whole line of its fellows so that liquor gushed like water leaping among the clinking particles of glass.

By this time six or eight of the other Palm Ranch men had joined them, leaving their fellows to hold their horses and to keep an eye on the gawking, bewildered onlookers as yet rooted like so many trees in their places. They went to work busily and for the most part in silence. They gathered scraps of paper, smashed flimsy tables and benches, made neat little piles of inflammable materials in a dozen places where they would do the most good. There were a dozen kerosene lamps in the place; they emptied the oil on their fuel piles. One of them, a long-throated, thirsty-looking new hand named Phil Bowton, looked longingly at the array of bottles, then yielded to temptation and started to help himself. Duke Jones happened to be close by and knocked the thing out of his hand.

They did their work swiftly yet methodically. Never a fire was lighted until Bill Dorn said the word. His was the first match to start a rush of flame up a dry pine wall. He said, "All right, boys. Let her go."

As flames caught everywhere the Palm Ranch men made haste to retreat as far as the doorways. There they stood a while watching. Dorn lifted his rifle and started shooting holes in whisky barrels. It was too rare a sport not to be entered into by the others. Bullets raked down lines of glittering, rosily flushed bottles, and the tongues of fire lapped up the spilled liquor and seemed to go drunk on it.

"Let's go," commanded Dorn, and they hurried out just as a tremendous roar burst from the no longer sleepy-eyed, no longer mystified and uncertain denizens of County Line. They saw what they knew now to be a pretty severe body blow directed at Mike Bundy, and scarcely a man of them cared about that; it was a joke on Bundy for them to guffaw over. But in the same act, once their awakened brains started functioning, they saw a punch in the thirsty midriffs for themselves. Where in blue thunder were they going to get the next drink? Many were the throats which already, in anticipation of the first morning glass, grew scratchily dry. And so their complacency of one moment became an angry resentment of the next.

"Let's high-tail the hell out'n here," admonished Cap'n Jinks. "We've done our noble deed an' done it manful, but something sort of whispers in my good ear this ain't no fit place to linger in!"

They went to their horses and mounted, and for a moment the fourteen of them, in a small compact knot bristling with rifle barrels that shone emphatically in the enormous bonfire already bursting out everywhere through flimsy walls and shaky roof, sat where they were. They were going in a moment, but they were not exactly anxious to run away from anybody. If any here were over eager to start something, that must mean that they chose to side with Bundy. *Bueno*; let 'em start something.

The crowd, grown angry, yet lacking any motivating community spirit, lacked any leader to mold the flare of their wrath into one red-hot spearhead, and so they simply shouted and then muttered and all the while watched Dorn's party narrowly.

There was light aplenty now, and in it Dorn waved his hat over his head in a command for attention, then made the curt explanation which he deemed these men had coming to them.

"Tonight Bundy burned us out over at Palm Ranch," he told them. "One of his crowd killed Curly O'Connor. We had the luck to kill Hank Smith. Now we're burning Bundy out here or anywhere else we can find him.—Come ahead boys; let's go."

"Hi!" yelled a voice, and a man came elbowing, ramming his way forward. "Wait a shake, Bill."

It was Stock Morgan. He was wearing a long-tailed white flannel nightgown and a pair of boots and a rifle. Close behind him came Ken Fairchild, fully dressed save for hat and boots.

"You say they killed Curly?" asked Morgan when he and Ken had come close. Dorn nodded curtly. Morgan held his silence a moment, perhaps in brief tribute to a man for whom he had a great fondness, perhaps thinking what to say next. Before he spoke further, Dorn asked, "It's true that Bundy isn't here, Morg?"

"Yes, Bill. He's been keepin' himself under cover for a couple of days. We might have known he had something like this on the fire. Say, Bill, wait a shake for us will you? Until I can get some clothes on? Me and Ken are ridin' with you; so I reckon are Johnnie Sharp and ol' Middleton."

"We won't wait here," said Dorn. "We'll ride out a mile or two and wait there for you."

"Which way, Bill?"

"Toward Palm Ranch until we fork off. I'll tell you when you join us, Morg."

"Bueno," said Morgan, and went elbowing back through the crowd, the tail of his nightgown held up daintily in one hand like a lady's train, his hairy shanks showing about the tops of his cowboy half-boots. With him went Ken Fairchild without having spoken a word.

And now when Dorn said again, "Let's go," the crowd opened up a lane as he headed his horse out of camp, and he and his following went out of County Line as they had come, with the drum-roll of hammering hoofs. They splashed across Silver Creek and headed back down the valley and this time not a man of them, with neither Bill Dorn nor Bud Williams excepted, failed to turn his head and look back with grim satisfaction on the work their hands had wrought, a lovely giant flower of red and yellow fire in full blossom against the most beautiful cloud bank of smoke any man of them had ever seen, smoke as black as midnight, as white as snow, streaked in one place with rose lights, become opalescent in another, as crimson as blood where a certain petal of fire incarnadined it.

"I only hope Bundy was hidin' somewhere aroun' camp," sighed Cap'n Jinks. "I'd hate for him to miss seein' this."

The new hand, Phil Bowton, crowded his horse up alongside Duke Jones'.

"What'n hell did you want to do that for?" he asked petulantly. And when Duke didn't know what he was talking about he added, "Why'd you knock that bottle o' hooch out o' my hands?"

"Belonged to Bundy," said Duke. "He's no friend of ours."

Out of sight of County Line, a mile or two on their way as Dorn had promised, they stopped to wait for Morgan and Fairchild and any that might elect to join their party. Some of the men smoked and talked among themselves; Dorn neither smoked nor spoke but sat apart brooding. Again and again he turned his eyes toward the ruddy skyline over County Line, but the red glow there could no longer wipe out of his memory the destructive flame back at the ranch.

He pulled himself up out of a gloomy reverie only when he heard horses coming on. Here were Morgan and Ken, and with them were both Sharp and Middleton. Every man carried a rifle as well as his belt gun and on their faces was the same look that had stamped itself on the faces of the men already with Dorn; the day was bright enough now to read their expressions, and they boded no great good to Mike Bundy. Every one of these men, in one way and another, was interested in making a going concern of Palm Ranch and its freight lines.

As they pressed on again, eighteen men strong now, Stock Morgan rode at Dorn's side and the two had much to say to each other, talking steadily for a good half hour. Morgan wanted full details of the happening at the ranch and got them succinctly and in such fashion from a man whose blood was boiling that the hearer's blood began to simmer as well.

"Bundy wants killin'," said Morgan. "A trick like that—"

"I heard a horse squealing, Morg. I'm afraid some of our stock got burned to death in the barn."

They rode in the fresh new day, with the skies turning a soft light blue, to a spot within half a dozen miles of Palm Ranch. There they found the other set of wheel tracks, a sandy road running down through the low hills to the southwest, the new road made by Bundy's teams hauling from Liberty and Nacional, skirting the southern end of the ranch. They reined into Bundy's road.

"They camp overnight at the old Grapevine place, you know," said Morgan. "It's the only water they can get at handy on that pull."

Dorn nodded; yes, he knew. It was toward the Grapevine that they rode now. They didn't hurry; there was no call for haste, and their horses had already carried them a long journey; further, the men who rode without saddles were feeling themselves over for sore spots, although now and again their companions spelled them, swapping mounts.

Dorn had asked where Bundy was; Morgan didn't know. Bundy, with Hank Smith and Mex Fontana, had ridden out of County Line one late evening two or three days before and none of the three had returned, so far as Morgan knew.

"He's makin' himself an alibi, the fox! Mos' likely he'll have a dozen lyin' polecats to swear he was down to Nacional or some such place las' night and a coupla nights before."

"Sure," nodded Dorn wearily. "Sure."

They jogged along for a couple of hours and the sun was high and hot when far off beyond the billowy sand ridges they saw the dust cloud.

"If we was playin' this hand Bundy's way, if you'd played it his way at County Line, we'd wear masks for this job," said Morgan.

Dorn didn't even trouble to nod or shake his head. Already his eyes, beginning to show flecks of red, were straining into the distance, trying to make out the laboring teams. He was hoping that Bundy's whole string of wagons was on the road this morning, that every wagon was high heaped with a cargo of value. Most of all he was hoping that Mike Bundy himself might be returning with his teams.

The wagons swung into view, a long line of them, Bundy's entire string of seven freighters, each pulled by six sweating horses. They were strung out over a mile of sandy road; from the way the horses shoved their necks into their collars and strained in the traces it was clear to see that the fleet of big Studebakers was heavy-loaded. Across the distance could be heard the lazy swearing voices of the drivers and the pistol-like cracks of their writhing blacksnakes.

The first driver stopped his team when he saw that the riders who were almost on top of him had no intention of turning out. The sun was in his eyes and it was a moment before he made out any faces that he recognized. Then he said, "Oh, hello, Morg. Hello, Bill."

While the others stopped, Morgan and Dorn rode one on each side to have a word with him. He was a man both knew well, Jim Bedloe who had worked for other men all his life, easy-going, unambitious, generally dependable and likable.

"The wagons don't go any farther this trip, Jim," said Dorn. "Better get down and unhook your team."

There was a rifle on the seat by Bedloe. He must have understood from Dorn's tone and from the look on his face, if not from his words themselves, yet he made no gesture toward his weapon. It is unlikely that he even thought of such a thing.

"What's up, Bill?" he said, puzzled.

"Bundy has asked for a showdown. He's getting it. Where is Bundy, Jim? Do you know?"

"He was in Liberty when we left yesterday. Heard him say he had just come up from Nacional where he'd been two-three days on business."

Morgan laughed. "I'll bet he's been tellin' every man, woman an' child where he's been! He's lyin', Jim. His crowd burnt out Palm Ranch las' night. Better pile down an' pry your horses loose."

Bedloe stared a long while, at Morgan, at Dorn, then at the grave-faced quiet crowd in the road ahead of him. He shook his head, locked his brake, threw his reins, gathered up his rifle and coat and a quart bottle in a box at his feet, and climbed down over the wheel.

"If there's anything in the wagon that belongs to you, better snag it out," Morgan suggested.

"There's a saddle," said Bedloe. "I'll maybe use it, huh?"

A couple of the mounted men got down, said, "Hello, Jim," in a casual sort of way and helped him with his team. He got his saddle out, threw it on the back of one of his leaders and moved his horses some little distance away, stopping there to watch interestedly. Dorn too got down, climbed up into the wagon, accepted the handfuls of dry grass and brushwood that were passed up to him and started a blaze in the dead center of the load;

in this dry, hot country almost anything but metals and water would burn, and you didn't have to bother with fanning the blaze. The gray smoke stood straight up, the flames caught and Dorn jumped down.

"Better back off, boys," he said as he swung up to his horse's back again. "There may be powder kegs aboard."

As they had treated the first wagon, so, one after another, did they treat the six others. Their drivers were helpless; one or two took the thing rather tragically; a youngster who carried a shotgun on the seat by him caught it up and vowed he'd blow their damn heads off. But in the end no shot was fired; each of the six drivers mounted one of his draft horses and rode on toward County Line, leading the rest of his harnessed team. They saw their wagons left abandoned, the smoke standing aloft, the fire eating all that it could, spoiling everything. Only one of the wagons carried explosives; thunderously it burst into a hundred pieces and the roar was heard miles away. "It's a good job well done," said John Sharp. "Now what, Bill? S'pose we'd find Mike Bundy down to Liberty like Jim said?"

Dorn shook his head. The job, good or bad, was certainly well done. "We've got to go back to the ranch, John. After what we've pulled off this morning we can look out for a comeback from Bundy, I suppose. And that girl is there pretty much alone—and there's another job of work, not so pleasant, to get done."

He was thinking of Curly O'Connor. And for the first time he realized that these had not been pleasant hours for Lorna, with Curly lying there waiting ever so patiently to be carried to his long resting place.

"We'll ride along," said Morgan, and spoke for them all. "Looks like we're goin' to be up against a pretty stiff proposition, buildin' from the ground again."

"Let's go," said Dorn.

Their following broke down into small groups of two or three men riding together, stringing out a mile or more before they came to journey's end. Dorn waxed more and more impatient and soon he and Bud Williams were far ahead of the more leisurely riders. Thus the two arrived alone at the ranch house. Their eyes from afar had marked the faint smudges of smoke still staining the gray-blue sky, and from anear took gloomy stock of what was left of the barnyard buildings and of little Halfway. They noticed a saddled horse in the yard, its reins down over its head.

"That's a Villaga horse!" said Dorn, and the discovery did nothing to dissipate the frown dragging his heavy brows down. His thought was, "Now here's further hell to pay for last night, for Juan getting home half dead if he ever got there at all." And he was prepared to see Diana Villaga burst out of the house at the sound of oncoming hoofbeats.

Through the vines pendant from the wide eaves he glimpsed someone standing on the porch. It was a girl, but it was Lorna and she came running down the steps and down the slope to meet him. There was someone else there on the porch too, and this one followed more slowly into the yard, waiting there. It was Ramon Villaga, Diana's and Juan's brother.

Lorna fairly flew to the meeting. Her eyes looked enormous and Bill Dorn felt that it was not alone the loss and shock and horror of last night that put this look into them but some new experience—something perhaps connected with Ramon Villaga's visit.

"Oh, Bill!" she gasped, and reached up and twined her fingers in his horse's mane in such fashion that he, seeing how her hand shook, put his own down over it, hard and steady.

"You're all on edge, Lorna."

There was little patience in any Villaga at any time, none at all in Ramon this morning. Seeing Dorn stop he came forward, walking swiftly. A score of steps away Dorn read the desperation in the boy's face that was so white and drawn, and instantly he leaped to the conclusion that Juan was dead, that Ramon came now to square the deal for his brother. But then, so eloquent do human eyes and faces grow at certain moments of

212

the profoundest stress, another keen glance told him that, though there might well be murder in Ramon Villaga's heart, there was something else which bulked above it, which held the hot impulse in check.

"Hello, Ramon," he said evenly, and added, before Ramon had time to return his greeting or make clear that he did not intend to, "Is Juan all right?"

Ramon coming to a stop a few feet away was as stiff as ever a Villaga could be.

"My brother, Señor, is alive; thank you for asking," he said as formally as though to an utter stranger, and accompanied his words with as old fashioned a bow as even Don Francisco could have achieved. "Or perhaps I should say that he was alive when I left home." His eyes, for all their unwinking steadiness, were passionately charged with hate, with bitterness, with an unspeakable anguish. "But I did not come here to speak of him. It is hard, Señor Dorn, to ask a favor of you, yet that is what I must do. My sister sent me. She asks if you will come to see her immediately."

"Why should I come to her?" snapped Dorn. At another time he might have been patient with the boy, but not today. "What does Diana want? Why doesn't she come over here?"

"I had rather that you did not ask me those questions," muttered Ramon.

Dorn shrugged heavily. "Suit yourself. Anyhow

I'm not going. Good Lord, man!" he burst out angrily. "Can't you see I've enough to do here?"

Ramon swallowed, bit his lip and swallowed again.

"My sister, I am afraid, Señor, is dying," he said thickly. "It is only because hers is a dying request that I—"

Dorn's exclamation of utter amazement cut him short.

"Dying? Diana! Ramon, what are you talking about? Have you gone crazy?"

"Perhaps." Ramon in his turn assayed a shrug, but his weary shoulders merely twitched. "Now you have heard her request I will give you her message. She says that unless already you have taken your revenge on Don Michael, you are to hold your hand until you have talked with her."

"I haven't found Bundy yet, but I've burned his damned dance-hall gambling joint to the ground," Dorn flared out. "And I've burnt his whole string of freight wagons. Does that answer you?"

"It is going to make bad matters much worse, that is all."

"But you haven't told me what is wrong with Diana!"

Still looking him steadily in the eye Ramon said quite clearly: "Her trouble is like my brother's, Señor."

Dorn came down from his horse in a flash and

caught Ramon by both shoulders, glaring into his eyes with eyes no less terrible. "You mean that she too rode here to burn us out last night?" he shouted.

"You can ask her your questions, Señor—if you arrive in time to ask her anything. Or do you refuse to come?"

"Of course I'm coming! I'm on my way the minute I can saddle a fresh horse."

XV

AT THE Hacienda Villaga an Indian girl, red-eyed and distressed looking, ushered Bill Dorn into the patio, saying, hardly above a tremulous whisper, "Señorita Villaga is waiting for you there, Señor."

On a couch among cushions in the rim of the shade, with golden flecks of sunshine shimmering on the gaily colored flowers and the fresh clean shrubbery beyond her, lay Diana. He hurried to her and stood looking down at her, a pang of commiseration in his heart. Her cheeks were like magnolia petals for waxy whiteness; her large eyes now seemed altogether too big for her small face and glittered like black diamonds. She had some sort of scarlet robe wrapped around her and was covered to the waist by a silken spread, a gay thing of mixed oriental coloring. A crumpled white blossom lay on the pillow near her head; it had fallen from her rich midnight mane of hair.

"Diana!"

She lay very still, looking at him, without speaking, without smiling. One hand drooped at her side; it too looked to be carved of wax, and he could see the faint throb of a blue pulse.

"Diana! Tell me! Ramon wouldn't talk. I know so little. Are you badly hurt?"

Still for a little while she did not speak. She was trying to think clearly, she was gathering her strength. And she kept looking at him in that queer, intent way as though he were some strange sort of stranger and she was bent on making him out. So he drew a garden chair up to the side of her couch and sat down, waiting for her. He made a gesture as though to put his hand out to hers, but though she didn't move, being too weak for that, yet he saw that inwardly she winced. Perhaps her pallid mouth hardened ever so slightly or the muscles about her eyes tightened.

"I hate you so!" said Diana.

He scarcely caught the words, though he leaned closer as he saw her lips part; her voice, once such silver bell music for sweet clearness, was now little better than a faint harsh whisper. But had he missed the words entirely he must have read the hate in her eyes.

He said swiftly and very gently: "Never mind that right now, Diana. We can talk of such things later, when you're strong again. Will you tell me how you were hurt and how badly? Have you had a doctor, and—"

A faint angry shadow touched her jet black brows.

"I had them bring me here—down to the *placita*—to die," she said. "It is nice here, no? One of your bullets last night at Palm Rancho—maybe from your gun, Don Beel?And Juanito, too! They will not tell me, but I know my Juanito is dying like me. Did I tell you, Señor Dorn, how I hate you?"

"But, Diana," said Dorn, very patient with her and feeling heart-stricken to see all her dash and verve and brightly dark brilliancy brought to this, "I did not know you and Juan were with Bundy's crowd—"

"Yes, I hate you. I wish I did not have to die, so I could live to see you suffer and die! I have always hated you, ever since I first saw Don Michael. For you knew I loved him and that he loved me—and you were always taking him away from me. So I hated you."

"I am sorry," said Dorn. He looked at her a long while levelly and searchingly. He said to himself, "I mustn't stay here talking with her, letting her use up her strength this way." So to her he added in a quietly matter-of-fact way: "Believe me, Diana, I am sorry. Some other time you and I are going to get this all straightened out. Not now, for you've got to rest and hurry to get well and—"

"Fool! Do you think I am a baby? Give me some wine."

On a little green weathered table, with a napkin thrown over them, were decanter, water jug and glasses. He poured for her a glass of the ruby red Villaga wine and held it to her lips. She managed to drink four or five swallows and thereafter spoke a hint more strongly.

"I live now for only two things," said Diana. "To talk with you, to say good-bye to my Michael who loves me as I love him. I want you to know that you never fooled us Villagas. I first, then all of us, knew you for the cheat and liar and robber you are. And you have worked so hard to make it seem that you are the honest one, Don Michael the rogue!"

"I am going now, Diana. Later—"

"You sit still, Beel Dorn! If you move I'm going to jump up and run after you until I drop down dead."

"All right," said Dorn heavily. "What else do you want to tell me?"

"Many things. First, you, through that sheriff of yours, are trying to make people think Don Michael killed that old prospector, Jake Fanning. He did not and you know it. One Eye Perez killed Fanning."

"That wouldn't surprise me. And someone killed Perez—"

"And that was not Don Michael! He did not even have his gun that night. But *you* know who killed Perez; it was that dance hall girl who lies when she says she is Lorna Kent."

"You seem to know—"

"Both Hank Smith and Mexico Fontana saw her kill him!"

"They're liars both, Diana, and you know that."

"Yes, *seguro*. But liars at times tell what is true. And now there is another thing which you have started people to say: That somebody killed the old lady Kent—and you will have them think that that too was done by Don Michael! And so I ask you this: How did it happen that her death came so quick after she made her will, leaving everything she had to her niece?"

"What do you know about any will?" he demanded.

"Was I not at her house the day she made it?" she shot back at him with a faint upflare of triumph. "When she sent the man to carry it to the banker in Liberty, did she not say to me: 'Well, that's done. I ought to have done it long ago. My niece Lorna won't have to be a pauper anyhow.'"

So that's where the will was, in Liberty at the bank. And now if Lorna Brown were only Lorna Kent—

"Then," said Diana, "this dance hall girl came. All that we know about her is that she's a cheap little liar and that in a fine rage she shot a man in the back. Had she been up at Palm Ranch before she showed up at Nacional? Who knows?"

"You mean that she killed Mrs. Kent?"

"Of course. Anyhow, Don Michael did not do it."

Bill Dorn meant to spare her everything, yet looking at her curiously he said involuntarily, the words slipping out:

"To you Bundy is perfect; above all crimes?"

"Yes! He is *muy caballero*. A good business man, yes; hard, yes. But every act of his is by daylight in the open!"

"Even the raid last night on Palm Ranch!"

Instantly he said it he was sorry. The look of death was in Diana's eyes and no matter what she said he was going to get up and go. But the instant she started to answer him he realized that this subject could not possibly have been avoided. For it was to speak of this more than anything else that Diana Villaga had summoned him.

"Michael Bundy did not raid Palm Ranch last night! He had nothing to do with that, and he did not know anything about it. It was I, Diana Villaga, who loves him so much and who hates you so much, that raided Palm Ranch! I and my brothers whom I made come along; I and the men that I talked to and used to my purpose. And if there hadn't been a blundering fool among us to start things before I gave the word, we'd have made a better, cleaner job of Halfway, and would have got away without a drop of our blood being spilled. But if you get ten men together you can be sure of one fool, maybe nine!"

He stared at her in amazement which was being slowly up-gathered into consternation. What she said was preposterous, and he wouldn't believe a word of it—yet when he watched her and listened to her and then sat staring into her eyes, he did believe every word. "It was not Michael Bundy. He had nothing to do with the raid on Palm Ranch. He was away and did not know anything about it. It was I, Diana Villaga! Because I love him so much, because I hate you so!"

"No!" said Dorn. "No! You may have gone along; that would be like you after all. But—"

"It was I! I alone who thought of it, who arranged it, who did it with a few blundering men to help. And I am glad!"

He did not want to be convinced. He was thinking: "Good God! Look at what I've done to Bundy today! And if he really had nothing to do with the raid—" His mind groped wildly, almost blindly for something to assure him that she must be lying. Then he thought of Hank Smith lying there at Halfway, his head split open by Wong's horrible weapon. He said sternly:

"Diana! You can't tell me this. I know! You see, one of the men left behind dead, was Hank Smith, Bundy's right hand man for all devilment—"

"Don Michael was away on business, I tell you. He has been away several days. He went to Nacional, to San Marco, to Liberty, to get more money. Hank Smith was left behind. And don't you think anyone can buy Hank Smith with a handful of pesos?"

Again, stubborn against believing what he already believed, he snatched at a straw. He said quietly, not wishing to be curt or stern, yet being both: "Anyone could buy Hank Smith with money, yes. But—"

"But the Villagas have no money! Not *una centavo*! Did you ever see Diana Villaga, Señor, when she was all dressed for a dance maybe, looking pretty in a white dress and wearing a long string of pearls? When the money of the Villagas went, did they not keep their fine name and their honor—and their few jewels? Those came to me from my great-great-great-great grandmama. I tore the string apart. Did you look in the dead Hank Smith's pockets?"

"If this is true—But it can't be! Why should you, you and your brothers—"

"My father, too, if he had been young like us! Why? I am going to tell you why. You stole Don Michael's thought. He was going to have a town there at Palm Ranch. He was going to have his freight wagons come that way. But you drove him out; you made his wagons go the long, long way around. *Bueno*; that hurt but it did not beat him! No one can beat my Don Michael! He is like a king. So he is going to make a change in his plan; he is going to bring freight down from the north, from San Marcos, and his wagons will come through Villaga Rancho! And so it is here, at Villaga, that we will have a town and all the things Palm Ranch is stealing from us! And I knew, if I burned your dirty houses to the ground and ruined all you had done, you would have no more money to go on with; and there would not be any town there to be a rival to our town. That is why, Señor Dorn!"

Her voice had sunk lower and lower so that at the end he could scarcely hear her; had he not watched her lips so intently some of the words must have escaped him. As it was he missed nothing. And when she had done he saw her eyes close, white wax lids with the faintest blue traceries, and he could see no pulse in throat or wrist or any stir of her breast in breathing. He feared her dead, slipping away so softly.

He wanted to ask, "Why do you tell me all this, Diana?" But already he saw her exhausted; that she was not dead he knew because her eyes came open again and were fixed on him as cold and black and unwinking as the eyes of a lidless snake. Such malevolence he had never seen; it put a chill ripple in his blood; he remembered with a start what Lorna had said once—it seemed long years ago! "She must carry a knife in her stocking! If some day she stabs you in the back—"

"I know," whispered Diana harshly. "I know your thought, Don Beel! You wonder why I tell you these things! It is because I want you to know and to remember always that it was I—I!—when you were making your last stand, who cut the ground out from under your clumsy boots! I who have ruined you and helped my Don Michael to victory. And—and—Go! Go away! Get out of my sight. Never come back to Villaga even when I am dead!"

He rose slowly. His face had grown almost as white as hers. In his heart were anger and a newly born despair and a deep pity for her. He rather guessed she had ruined him, doing a better job of it than she knew! Yet even at that moment of inner confusion he was granted a flash of true vision, seeing perhaps more clearly into her troubled bosom than she could ever have seen. He wanted to say a gentle, "Good-bye, Diana." But he said nothing.

He returned straightway to Palm Ranch. In the corral he left his horse with Bud Williams and Duke Jones, two quiet, dull-eyed figures sitting on the fence.

"Saddle another horse for me, will you?" he asked. "I'm getting a bite to eat, then I've got some more riding to do."

"We just found out, Bill," said Bud, "that anyhow two or three of the horses were in the barn and burned along with it."

Dorn went straight on to the house. Lorna was sitting on the top step, her slim body bent forward so that her face was on her crossed arms. Cap Jinks leaned droopily against a post supporting the porch roof, looking down upon her curly head abstractedly. Both figures stiffened into attention when they heard his footsteps. "Have you had a single thing to eat today?" were Lorna's first words.

"I'm eating now, if Josefa can dig up something, and then I'm riding."

"You're the ridin'est man I ever knowed," grunted Jinks. "Didn't you get enough las' night an' this mornin'?"

"I'll go tell Josefa," said Lorna, and went into the house. Bill watched her and shook his head. She didn't run as she always did; there wasn't much spring in her step today.

"What about the Villaga girl?" Jinks wanted to know.

"Wait until Lorna comes out, Cap. It's not the kind of a story a man wants to tell twice."

The three sat on the steps in the sunshine—they felt that they could do with a lot of sunshine today!—and Dorn got through his story the shortest way, after having eased himself into it by saying, "By the way, Diana says that Mrs. Kent did make a will; that she sent it out to Liberty to the bank."

Lorna and Jinks looked at each other. Jinks said drily: "We knowed it already, Bill, though I ain't seen it yet. Remember I tol' you I was goin' to do me some detectin'? Well, I guessed it might be at a bank an' I asked Roger Rutherford an' he said, Yep, he was holdin' it. An' I been helpin' the sheriff to find out things, too. Which reminds me, Bill. MacArthur rid by here about an hour ago, an' say! he's sore as a saddle boil!"

Dorn cocked up one eyebrow. Jinks explained:

"He says he ought to throw our crowd an' Bundy's crowd all in jail, but where'll he find room in any jail that's handy, an' besides mos' likely we'd tear his jail down."

"What about Diana?" asked Lorna eagerly.

"She says she's dying. I guess she is." He went steadily on and finished all he had to say without an interruption. At the end he added bluntly and without lifting his head to look at them, "And if anyone asks you, folks, you can tell him we're through. After what happened last night and this morning—No use not looking it in the face. We're licked."

Lorna sat rigid, staring at him incredulously. Of a sudden she sprang to her feet, the blood rushing hot and red into her cheeks that had been so wan, and cried vehemently:

"We're not! We're not, I tell you, Bill Dorn! Nothing is going to stop us. We're going to start right in now, today, to clean up and build all over again!"

"Is *that* so?" Dorn snapped back at her, as cross-tempered as an old bear. "Go ahead then. Don't let me stop you. Do all the cleaning up and rebuilding you like." He too got up. "I'll step in and see what Josefa's got to eat. The coffee smells good."

But Lorna caught him by the sleeve and tried her best to shake him. "Bill Dorn, you great big coward! You great big quitter! You—you—you—"

"Have it your way," said Dorn gruffly. He put his hand down on hers, trying to pry her loose. But she clung tight and her cheeks were hotter than ever, and her eyes were blazing when she demanded: "What are you afraid of? Why won't you go on? What's happened to you anyhow?"

"We went into a pretty big project when we started all this," he told her, and seeing how upset she was he forced himself to speak more calmly and even gently. "We knew it was a gamble all the time: give us luck and we'd maybe win; let luck run out on us and we'd lose. Well luck ran out and we lost. Now wait a minute! To go on would take money, wouldn't it? A lot of money? New buildings, a new dam, new wagons; everything to be done over. May I ask, without prying too deeply just how much money you stand ready to chip in with, Miss—Miss Brown?"

She let her hand fall from his sleeve.

"You mean—you mean your money is all gone? That we can't raise any more?"

"Course he don't," put in Jinks sharply. Probing

227

at Dorn with those shrewd old eyes of his he said tartly: "You tol' me yourse'f, Will, an' not over four-five days ago, you'd fixed things with Roger Rutherford for enough to keep us runnin'. Shucks, Will, I know you got anyhow ten-twenty thousand—an' me, I ain't throwed in every cent I got yet, an' there's Morg and ol' Middleton an' John Sharp that ain't ready to throw the sponge, an'—"

"You two don't seem to have got the gist of what I've just been telling you," cut in Dorn, again grown curt and hard. "We were all willing at the outset to tie into a fight with Mike Bundy, a rough-and-tumble, catch-as-catch-can, give-no-quarter battle. Ever since the day I met Lorna down in Nacional she knows that that's the way I felt. But there are some things a man just doesn't do, no matter how he hates the other fellow, no matter what the fight is for. You don't put poison into his soup. You don't sneak up behind him and jab a knife into his back.—Or do you?"

Jinks rasped out: "What'n hell you drivin' at, Will?"

"We went out last night and burned Bundy's place at County Line when Bundy wasn't even there. We swooped down on his wagon train and burned the whole works, cargo and all. At the time we thought that that was what he had done to us. Well, we know now that he didn't do it."

"I still don't figger you, Will."

Dorn shrugged heavily and turned toward his meal.

"Bundy's in Liberty. So is my bank. I'm on my way now; I'm going to pay Mike Bundy every damned cent his whole outfit was worth, and when I get through, if there's a dime left in the bank, we'll sink it in Palm Ranch to build a new dam, new barns, new houses!" He stalked into the house.

"You're crazy!" Jinks shrilled after him.

Lorna cried hotly: "I don't believe a word those Villagas say! I don't believe Diana is dying and I doubt if she was hurt at all! I don't believe—"

Dorn gulped a cup of hot black coffee, took a big beef sandwich in his hand and escaped to the corral. He rode away, Liberty bound, without another word to anybody.

"That Diana Villaga!" cried Lorna passionately.

That night Diana Villaga died.

XVI

WHAT in thunder have you been up to this time, Bill?" demanded Roger Rutherford, staring in a fascinated sort of way at the tall, gaunt, dusty figure striding into the bank with spur chains jangling.

"What are you talking about?" Dorn countered. He dropped into a chair in a corner of

Rutherford's private office, let his hat slide to the floor and started making a cigarette.

Rutherford continued to regard him curiously.

"Rumors are flying around as thick and as black as a flock of crows," he said, and emulated Dorn's activities to the extent of reaching for his pipe. "Have you run amuck or something? Have you gone crazy with the heat and turned bandit and general menace to life and property? Or have you just been blind drunk and having a good time?"

"I don't get you," frowned Dorn.

"They're saying you came down on County Line like the wolf on the fold. That—"

"Oh, that!" said Dorn, and licked the edge of his wheat straw. Then, slightly puzzled: "Say, the news did travel! To get to you so soon."

"That sort of news always is out for short cuts and speed records. What's the truth, Bill?"

"I'll tell you some time, Roger. I'm here on business now. First, do you know whether Mike Bundy is still in town?"

"He left a couple of hours ago. I saw him! He went out of town rarin' and pitchin' and pawin' the ground like a young bull in springtime. If I'm not mistaken he was headed two ways at once— to see how much hell-to-pay there really was at County Line, and to have it out with you."

"I'm sorry I missed him. Like him, I'm on a double errand. First to see you, then to see Bundy."

"Well, you see me, Bill, and I'm glad you dropped in. I was going to send word to you. As for Bundy, watch your step. If you ever saw a man with murder in his eye, it's Mike Bundy."

"That's all right. This time we'll get along."

But Rutherford shook his head. "He's trigger-set, Bill, and you better know it. When he got word of what you'd done to him at County Line he was already just ripe to go on the warpath." He paused a moment; reflectively he polished the warm bowl of his pipe against the side of his nose. "I violate no confidences," he resumed. "Bundy's no friend of mine; he has never done any business with my bank. So it struck me as odd that he should come to me, trying to borrow a hefty chunk of money. I said to myself, 'That long-legged Dorn boy is somehow getting Bundy down flat on his back the way he said he would.' And in a nice polite way I told Mr. Bundy he could go to hell. There was no gleam of joy in his eye at all. Then on top of that he got word of what had happened to him at County Line while he was chasing around after fresh ammunition."

"But look here, man," said a puzzled Bill Dorn. "He's got a gold mine that's worth a mint—he ought to be able to borrow all the money he needs on that."

"Later, no doubt," returned the banker, "but not right now in a hurry. It's a big proposition; he is consolidating a lot of interests; also he's forming a corporation, I understand, planning to sell stock. He can't pledge the thing until his papers are all in order, and that takes time."

Dorn's jaw hardened; his compressed lips made a rigid, slowly whitening line and his brows came down into a black scowl. To himself he said, "We did have Bundy worried—and now I'm getting ready to go broke in order to give him a leg up!"

But that was his own private grief and none of Rutherford's affair.

"On the subject of money, Roger," he asked, "how much am I good for right now. Cash on hand, I mean."

Rutherford went for a sheaf of papers and glanced through them. "I've cleaned up a few odds and ends as you asked me to when you gave me your power of attorney; the items are all here."

"Slide over them. Later, Roger. Just the total I can write a check for?"

Rutherford went for the current balance sheet, juggled a moment with figures and announced: "Twenty-one thousand, about. Maybe a few hundred more, maybe even a couple of extra thousand when this is all cleared up."

"Twenty-one thousand now?"

"Right, Bill."

"*Gracias, amigo,*" said Dorn and stood up. "*Y adios.*"

"Back to the ranch? Why not have supper with me and we'll talk."

"No can do. I'm off to the hotel; I'm going to eat and then I am going to crawl into the best bed the place has got and sleep the clock round."

"*Mañana*, then?"

"By the time the rosy fingered goddess gets busy letting the bars down I'll be on my way. Back to the ranch and to County Line. So long."

And Rutherford said, "So long," and Dorn was off to the hotel and to bed before it was dark. He awoke before dawn and lay on his back a long while, hands clasped behind his head, frowning eyes on the vague blur of a ceiling which slowly lost its vagueness in the new day. After a while he shook his head and got up and dressed. There was no other way; there was just one thing to do and he was going to do it the quickest way and get it out of his system.

He meant to stop at the ranch only long enough to change horses, but remained some hours instead. The sheriff was there again and, as Dorn promptly discovered, was as mad as a hornet. Why in blue blazes, he demanded right and left, did they have to go and kill Hank Smith anyhow?

"Drat your pesky hide, Bill Dorn," was his irate greeting when he met Dorn out at the corral. "Why do you have to let this happen? Hank Smith knew a lot that I want to know, standing closer to Mike Bundy than anyone else. Now you've got his mouth shut for good, just when I hit on the way to make him talk."

Dorn demanded quickly: "What have they done with him? Buried him yet?"

"The boys figured he wouldn't improve any with keeping," MacArthur snorted, "so they carted him off just over the edge of the ranch and scooped a hole and popped him in it. Did you want to hang some flowers on him?"

Dorn was thinking of something Diana had said. "Did anyone think to see what he had in his pockets?" he asked.

Up shot the sheriff's brows at the same time that the corners of his shrewd eyes contracted.

"I did," he retorted. "And I found something. What do you know about it?"

"What did you find?"

"Some tobacco and papers. A few extra shells for his gun. More money than you'd think to look at him that he'd have. And something else!"

"Let's have it," said Bill.

The sheriff extended his leathery palm. In it, like plump lovely eggs in a rude nest, were two satiny, softly glowing pearls. Dorn nodded thoughtfully. Here, if a man needed it, was corroboration of Diana's story.

"Tell me, Bill," said the sheriff. And when he had listened to the recital and had returned the Villaga pearls to his pocket and had rolled a thoughtful cigarette, he said, grown brisk again:

"*Bueno.* Now I'm off to have a chat with Mex Fontana. Maybe I can't make that hombre talk! The two of them, Mex and Hank Smith, have been sticking pretty close side by each. If she gave these to Hank, maybe she gave likewise to Mex. And I've got a hunch that I can persuade Señor Fontana to open up."

"If you're headed for the Blue Smokes, wait a shake and I'll ride along."

"Still looking for Bundy?" Dorn nodded. "Well, you won't find him there right now. He was at County Line last night; busted in on the place like a crazy man, he was that mad. He was starting out to meet you halfway, Bill, when word came for him to hurry over to the Villagas'. He went over right away, got back late, and again late this morning buzzed back there. I heard him tell some of the men he's got cleaning up the mess you made of his gambling joint that he wouldn't be back until some time tonight."

So the sheriff rode on his way alone, and Dorn remained a while at the ranch. He saw two men on a gentle slope digging; they were Duke Jones and Bud Williams who had at last found a spot which suited them, a place from which a man could look far out over the gently rolling country, a place that would be gently touched by the first rays of the rising sun. "Old Curly would kind of like this place," they agreed.

He found Cap'n Jinks hunkering on the steps at

the house, looking like a sad old grasshopper. After a while Lorna came out, her eyes red and swollen; she had wept over Curly gone, over the ruins about her; had wept from general weariness and dreariness and brokenheartedness. They had little to say, no questions to ask. If he had cared to volunteer any information they would no doubt have listened listlessly; but he, like them, was content with silence. Once Jinks said in a mumbling way, as though talking to himself, "They're buryin' Curly at sun-up; he was a great hand for sun-ups, was Curly." Lorna merely dropped her face back into her hands; Dorn sat staring away across the green valley into the purpling distances.

At dusk, with no word said against his going this time, he rode away; in his shirt pocket was a blank check and a stub of indelible pencil. And in the early starry evening he came to Bundy's town.

Here, too, was a heavy pall of silence. It seemed that with the destruction of Bundy's casino the heart had been cut out of County Line. There was nowhere that men could gather in large numbers to drink and carouse, to dance and gamble and in general make merry; furthermore County Line knew for the first time in its hectic young life a shortage of fire-water. The town drowsed in semi-dark; here and there a light shone in cracks about a door or window. Men went early to bed that night.

Dorn inquired of a man he chanced upon idling down by the ford for Bundy, heard again that Bundy had gone over to the Villagas', but learned where he might be found when he returned—the cabin which he had occupied while his main building was being erected stood on the bank of the creek a little higher up-stream. Dorn went to it, found it dark, the door unlocked, the one room untenanted. Thereafter, with growing impatience, he set himself the task of awaiting Bundy's return.

One would have thought County Line unusually well policed that night, for the law enforcement machinery of two counties was present in the persons of those counties' two sheriffs, MacArthur and Martinez. While Bill Dorn in growing impatience was awaiting the arrival of Mike Bundy, MacArthur and Martinez were sitting with a rickety homemade table between them, with a bottle on the table, with the air blue with their smoke. The cabin belonging to Stock Morgan and John Sharp, neither of whom had yet returned to the camp, housed them; presently they meant to roll into the two bunks. Now a bit of talk and a drop or so sufficed them.

Martinez had just been saying, with a vast and complacent chuckle, "Well, old-timer, I guess we were both in luck not being here when Here-We-Go Dorn and his pack of wolves hit this place to do a bit of old fashioned hell-raising. It would have been a tough job to handle, huh?"

"No handling that gang in the mood they were in then," agreed MacArthur. "And now?" He shrugged. "Bill and all the rest of 'em would come along gentle, I reckon, if the law called to 'em to do so. But so far Bundy hasn't said anything to me. Has he to you?"

"Hell no; why should he? I'm here tonight just as a private citizen, to talk to a man tomorrow about a claim he staked for me and—" He chuckled again, good-humored and mellow tonight. "And to watch what happens." He leaned forward and grinned into his brother sheriff's face. "I've been going over things with our county surveyor since I saw you. The good news is that this whole damn place is clean over my line and in your county. I haven't any more authority here than you have in China."

"The hell you say!" growled MacArthur. He was tired where Martinez was rested, testy where Martinez was a cricket for cheer. "That green kid of a Rincon County surveyor is as crazy as he's cocksure about everything. Me, I've been going into this too. Had a talk with Dad Milburn, our surveyor and he says—"

Martinez hooted at him. "Dad Milburn! That old bozo is in his second childhood; seven years ago he got so he forgot where he put his spectacles when he had 'em riding his nose. And you can take it from me—"

MacArthur reached for the comfort of the bottle. "I'm sheriffin' south of the creek," he said emphatically. "What happens this side—your side—is none of my give-a-damn. Here's happy days, Martinez."

Martinez reached, said, "How, Bart," and drank. Then they started preparing for bed. They were just about ready to turn in—in other words each of them had discarded coat, belt gun and one boot—when they heard a pistol shot.

"There she goes!" muttered Martinez and through force of habit reached for his gun even before he yanked his boot back on, just as MacArthur, his involuntary gestures dead ringers for Martinez', growled deep down in his throat, "They're taking the lid off hell again." They jostled each other in the narrow doorway and raced down to the creek whence the single shot had resounded.

They and sundry others arrived at the scene of action just in time to see two men, gripped in each other's arms like two wrestling bears, burst out of Bundy's old cabin, trip at the threshold, lunge staggeringly and fall to roll almost into the creek.

What had happened before any witnesses arrived had occurred in a space of time in which a wide-awake cat might have blinked its eyes twice. Dorn sat there waiting for Bundy, perched on an uncomfortable stool to keep from nodding, lighting no lamp, since he saw wisdom in taking

239

the other man by surprise. As Bundy came into the dark room, Dorn spoke, saying simply: "Bundy, this is Bill Dorn. I want a word—"

Save for a rip-snorting oath from Bundy, that was as far as any talk was to go just then. Bundy was all set to go for his gun, and went for it in a flash. Dorn, too, was alert, and brought his fist smashing down on Bundy's wrist. The weapon exploded harmlessly and flew out of Bundy's hand; Bundy leaped for it; Dorn grappled with him—the rest happened out in the open. It wasn't that either consciously made for the door; the place was simply too small to confine them and they shot out through the most convenient opening.

They broke free from each other, got to their feet, and Bundy made a lunge back toward the cabin door, headed toward his gun. Dorn roared at him: "Damn you, Bundy—I just want to talk—" and then made a lunge as wild as Bundy's to grapple with him again, to keep him from the cabin.

Bundy's answer was the grunt of effort accompanying a fist swung like a mallet into Dorn's face. Men already gathering, some demanding, "Who are they? What's the trouble?" heard the impact of the blow. Dorn went reeling backward and Bundy plunged into the cabin again. But in the dark there, not knowing exactly where his weapon had fallen, he could only grope, and before he found it Dorn came leaping in on him.

MacArthur said to Martinez, "If you don't want one of those men killed heap quick, you'd better step in pronto."

Martinez shot back at him, "It's your job, not mine."

"I wish they'd come outside to finish it," said MacArthur, trying to peer into the darkened room. "I'll bet Bill Dorn knocks hell out'n him."

"Bet you ten dollars," said Martinez.

Then the two men, after wrecking the cabin's interior as sounds of crashing and splintering amply testified, did emerge again. This time they did so because, while Bundy was stooping, still groping with both hands, Bill Dorn caught him by the middle, lifted him clean off the floor and hurled him through the door. Where his enemy was flung ahead of him Bill Dorn followed like a lean mountain cat making its deadly pounce.

They stood up to each other then and slugged. Those who watched could not see everything that happened, could judge best of blows by the sounds of fists on muscle and bone, for the night though starry and cloudless hid more of all this than it revealed. But Dorn and Bundy seemed to see well enough. There were men who, after that fight, swore that they could see the two men's eyes gleaming like cats' eyes!

Twice, between blows, Dorn tried to gasp out that he came just for a talk. Bundy roared him down and landed another good smashing fist into his face and made a wild grab at the gun at Dorn's belt. Bundy's fingers closed on it, yanked it away, jerked it up as he whirled on Dorn and roared, "Take that, you—"

But Dorn again had leaped swiftly after him, was pressing so close that Bundy was thrown off his balance, and before Bundy could make any use whatever of Dorn's gun, Bill Dorn used his own and most effectively. He brought it down forcefully on Bundy's head, then stood back grimly satisfied with the result.

When Bundy came to, he lay on his own bunk to find a lamp burning, his head and shoulders sopping wet and Bill Dorn sitting on the stool and leaning close over him.

"You—" began Bundy, and tried to surge to his feet. But Dorn shoved him back, flat on his back and menaced him with a Colt 45, clubbed by the barrel. Bundy looked beyond him, saw that there were many men just outside, peering interestedly in at the open door. His face reddened with shame to be seen like this.

"Shut up and lie still!" Dorn commanded him angrily. "I didn't come here tonight to fight with you. I told you at the beginning I had something I wanted to say; now you are going to listen. If you make a stab at getting up or if you open your trap, I'll bat you over the head again."

Bundy lay quite still, but Dorn could see that he

was only gathering his forces, getting his thoughts in order. After a blow like the one he had so recently taken, though consciousness had fully returned, a moment or so was required to pull himself together. Dorn took advantage of the brief quiescence.

"We got burnt-out at Palm Ranch," he said slowly, making sure that Bundy got every word he had to say. "The crowd that gang-jumped us left us pretty much in ruins, buildings gone, freight wagons burned, darn blown up. I naturally supposed I had you to thank for that. So I hotfooted over here to do the thanking while my gratitude was still warm. You know what hell I raised here with you, and you know what I did to your freighters. Then, the first thing I learn is that it wasn't you at all who raided us at Palm Ranch."

"It's pretty damn late now—"

"Shut up! It was my mistake, my blunder. I like to pay for my own damfoolishness. I came over tonight to pay you for the damage I've done."

A curious gleam came into Mike Bundy's eyes. Suddenly he let his taut body go limp on the bunk and burst into laughter.

"Damfoolishness is the word, and of all the damn fools—"

"Shut up!" roared Bill Dorn. He yanked his pencil and blank check out of his pocket. "Up to twenty-one thousand dollars I can pay you whatever you say your junk was worth—"

"Make it exactly twenty-one thousand and we'll call it square!" Bundy said promptly. "My losses, as anyone will know, are a lot more than that. Not counting wagons and freight."

XVII

IT WAS just sun-up when Bill Dorn came back to Palm Ranch. He saw the little procession, looking infinitely small with the wide sweep of hill and desert and soft green fields extending into such remote distances, as they came slowly up the slope. He joined them there at the open grave. There were flowers, all the prettiest, gayest flowers Lorna and Josefa could get.

Lorna knelt and murmured, so low they could scarcely hear her, the twenty-third psalm—"The Lord is my shepherd." There was a silence. Old Cap Jinks cleared his throat and started singing, the best he could, "Nearer My God to Thee." The others joined in. Some of the men had fine, clear voices; the others, though they did not sing so well, sang louder. Before they were done every face was unashamedly wet with tears for good old Curly O'Connor—every face except Bill Dorn's. His eyes were dry and hard; they looked as though a desert wind were blowing across them; inside, too, he felt dry and hard.

When Lorna and Josefa went back to the house the men congregated in the now dismal barnyard, a place of black char and wreckage and ruined hopes. They were all there, even to Wong; Stock Morgan, John Sharp, Middleton and Ken Fairchild were among them. Bill Dorn said: "Boys, I've got something to tell you. When I'm done you can line up and take your turns kicking me if you'll feel any better. I wouldn't feel any worse." Then he told them of his payment to Bundy. "I've been doing damn fool things all my life," he admitted at the end. "I can see that plain enough now. If this is just another of my damn fool plays, well anyhow it's done. I played it low-down on Mike Bundy when I said, 'Come along; let's burn him out.' Now I've done what I could to play square. The result is that I'm busted flat. If there's going to be any rebuilding here, any new string of wagons, somebody besides me has got to do the job."

Then, his face still stern and grim, his eyes still hot and harsh, he went straight to the house. Lorna was in the front room, lying back listlessly in a big chair. Dorn scarcely glanced at her; he went on into the kitchen where he found Josefa starting breakfast.

"Never mind breakfast for a while," he said tonelessly. He took the coffee pot out of her hand, set it down and escorted her to the back door. "You go outside somewhere and don't come back until I call you. I want to talk to Miss Lorna, Josefa, and I don't want you close enough to hear what I'm saying. Understand?"

Josefa looked at him in dull amazement, muttered, *"Si, Señor,"* and went out. Dorn closed the door after her.

Returning to the living room he found Lorna sitting bolt upright, staring wonderingly at him. He had not lowered his voice; she had heard not only the emphatic closing of the back door but every word he had said to the Indian girl as well. She couldn't but wonder what on earth Bill Dorn had to say to her that he didn't want Josefa to overhear.

Instead of waiting to learn from him she jumped to conclusions. There was such an air of gloom about the man, a most unaccustomed thing with Here-We-Go Dorn, and his face was so stern with a sort of sternness that suggested a relentlessness of solidly taken determination, that she was sure she read his thought aright and knew perfectly well what he was going to say. A sudden deep pity surged up within her for the man. She knew so well his strength of will, she so well understood how his whole heart and soul had gone unreservedly into this long-waged battle with Mike Bundy, that suddenly it dawned on her that defeat meant far, far more to him than to her! And here all along she had been thinking only of Lorna, poor little hurt Lorna who had lost her pretty playhouses and a lot of new-born dreams.

Of a sudden too she snapped out of her listlessness. She sprang to her feet, on the instant become the old impulsive Lorna, and a flush came into her cheeks and her eyes grew sparklingly bright. Astonishing him she caught his hand in hers and gave it a good hard squeeze.

"Bill Dorn!" she exclaimed excitedly as though she had just chanced upon some glittering discovery, "I've called you all the things I could think of—a brute and a beast and a fool. And it just dawns on me you're magnificent!"

Never did a man's facial expression present a stranger study in contrasts. Stamped as it were on top of the look he was wearing was a new one of profound puzzlement. What the devil was this girl saying anyhow?

Considering that he had made all arrangements, even to the evicting of Josefa, to get something said the straightest, swiftest way, it is not without interest that he got never a single word in edgewise until Lorna had said her say. She ran on swiftly: "When you started out to give that money—all the money you've got—to Mike Bundy I could have killed you! And do you know it's not until this minute that my own personal feelings in the matter have stood aside long enough for me to see that—that you did the only thing a gentleman—yes, darn it! a real gentleman like Sudden Bill Dorn—could do; that you did the—*the most splendid act* I ever heard of!"

"Forget it!" said Dorn, and snapped the words at her so that she jerked her hand from his and was for a second afraid of him. "I did that because I had to; think I wanted to? And after a while, I suppose, I'll see I was just a jackass for doing it. I do everything wrong-end-to, but at last anyhow I know it. And now are you going to keep still and listen to what I am saying to you?"

"I'll listen," said Lorna, and went back to her big chair. "But I know ahead what you're going to say."

"The devil you do! And what is it then, Miss Know-It-All?"

"It's what you've said already. I didn't have sense enough to see the truth of it then; rather, I was just too pig-headed to let myself see the truth—that we're done, finished, licked. That all we've got to do is clear out and let Mike Bundy do what he likes. That—"

"What do I care about all that!" cut in Bill Dorn, almost shouting at her. "I wasn't even thinking of it. I tell you, as long as I have been a fool all my life anyhow, I'm going on being consistently a fool, and right now I'm going to do the damnedest fool thing even a man born a Dorn ever did! I'll be on my way somewhere else before long, but before I go, you listen to this: I don't care a tinker's dam who you are or what you are or where you came from or why. I love you! Hear me?" He came to stand towering over her, glaring down at her. "Dammit, I love you!"

He turned to stalk to the door. The last thing he

had expected was that she would laugh at him. And when out of a startled silence all of a sudden Lorna's laughter burst forth merrily, Bill Dorn's face went brick red and his teeth were set hard and the hand he had lifted to the door knob showed knuckles gone white. He didn't turn. There wasn't anything else to say—

That is he thought there wasn't! Lorna jumped up and ran to him and, still laughing as he had never heard a girl laugh before—for that matter, neither had she!—she caught his rigid arm with both hands and began shaking him.

"The funniest part of it, Bill Dorn," she gasped, "is that I—I love you, too! W-with all my heart; with all my soul; w-w-with everything that's in me! And I have loved you like that—you great big lummox—ever since the night we fought each other like cat and dog at Nacional! And if you don't k-kiss me before you growl another growl—I'll bite you!"

Bill Dorn kissed her.

"Oh, Bill!" gasped Lorna.

After that the world was altogether a different sort of place.

Breakfast was late that morning. Josefa, forgotten, sat with her back to a rock in the sun and gave over wondering what was happening there in the house. Once a loud voice had startled her; after that, though she listened with all her ears, she couldn't hear a sound.

Lorna said after a while, a perfectly radiant Lorna: "What if we are done, finished, licked? Who cares a hoot, Bill Dorn?"

Then he amazed her a second time. He swept her off her feet, high from the floor, and, as Lorna vowed later, "brandished her!"

"We're nothing of the sort!" an amazing Bill Dorn flatly contradicted her. "And if you want to know why, I'll tell you in plain logical terms that a child could understand—"

"I'm no child," said a squirming Lorna. "You put me down, Bill Dorn, or—"

"Or you'll bite me? Go 'head and bite." She nibbled at his ear and he laughed at her and put her down, but kept both her hands locked tight in his. "Here's the why of it, Miss Lorna: You say you love me? *Bueno, Señorita!* If *that* is possible, then I tell you anything is possible! What can you think of more wonderful than that Lorna Whatever-her-other-name is—and it makes no difference because I'm going to change it quicker than a cat can wink its eye—loves old Bill Dorn? Now if a thing as wonderful as that can happen— Pshaw, girl, to lift ourselves up by the bootstraps and lick the stuffing out of Bundy would be the minor sort of matter you'd stick in a postscript. You love me? Come ahead then; we can lick the world."

"Oh, Bill, you *are* crazy! And I love you for it. But how?"

He grinned at her. "I haven't the vaguest idea. Who cares how we do the job, just so we do it? Come on!"

"Where?" He had started drawing her along in his wake toward the front door. "Where are we going?"

"The boys have been loafing on this job long enough," he told her vastly good-humoredly. "They're going to start cleaning up the mess, and they're going to start now. And do you know, I, for one, haven't even walked over to the dam to see whether it's a total loss or only half of that! We'll have it looked at. Then we're going to scare up some wagons and start freighting again."

"How *can* we?"

"I don't know," he laughed at her. "What do we care how, just so we do it? And later I'll pop in for another visit with Rutherford. There should be a few hundreds left anyhow; maybe, he said, a thousand or even more. We don't want any more until after we've shot that, do we?"

"Bill, don't you dare get my hopes up again!"

He looked at her in a brand new way, such a way that it made her blush. His eyes worshiped her.

"Listen you to me, Lorna girl," he told her in the tone of a man who knows what he is talking about. "Your hopes are already up so high that they're shining out of your eyes right now—and we're back in the fight to stay, in spite of hell and high water, until we get what we're after. And now—"

"Now," cried Lorna happily, "I am going to tell *you* something, Mr. Bill Dorn. It is something I vowed I'd never say another word about—that is, to you; I have already told dear old Cap—"

"Jinks has been going round looking ready to burst, stuffed so full of your secrets. From now on, young lady—"

"Do you want to hear or don't you? You said just now you didn't care a tinker's dam who or what I might be, so maybe—"

"I said I'd love you no matter who or what—"

"You were an old darling to say that, too! Now listen: I told you who I *wasn't;* I'm not Lorna Kent. That's just because—and I told you that too at the same time—there really isn't any Lorna Kent. You see if there were a Lorna Kent, then that's who I'd be. But—"

"Whoa!" said Bill Dorn, and began to laugh. "To make a fellow an explanation of some sort do you have to start in getting him all mixed up? After all, if I asked you anything about yourself— and mind, I'm not doing anything of the sort!— I'd not ask who you're not, but who you are."

"And that, I've told you already. I'm Lorna Brown. And—"

There was the sound of heavy boots coming flying up the steps; the door was flung open so heartily that it banged back against the wall and Cap Jinks burst in on them like a shot out of a gun.

"Talk about the devil and here he comes," said Dorn as he and Lorna fell apart. "Just a minute ago, Cap—For the love of Heaven, man, what's happened? You look—"

Jinks came cavorting down upon them like an Apache on the war path; his first vocal utterance might have been that same gentleman's war whoop; he carried his disreputable old hat in his hand and in one flourish managed to wave it high over his head and bring it slapping down on his dusty thigh. In his eyes was such a gleaming as no one had ever suspected Cap Jinks' eyes could harbor.

As his mouth opened for understandable words they were prepared for nearly any announcement other than the one he made. He had all the ear-marks of a man bringing the gladdest of glad tidings, and what he said—he couldn't keep his voice from ringing exultantly—was:

"Mike Bundy's comin'. He's up by the corral already. He'll be here in a split second."

"First time I ever knew Bundy's arrival to make you as gay as a Christmas tree," said a perplexed Dorn, while Lorna just looked searchingly at Jinks.

"Hell, it ain't that that's got me doin' Maypole dances. It's something else, an' when you two hear it—But it'll have to wait till Bundy's gone." He heard footsteps outside, and pressed closer, whispering the last few words: "For the love of

Pete, Will an' Lorny," he begged them, "get Bundy out o' here quick, so's I c'n tell you. Else I'll bust! You'd never believe—Sh!" He commanded, as though they had been shouting at him. "Here he is!"

He had left the door wide open and now Bundy looked in.

He was a Bundy hard to make out. For one thing it was obvious that he meant to appear friendly. He smiled in on them; he said quite cordially: "Hello, Bill. Good morning, Miss—Miss Lorna. Hello, Jinks." But one had the odd impression that this new geniality hurt him; as though it were all on the outside while within a secret interior his mood was downright ugly—murderous almost.

They only sensed that something galled the man; they could not guess what it was, since they did not know what had happened in County Line. Mike Bundy, though many men hated and not a few feared him, had held men's respect. He had done big things, done them in a big way, and there was a dignity about him which others recognized and, in one way and another, paid tribute to. But in an instant, like an over-proud Lucifer, he had fallen from his high estate in the estimation of his fellows. And the thing that had brought him down headlong was the roaring laughter of the rude mining camp. And it was Bill Dorn's errand of last night that had worked the change.

Men told the tale over and over among themselves, and the inevitable trimmings were added. The episode became a gigantic bit of slapstick, with Mike Bundy playing the part of the man who gets the custard pie in his face.

"Ol' Sudden Bill Dorn, the son-a-gun," men were saying, "come over an' jumped Mike Bundy an' knocked hell out'n him, an' then hel' him down whilst he shoves twenty thousan' bucks in Bundy's mouth, an' says to him, 'I pay my debts, you skunk, even if it's a skunk I owe 'em to!' Ol' Sudden Bill's shore a case, ain't he?"

Sudden Bill right now was saying curtly, "What are you here for, Bundy?"

"I've been thinking things over, Bill," said Bundy without seeming to note Dorn's curtness. "You started me thinking. You took me off guard yesterday; I was sore as a saddle boil, too. But I'm here today to tell you that when you toed the scratch the way you did—Well, Bill, it was a damned fine thing to do, and I don't know any man on earth who'd have been the man for it except old Sudden Bill Dorn!"

Dorn looked more puzzled then ever.

"What's back of all that talk, Bundy?" he demanded.

Bundy shrugged. "I'm not here to fall all over you and kiss you," he said bluntly. "But I am here to tell you I have sense enough to appreciate a thing as big as the thing you did last night. So much for that. Now I want to say a word about the

255

future: I'm getting no particular satisfaction out of fighting you. Suppose we draw off and let each other alone? Call it a draw and quit; what do you say?"

"And what's back of *that?*" snapped Dorn, suspicious now as he would be suspicious always of any act or word of Bundy's.

"I've got you licked and you know it," said Bundy evenly. He seemed determined to remain unruffled, good-humored. "But you've been square with me and I'll be square with you. First, there has been the question of ownership of this ranch—"

"There is no such question. It belongs to this young lady and me," said Dorn. "We hold it now in partnership."

"But only theoretically; you might say, sentimentally," smiled Bundy. "I think you must know by this time, Bill, that this young lady is not Lorna Kent. The real Lorna Kent was at Liberty some time back. She vanished one night—"

"Lugged off by Smith and Fontana," said Dorn.

"Yes. Though I'd say 'escorted' rather than 'lugged.' Well, I have known all the time where she was to be found. A couple of days ago I had a long talk with her. She will be showing up whenever I send for her to come. She will have no trouble establishing her identity as Lorna Kent, old lady Kent's heiress. And meantime I have a deed from her, making over to me all her right, title and interest in Palm Ranch as it may appear. So you see this place is mine in more ways than one now."

It was Dorn's time to shrug.

"I won't call you a liar because maybe you're telling the truth. Maybe you are not. Time will show. But why come to me with all this?"

"Because you came to me as you did last night. I'm not much given to gestures of charming sentiment as you know; just the same I'm willing to give you a chance to get out with your shirt. To get out before you are evicted through due process of law."

"Thanks," said Dorn drily.

"You're licked already, remember," said Bundy, and they could see that it was only with an effort that he held himself in check. "You and this girl and Jinks and the whole outfit, you're licked. But I'll do this and I'll tell you why: First, I want to let you down easy—"

"Skip that part of it, Bundy!"

"All right. Second, I am as anxious as any other man to avoid litigation. I want this thing cleaned up in a hurry. I want to use Palm Ranch myself just as you were using it. For a while I thought I'd change my plan and work from the north, hauling from San Marco through Hacienda Villaga, establishing a midway station at the hacienda. I've given that up.

"So I come back to my original scheme which

you folks for a time have done me out of. And I realize that this charming young woman may just possibly make a bit of trouble for me, phony though her claim is bound to be proved to be. To make a clean sweep here and get it done like that—" he snapped finger and thumb—"I'll pay this aforesaid charming young woman, and you too, Bill, a round sum for a quit claim. You move out and I move in."

"How round a sum might it be, Bundy?" piped up Cap Jinks. "How much did you say you'd pay?"

"Do you come in on this too?" said Bundy, edgily.

"Yep, shore do. We're all like one big happy fam'ly."

Bundy ignored him and returned his attention to Dorn.

"How about it, Bill? Right now I'm on my way into Liberty. Shall I cash this?" He pulled a paper out of his pocket and displayed it; it was Dorn's check for twenty-one thousand dollars. "Or shall I tear it up?"

"You mean me to believe that you're willing to spend twenty thousand dollars for what you claim will be a worthless deed?"

"Did I ever shoot nickels?" demanded Bundy. "If you could afford this much money just to show the world you could shoot square, and at a time when your back was to the wall, can't I afford it now to get what I want when I want it instead of waiting months for the damned legal wheels to get turning? I've got a gold mine that's going to be worth a million; in six months I'll be in a position where I can cash in for twice that and—"

"You're a damn liar an' ever was, Mike Bundy," snapped Jinks who refused to be ignored.

"I'm talking to you, Bill," said Bundy.

"Go cash your check," said Dorn. "And now we're going to have breakfast—and we're not asking you to stay."

Bundy's mouth opened for a tirade that never came. Instead his jaws came together with a click of teeth and he turned on his heel and went out. Cap Jinks followed him to the door and as Bundy strode away to his horse called shrilly after him: "Nex' time I see you, Bundy, I'm goin' to have something awful funny to tell you! Get ready to laugh your head off—damn your eyes!"

Cap'n Jinks, having shot his taunting yell after the departing Bundy, came charging back into the living room. Once more the gleam was in his eye and shone brighter than ever.

"Gather roun', you two," he began jubilantly, "an' stretch your ears to get 'em full of such words you never hoped to live to hear. An' me, I'll the tale unfol' that'll make your eyes stick out seven mile an' maybe seven more. When them jaspers raided us—"

"Whoa, Cap!" Dorn stopped him just as Jinks was going strongest. "Lorna has already started unfolding a tale that comes ahead of yours. Just you keep your shirt on, old party, until her story is done."

For an instant it was clear that Jinks was of a mind to override all commands and blurt out his news. But, becoming the smuggest man they ever saw, he said only, "Mine'll keep." Then he giggled and said in high glee: "There's a joke in that! 'Mine'll keep!' You'll get the joke when I spill the yarn."

"What I started telling Bill, you know already," said Lorna to Cap, and Jinks for the first time remarked a new radiant quality in her smile and took stock of her bright, high color and the sparkle in her eyes. To himself he said, "Humph! They've got to it as las'." Lorna turned again toward Dorn.

"You see," she went on, "Aunt Nellie Kent was really my aunt. My mother was her sister. Mother married Charles Robert Brown who, when they were married, was a not very successful musician. Aunt Nellie had always mothered my mother, who was several years younger; she took a very strong dislike to Charles Robert Brown, and Mother and he had to elope. They were both very young; I think they were both a little bit afraid of Aunt Nellie. Well, after that she would have nothing to do with either of them. She never saw either of them again; never even wrote to them. They remained in the East. She came West.

"I lost my mother when I was very little; I can scarcely remember her. Then, four years ago, I lost my father. He had never done very well financially, but he did leave enough insurance to send me to a very good if inexpensive girls' school. About two years ago the money ran out. I was doing the best I could; I had learned a little music and how to dance; I had small classes. Then I got a most surprising letter from Mrs. Kent.

"In it, first of all, she scolded me for being my father's and mother's daughter. But she was kind, too. She wanted to help me. But her letter had made me *mad*—"

Jinks chuckled, "You're good at that, Lorny. I'm warnin' Bill Dorn right now it ain't all goin' to be smooth sailin', him an' you."

"What has Bill Dorn got to do with it?" demanded Lorna, and tried to stare him down.

No staring Cap Jinks down this morning! "When I see folks look at folks like you two folks is lookin' right now—do you reckon I need to have you write it down on a slate? Hell no! Faces of two silly young geese when they're crazy in love is so easy to read a Chinaman could do it."

"Never mind Cap here," Dorn grinned at her. "He passed the age of discretion about the time he went into senile decay—which is to say about forty years ago. Sail on, Lorna. But I guess I've got it already."

Lorna sailed on.

"We wrote back and forth for a while. I was lonely for some of my own, and her letters got kinder and I got to understand that she too, in her own way, was lonesome for some of her own flesh and blood. The first check she sent me was on my birthday; you can't guess how it surprised me. She must have known about me ever since I was born. Then not very long ago she asked me to come out here. And she said that she was going to try to make amends for having been so seemingly forgetful of me all these years. But she made one thing clear from the start: If I came to her I must call myself Lorna Kent and never Lorna Brown.

"Later she wrote again. She told me that she wanted me very much; that she was going to make her will in my favor; but that before I could ever touch a cent of hers I must have my name changed legally to Kent. Well—well, I came. You know the rest of it."

Dorn nodded thoughtfully. "And you got here just too late ever to see her. Tough luck."

"Anyhow," piped up Cap Jinks, "the will's made out an' is at the bank in Liberty. Roger Rutherford tol' me so."

"And with it, no doubt," added Dorn, "will be instructions to the effect that Lorna Brown must become Lorna Kent to inherit." He looked at her sideways. "Seems to me you're headed toward doing a lot of changing of your name, young lady." Having paused long enough to admire the effective manner in which Lorna could wrinkle up that saucy nose of hers, he added, again thoughtful: "All you've got to do now is to arrange to have your identity as Lorna Brown established here."

"I've already written a friend of mine back home, a lawyer who I am sure will help me."

"A friend of yours, huh?" said Bill Dorn. "Young or old, this lawyer?"

Jinks broke in with a hearty: "Aha! What did I say about smooth water ahead?" And then he added, hurried and eager once more: "You two done now? Ready to hear a tale that is a tale?"

Dorn laughed into the puckered, oddly boyish old face, clapped him on the shoulder—you never could smite Cap'n Jinks on hip, thigh or back without starting up a small cloud of dust—and gave him his permission to go ahead and do his worst.

"If you don't get it out of your system in a hurry," said Dorn, "you're sure to go 'pop' like a toy balloon on a hot day. Shoot, Cap."

"Here goes," said Jinks. "Firs', since you wouldn't listen when I was ready to bust out with it, I'll make you wait until I mention something that has popped into my head since I come a runnin'. Yestiddy, Will, when you chased off to play square with Bundy, well, I thought you was a damn' jackass same as usual, it bein' my hunch that it was Mike Bundy an' not the Villagas that planned an' plotted that raid on us. Now, I know different. You c'n make dead shore Bundy didn't have any hand in tryin' to blow us off the map."

"That's no news to me, Cap. But what brought you around to it?"

"That comes later. Bein' a sort of Nick Carter, I sort of figger out things like that. To resoom, as the feller says: Lorny here's lucky for bein' Lorny, an' Will Dorn's a lucky dog that he chipped in with Lorny, an' all us other fellers is maybe lucky fellers we chipped in with Will Dorn. Fu'thermore, we got the worl' by the tail, the drag is downhill an' the skids is greased, an' Mike Bundy's a louse. Add to all of which, I c'n up now, soon's I get ready, an' say to you folks, like folks likes to say to folks, 'Me, I tol' you so!' Only I'll bet a man you don't even rec'lec' what I did tell you! You upped an' made light o' me then, but I'm danged if you're goin to make light o' me now."

"Cap Jinks," cried Lorna, "if you don't say what you've got to say—"

"Ain't I sayin' it?" chuckled Jinks. He stopped, drew a deep, slow breath and fairly exploded his next words at them: "I said long ago, why was Mike Bundy so crazy anxious to get this place? An' I said right then, 'Maybe the gold's on Palm

Ranch 'stead of bein' in the Blue Smokes.' Mike Bundy's gold mine ain't Mike Bundy's gold mine a-tall, but it's our gold mine and it's not over a half mile from where we're standin', spang in the middle o' Palm Ranch! An' me, Cap'n Nicholas Carter Ashbury Jinks, I found it this mornin'. An' if them hyenas, which now we oughter call good Christian frien's of our'n, hadn't blowed up our nice new dam, we'd never have knowed a thing about it! An' if you ain't got an ear full now, say so!"

Cap Jinks, no matter what his expectations, could not conceivably have been disappointed in the effect of the tale he blasted into their ears. The two young, happy faces of a moment before grew absolutely blank as two pairs of wide-open eyes stared at him. Dorn and Lorna didn't even look incredulous; they appeared simply stunned.

Lorna gasped and sank down into her big chair and forgot even to close her mouth which had involuntarily opened at some stage of his racing announcement and thereafter had remained in the status quo. She looked up at him as a child of four might look up into the actual, real, first-seen Santa Claus, spellbound, perhaps a little shocked and with a hint of fear pounding at her heart, bereft equally of words and of the power of thought.

As for Bill Dorn, he looked grimmer and grimmer and the muscles corded along his lean, hard jaw. There was so much at stake; they were, despite brave words, in such a hopeless mess altogether, that such news as this, so utterly unexpected, took a man in the short ribs like a fist. If this were true—if Jinks had made some idiotic mistake—

"Jinks," said Dorn at last, out of a silence of considerable duration, "if—if—"

And Lorna at the identical moment got control over her own speaking muscles and said, "Cap Jinks, if you—if—"

"Two hearts without a single thought!" yipped the delighted Jinks.

Dorn bore down upon him, Lorna swooped up to pounce on him, they got him one by each arm and held on to him as though they feared he might sprout wings and soar up through the roof to vanish for all time.

"Let's have the whole thing now," said Dorn. "Slow, Jinks; in words of one syllable, so we can get it. You've got us sort of dazed."

There was behind them a hesitant creak of the kitchen door, a soft, also hesitant footstep, and then Josefa's face looked in on them.

"I hongry," said Josefa. Her voice, too, was hesitant, yet there was a hint of sullen, Indian defiance in it. "Brikfuss now? Huh?"

Given carte blanche in the matter of disporting herself with abandon among the bacon and eggs and hotcakes and coffee, the long-enough forgotten Josefa withdrew with alacrity and what was almost a smile.

"You see," continued Jinks when the door closed, "that I got reason for admittin' at las' that you was right, Will, sayin' as how Bundy didn't have a thing to do with raidin' us. You see, it's like this: We had a mighty sight o' water piled up in that dam, an' when them good S'maritan frien's of our'n blew up the dam, they cut loose a ragin' mill race like a cloudbust roarin' down a mountain gully. That torrent ripped an' roared along the sides the ravine, gougin' an' scoopin' for Sam's sake. An' that way it brought to light what would have been hid until somehow Bundy got the ranch in his own claws. Sooner or later he'd of got it. He'd of knowed too much to take the chance o' that happenin'."

"You know gold when you see it, Cap—"

"Reckon. An' there's a ledge clean uncovered, maybe eighteen foot of it, that looks like some feller had stood off an' plugged gold into it with a shotgun."

"Yet that doesn't necessarily mean that this is Bundy's discovery. How about the strike up at County Line?"

"He's got a fence aroun' most of it, ain't he? Ten bob-wires, high as your head! Now you look a-here, Will; Bundy's a gam'ler an' a poker player, an' he never went into any sort of business deal in his life that he didn't make it into a poker game.

You know that well's I do. An' right now it's my one best bet he's playin' the biggest game o' bluff over to County Line he ever played in all his life."

"But there's gold there, Cap. Everybody knows that."

"Shore. An' when a man bluffs he's always got something in his hand, ain't he, if it's only a seven high. Shore there's gold in the Smokes an' we've knowed that for forty-fifty year. Only it's in no such bonanza quantity as Bundy makes out. A pocket here an' a pocket there, yep. More'n one shif'less ol' desert rat has clawed gold out'n them hills, sometimes a pocket worth a hunderd dollar; an' I rec'lec' when ol' Jimjam Rafferty once opened up a pocket that went better'n a thousan'. But it's always found all scattered from hell to breakfas' an' nothin' ever to call a mine."

"Then Bundy has simply salted what he calls his mine up there?"

"Reckon," said Jinks, as one who knew. "An' you'll find out he's done him the fancies' job any man ever did in that line. He's fooled some fellers that mos' generally would know better. But you'll note also he bought in all the surroundin' claims quick's a cat could wink, an' then that he built him a high bob-wire fence. An' with all his shoutin', he ain't done any development yet, has he? He's got excuses, shore—he's incorporatin'; he's fixin' to sell as-is for a coupla million; he's this-an'-that-in', jus' stallin' for time."

"Maybe," said Dorn, very thoughtful. "Maybe, Cap."

"Maybe your foot!" snorted Jinks. "It's common talk, ain't it, that Bundy's tryin' to raise money? Why'n't he raise him anyhow half a million on his mine? He ain't got any mine, that's the answer!"

Lorna began tugging him toward the door.

"Oh, you two!" she exclaimed. "What do we care about whether there is gold in the Blue Smokes or not? I want to see what we've got! Come show us, Cap."

"Right!" agreed Dorn. "First, call all the boys. There'll be a crowd of us, Jinks, and if you've just had a beautiful dream you better start running while you can; they'll lynch you, sure as shooting."

"Don't go an' tell anybody yet, Will," pleaded Jinks as the three went out on the porch. "Take time to think it over. We're out to bust Bundy, an' for a spell it might be a good idee to keep him from findin' out that we're on to him. Maybe he'll bust himself for us and save us the trouble! He's still tryin' to make his bluff good over to County Line; let him go dumpin' money in that sinkhole a while longer. Maybe you'll learn some day, Sudden Bill, not to be so danged sudden."

Lorna laughed. "Imagine Bill ever learning that! Anyhow, I won't have him spoiled, Cappie darling."

"Hmf!" said Jinks.

By now they were on the steps, but before they went down into the yard they were hailed by a rider who was just coming down from his saddle by the corral gate. It was Sheriff MacArthur. They saw another man with him; this one sat stolidly in the saddle making no move toward dismounting, his head down, his hat pulled forward as though he wanted to hide his face. Still Dorn recognized him.

"It's Mex Fontana!" he said. "Looks like the law had him in tow. Now what?"

MacArthur hung his spurs over the saddle horn, left Fontana with the two horses and came on to the house.

"Seems like I smell bacon, coffee, too, maybe," he called to them, and seemed cheerier than they had seen him for a long time. "Morning, Miss Lorna. Hello, boys."

They returned his greeting as cheerily as it was given. Then he looked at them and they looked at him, a noticeably beaming quartette, and MacArthur demanded: "Say, what's happened? Where are all the long faces gone? You three look like folks that had just found a gold mine or something!"

They laughed at that, thinking what a surprised man he was going to be when he came to learn how his offhand diagnosis had rung the bell. Dorn shot back at him, "You, too, Mac. Found a bonanza? Or just a diamond mine?"

"Pearls," chuckled MacArthur. "That's all. Two kinds, though. Pearls of wisdom along with some of the same sort Hank Smith had in his pocket. If you'll ask me in I'll help you track those bacon and coffee smells to their den, and we'll chin."

So they turned back into the house. Over their late breakfast they alternated moments of brisk, inconsequential chatter with sudden profound silences; that was because MacArthur had jerked his head toward Josefa as much as to say; "Wait till she's out of the way." When they had finished she was dispatched to the barnyard with eggs and bacon and coffee for Fontana, and instructed by Dorn to amuse herself outside until called. Then MacArthur got his cigarette going and his elbows on the table and treated Dorn and Lorna and Jinks to a frank, probing scrutiny. He saw Dorn and Lorna look at each other—and suddenly MacArthur grinned and fancied that he knew now what had put that sparkle into their eyes. He winked at Jinks. And then his puzzled frown came back.

"That would explain why these two youngsters are all wreathed in smiles," he conceded. "But what's come over Jinks here? A girl can't fall in love with two men the same time, can she? Anyhow no girl, no matter how good she was at it, could fall in love with you, Jinks, old boy."

"Think you're smart, don't you, Mr. MacArthur?" said Lorna, and she wrinkled up her nose at him.

"I do feel sort of smart this morning," admitted the sheriff complacently. "All puffed up about it, too. Here I've been running around in circles ever since the day when Mike Bundy butchered Jake Fanning—"

"What!" burst incredulously from Dorn. "Bundy did kill Fanning then? You're sure of it? Not just guessing?"

"I've got my rope on Mex Fontana at last," said the sheriff. "It's out of him that I squeezed the two kinds of pearls. What I was gladdest to get were some few words of the truth. Yes, Bill, I know Bundy killed old Jake. But the devil of it is I don't know that I'll ever prove it. I have felt it in my bones all along, but somehow it does take a good bit of believing to believe that of Mike Bundy. He ought to have had more sense. And even yet I can't quite get why he did it."

"There's the gold mine in the Blue Smokes," suggested Dorn, tentatively. "Jake knew about it, found it himself, no doubt. And Bundy—"

"Only there isn't any gold mine in the Blue Smokes," grunted the sheriff. "I permitted myself the luxury of dropping the boys up at County Line a little hint this morning. It's just the biggest, rawest, most beautiful hoax this neck of the woods ever heard about."

Lorna and Dorn and old Cap'n Jinks were so silent, their faces so blank, their eyes so guarded against trafficking with one another's, that it would have been hard for a man far less shrewd than Bart MacArthur to have failed to sense their constraint. He knew that what he was telling them about County Line did not in the least surprise them. He realized instantly that something had happened to make this trio stand on its guard against him this morning.

Promptly he shoved back his chair and stood up. "Thanks for the hand-out," he said curtly. "I'll be shoving off."

"Hold on a shake, Mac," said Dorn.

"Nope. I came here to chin, like I said. I hoped I'd bring news that somehow might help along. You three knew already that Bundy's mine was a colossal hoax. You haven't said as much as damn-your-eyes to me. So *adios*. I'm going,"

And now Dorn and Lorna and Jinks did look at one another, and the sheriff saw them out of the corners of his eyes, saw them nodding, too. So his old smile came back and he dropped down into his chair again and said: "That's better. Now what?"

Jinks' tale of his discovery lost nothing in being twice told. MacArthur heard him out without a word, then sat silent save for the drumming of his big blunt fingers on the tablecloth. Of a sudden he jerked his head up; he sat staring straight before him at a blank wall which, so far as he was concerned, fell open before him to reveal a long vista between solid facts clicking into place. His fist came crashing down into an open palm.

"It's all as clear as a hole through a plate glass window!" he boomed out at them in a sort of jovial thunder. "There were a dozen questions I kept asking myself, questions that stood up in my way like barb-wire fences, and now this answers every one of them! Oho, Mr. Mike Bundy, have I got you by the scruff of the neck!"

"I guess by now I know Mike Bundy pretty well," said Dorn, frowning. "Somehow I can't figure him as a killer, MacArthur."

"I know. Me, too, at first. But ask yourself this: What keeps him from being a killer?"

"He's too big a gun. He's too wise. He takes chances, all right, but he wouldn't take a chance like that. Not unless—"

"That's it! *Unless!* That was as far as I got, Bill. Unless, let's say, the reward was enormous. Or unless the man was desperate. And desperate is what Bundy's been for a good long while, and enormous was what the reward promised to be! Out on the end of a limb with it about to break off under him, he saw his great big chance. Would he turn killer with things like that?"

Slowly, even reluctantly, Dorn nodded.

"Bundy killed Jake Fanning," said MacArthur, and folded a finger down into his palm. "He killed One Eye Perez." He folded a second finger over to join the first. A moment he sat looking at Dorn, then slowly he brought a third finger down. "And he killed Nellie Kent. It was all because Bundy was in a jam to begin with, then because Jake Fanning found gold right here. A part of this I know; a part is easy to guess. Later, after we've had time for some thorough investigating, the whole thing will come out."

He knew whereof he spoke. And the time was boiling up when, as he predicted, all this would be as clear as that hole in his plate glass window.

"Of course I thought of Bundy as soon as Fanning was killed," he went on. "But it didn't seem reasonable. Bundy could have shut Jake's mouth some other way, or anyhow he could have gone ahead and done what he did do later at County Line, grabbing what folks thought was the cream. Next, One Eye Perez got knocked over. Now there were two funny things about that. One was that Bundy, when he showed up right afterward, didn't have a gun on him. The other was that two of Bundy's men, Smith and Fontana, grabbed Miss Lorna here and put the job on her. I'd have said right off one of those two boys did it—only it stuck in my craw that Bundy didn't have a gun on him! He just overplayed his hand that time. He was so anxious to get himself out of the picture that he stepped square into it. I knew he'd been carrying a gun everywhere he went for a long while. I started looking for it and I found it. Behind One Eye Perez's place there's a well; in the bottom of the well was Mike Bundy's gun.

"And here's something. I got the bullet out of Jake Fanning's skull; I dug the One Eye Perez bullet out of the wall; they were both thirty-eights—and so is Bundy's gun!

"Did all that point straight enough? Sure it did. Any real evidence in it though? Nary. And never a motive strong enough to make it seem reasonable. Hell's bells, it didn't sound reasonable even to me that a man like Mike Bundy would pull those two jobs.

"Then Lorna's aunt here falls off the back porch and breaks her neck." Lorna shuddered and under the table put her hand into Bill Dorn's which went sympathetically half way to meet it. The sheriff, engrossed in his solution of a problem, did not notice. He went on: "Mrs. Kent was always hiring and firing her household help; at that particular time she was doing her own inside work. The two men working outside were off at the upper end of the ranch with a wagon, hauling firewood. So as far as we could tell she was all alone when she got her fall.

"When they got back they found her like that. I asked them what they supposed she was doing, leaning against the railing on the back porch. They said she was leaning over to water some flowers just below, because there was a watering can lying right close to her, some water left in the bottom. I asked what time they got back and found her. They said they got back early, three or four o'clock in the afternoon. They figured she had been dead quite a while—"

"Why," cried Lorna, "you water flowers either very early in the morning before the sun is hot, or about sundown!"

MacArthur nodded. Jinks came over and patted Lorna on her curly head.

"Nick Carter used to have a lady assistant, Miss Lorny. You an' me could go places together, detectin'!"

"So," resumed MacArthur, "the coroner and I came out here one night to sort of look into things. All we found, as you know—"

"Lorna doesn't know," said Bill Dorn swiftly. "We didn't see any use telling her."

"Well, she's got to know sooner or later, and it might as well be now." When Lorna heard how they had found the grave empty, she cried out, "Oh, it's too horrible!" and clung tighter than ever to Bill Dorn's hand.

"And then for a time," continued MacArthur presently, "I was up a stump. But I figured that if Bundy had had any hand in this, too, he would have required other hands than his own. Smith and Fontana, as a good bet. Already they knew a lot; they were pretty sure to know about Perez. So I was hunting a way to make them talk when Wong's cleaver put Hank Smith into the silent squad. But at last I've got Fontana, and I found the way to make that half-bred snake open up wide!"

He had to stop and chuckle over it, and to admit that he had played it pretty low-down on Mex Fontana! Here is what he had done: He had rounded up a dozen men in County Line known to be friends of Bill Dorn's. After he had coached them in their parts they ambushed Fontana, gang-jumped him when he came riding into camp, smuggled him off into a convenient lonely cañon and proceeded to make it clear to him that he was about to be swung off into eternity on the end of a rope under a pine tree. They said to him: "We know you're one of the gang that raided Palm Ranch. Well, it was your last raid, Mex." And only when the rope was tight and a screaming, terror-maddened wretch was at the end of hope though not of frenzied struggling, did the law, as represented by Sheriff MacArthur, put in an appearance.

"They're all rats, these killers," said MacArthur disgustedly. "A dirty coward is Fontana. When I told him I'd save him from that gang only in case he'd tell every damn thing he knew, and that if he did come clean I'd promise him a chance to skip south across the border, he started spouting like a geyser. I was right about it being him and Hank Smith who had done the grave robbing. And he led me straight to the new grave, about two miles north of here."

The sheriff did all he could to spare Lorna, touching only lightly on the essential details. Mrs.

Kent had not died of a broken neck; her skull had been crushed. And, considering that she was a small, slight woman weighing but little over a hundred pounds, and that the fall from the back porch was inconsiderable, it was rather more than merely likely that her death had been caused by a tremendous blow, such a blow as a man might have delivered with a club or the heavy barrel of his gun.

"Bundy killed her. Now that Jinks has found where Bundy's gold mine really is—and that it was never Bundy's at all—I'm going at last to be in a position to slap Mr. Bundy in the hoosegow, and to give the County Attorney enough facts to get him started on a chain of evidence that'll hang Mike Bundy as high as a kite. And just think!" He glared at them. "You three confounded conspirators were going to hold out on me, cheating me out of knowing the one thing I had to know to make sense out of the whole mess."

"Even yet," muttered Dorn, "I don't see how—"

"Look, Bill; here's what happened. Mike Bundy was a big gun, but he never was as big a gun as he thought he was. From the jump, in everything he did whether straight or crooked—and most of it was crooked—he overplayed his hand. He can't help that sort of thing any more than a rag can help fluttering in the wind."

Then, casting back for a beginning to the time when Mike Bundy began his career here in the

Southwest, and advancing gradatim to the present crisis, the sheriff pictured for them a line of action which could hardly have failed soon or late to swing into an outright criminal trend. Many facts he had gleaned, many were pure, though logical, deductions. Later when they knew the whole story they saw that the shrewd sheriff, though in error here and there, was in the main as right as rain.

"Here's what happened," to quote MacArthur. Jake Fanning, grubstaked by Bundy, had really found gold in the Blue Smokes, but, when Bundy had looked into it carefully, it was nothing to get excited about. Fanning kept on prospecting. On one of his trips, returning to Nacional, he camped in the afternoon in the ravine at Palm Ranch. And there, by sheer chance when least expecting it, he had come upon the bonanza which in his shiftless way he had been hunting all his life.

Hastily he covered all traces of his find and hurried along into Nacional. Bundy had recently gone into partnership with One Eye Perez, seeing big profits in the gaming tables. Jake Fanning burst in on the two of them, talking in Perez's back room, and blabbed the news. So Bundy had two men to bribe to keep their mouths shut, promising them all sorts of things when once he got his hands on Palm Ranch. He managed for a time to keep Fanning sober and busy; he had slightly less trouble with Perez. And Bundy bent all thoughts toward getting hold of the ranch.

Meantime Jake Fanning couldn't resist the temptation to return to look at the ledge he had uncovered once. Again he got permission to break his journey at this halfway place, camping over night. Greed got a mightier strangle grip on his covetous throat than ever before. Perhaps he thought he could make a better deal with Mrs. Kent than he could with Bundy; he always was a doublecrossing dog. At any rate he was a man who had a profound scorn for a woman's intelligence and who estimated his own acumen vastly higher than facts warranted. He talked with her in his sly way and Mrs. Kent's suspicions awoke.

The next day Bundy called. How much she told him of her talk with Jake Fanning remains matter for surmise. Perhaps she said outright: "I know why you're trying to get my place. There's gold here and Fanning found it and told you. I was talking with him last night." Bundy killed her. Later it was a simple matter for him to break through the flimsy back porch rail, to make it seem that she had fallen, to ride off without being seen.

"Bundy killed her," MacArthur droned on, "because he flew into a rage and because he was desperate anyhow and figured he pretty well had to. Desperate; yes, that's the word. At the time when you and I and everyone else thought he had the world by the tail, he was on quicksand. He had spread out over too much territory, covering it too

281

thin. On top of that he had been gambling his head off in mining shares, gambling and losing, and he was using not only his own money but funds he'd have to account for in the course of time, sums put up by other men he had drawn in with him."

Bill Dorn could understand this. He knew Bundy was essentially an adventurer, a gambler. Proud, arrogant, always sure of his destiny, obsessed by the idea that he was a sort of giant among pigmies and therefore unbeatable, he took chances another man would not take. His strength lay in his boldness, recklessness, courage, assurance, arrogance. But also in these qualities lurked the seeds of his weakness. He was impatient of the slightest delay or obstacle; he wanted results; he wanted them *now.* He was a crook and he was a hog. He was so big-headed, so pig-headed, that he had no fear either of other men or of mischance. He was of the sort of stuff of which the world's dictators, especially the inefficient ones, are made.

"I've noticed," said MacArthur, "that a lot of crimes get committed because a first crime makes subsequent ones pretty darned near compulsory. He killed Mrs. Kent. Then maybe he saw that Fanning guessed it. He killed Fanning. There was Perez left. Perez wasn't exactly a fool. Well, Bundy came to Nacional that night in time to see Lorna and One Eye, and maybe Bill, all squabbling in One Eye's back room. Bundy shot him, hid his gun, had Smith and Fontana swear they saw Lorna do the shooting. It must," he added with a wry grin, "have seemed a good idea at the time!"

"Do you suppose he knew then who Lorna was?" asked Dorn.

"*Quien sake?* Offhand, I'd say yes. He had had many talks with Mrs. Kent; maybe she had told him her niece was coming, and he may have been on the lookout for her. It seems rather more than coincidence that he should have picked on her to take the gaff; whereas in case he did know who she was he would figure that in incriminating her he was killing two birds with one stone. Had she been charged in Nacional with One Eye's murder, I fancy he could have fixed things so that she would never have bothered up here."

"Diana knew that she was Lorna Brown. Did Bundy know, too?"

Again MacArthur could only say, *"Quien sabe?"* This time he added, "Diana might have learned from Mrs. Kent her niece's real name."

"You knew?"

"Jinks told me."

Dorn pretended to glare at Lorna though under the table her hand, a willing prisoner to his, got a lover's squeeze as he said, "She let everybody know but me!"

"You were horrid, remember," said Lorna.

"And that other girl, down at Liberty?" asked Dorn.

"Scared up for the occasion by Bundy. Taught her part by him. He no doubt had Lorna's suitcase, the one that vanished in Nacional. There were odds and ends in it that went to the other girl, the handkerchief and letter Jinks found. He was doing what he could to cloud Lorna's claim here in the eyes of all who were interested; he even had us worried, didn't he? Then he had his hired watch dogs cart her off and put her on a train, done with her; made us think he had her corraled somewhere so that he could prove her claim when he got ready and buy from her."

"Shore," piped up Jinks. "Me, head detective on this job, I figgered that an' tipped the sheriff off. Huh, Bart?"

MacArthur grinned and saluted. "Right, Nick."

He fell to drumming on the table again. Suddenly he stood up and reached for his hat.

"I'll drift now. I want to put Mex Fontana in a good safe place where I can have him on tap when I want him, which will be soon, and where Mike Bundy can't get at him, and where I can keep my promise to him and ship him back across the border when I'm through with him. By the way, Bill," he said curiously, "when I spoke of two kinds of pearls a while ago—well, I found one kind, the same that I found on Hank Smith, in Fontana's pockets. Two of 'em."

"Well?" demanded Dorn.

"What does it prove to you?"

"What we all know already. That one thing we can't lay at Bundy's door, though I did lay it there when I went off half-cocked, was the raid on the ranch. Those were Diana Villaga's pearls."

"Yep," snapped the sheriff. "They were. But once I got Fontana talking he pretty near talked his head off. Didn't I tell you Bundy was in a mighty bad hole financially? He was in deeper than even I guessed. And he had that girl crazy in love with him and—Anyhow, about two weeks ago Fontana saw Diana hand over to Bundy every damned heirloom the Villagas had that was worth a thin dime, and she handed the string of pearls along with the rest, and Bundy, short of cash, gave those pearls to Fontana and Hank Smith as overdue pay! Got it? It *was* Bundy who pulled that raid on you—and you galloped off, half-cocked like you say, to beat hell out of him just in order to hand him twenty thousand dollars for making a monkey out of you!"

Dorn's jaw dropped. But Jinks piped up first: "Bundy wouldn't have blowed up the dam, knowin' that thataway he run all kind o' chances uncoverin' that ledge!"

"Bundy wasn't with the raiders in person, I'll grant you," said MacArthur. "Blowing up the dam was no doubt just an inspiration on the lovely Diana's part. I guess she was sorry when she found out what she had done. Maybe that's why she sent for Bill and tried to clear Bundy altogether."

Bill Dorn came up to his feet like something jerked erect by a mighty spring, his eyes blazing. As he raced toward the door Lorna cried out after him: "Bill! Bill Dorn! Where are you going?"

Over his shoulder he called back: "I've got to get to Liberty before Bundy cashes that check!"

They hurried out to the porch and saw him running toward the corral, shouting as he ran to one of the boys out there to rope a horse for him. "He didn't even get his hat!" exclaimed Lorna, and ran back for it.

Old Cap Jinks tugged savagely at a lower lip.

"Bundy's got too much head start," he muttered reluctantly. "Bill can't make it in time." And at the top of his voice he began calling Dorn back while Lorna, Bill's hat in her hand, sped out to the corral.

XVIII

HARD-RIDING Bill Dorn was in the saddle again, bound this time upon an errand which he felt hopeless from the first jump of the lean, eager half-wild horse under him. Bundy should arrive in Liberty long before he could. But there was always the long chance, the thin, hundred-to-one chance, and Bill Dorn rode.

Bundy, too, rode hard that morning, for his mood was savage. Yet, he would have ridden even harder had he known how his bright Lady

Fortune, in whom he had ever so recklessly put his trust, was frowning. It was just that Bundy had no inkling of what hounds of retribution had been unleashed at his heels by Sheriff MacArthur.

At County Line that morning, the sheriff, departing with Mex Fontana all but hanging on to his coat tails, had done little more than drop a hint. "You suckers! A gold mine here?" He had laughed in their faces.

The thing which he hinted already lay close under the surface of more than one man's thoughts. In five minutes MacArthur's innuendo had flown like a croaking black crow all over camp; in ten minutes the place was bristling with the rapidly growing suspicion. Men, especially those who never had liked or trusted Bundy, exploded first into oaths, then into action. They broke through his high protecting fence, defying his guards with their preponderant numbers; they fell to with picks and shovels, prospecting for themselves on Bundy's claims, gouging at the prospect hole he had made so much of, saying among themselves: "Suckers, huh? Well, if there's gold here we're going to see the color of it." Two hours later the last man of them had hurled down his tools. "Where's Bundy?" a strapping big chap thundered. "Where'n hell is Bundy?" they began shouting.

In another ten minutes some two hundred infuriated men had saddled and mounted and buzzed out of County Line like a swarm of mad hornets. Bundy, someone had learned, had ridden over to Palm Ranch.

Thus behind Mike Bundy rolled a thunder cloud, one of those black clouds trimmed with lightning. And in front of him, no less, were events shaping little to his liking. In Liberty Roger Rutherford, banker and staunch friend of Bill Dorn's, was a much troubled man. Holding Dorn in friendly esteem, he hated the ground Mike Bundy walked on. And a newsmonger, one of the Antelope Valley boys, coming to the bank to borrow fifty dollars, had told him in detail of the recent fight and financial deal between Dorn and Bundy.

"It's just like old Sudden Bill," growled Rutherford disgustedly. "Here he goes spending his last nickel to give his worst enemy a leg up, doing it without taking five minutes to think it over. Of all the—"

"And the funny part of it," said the Antelope Valley man, "is that while about half of County Line agrees with Bill that Bundy had nothing to do with the raid on Palm Ranch, the other half swears Bundy planned and directed the whole thing, just arranging to have the job done while he was somewhere else. My hunch is that he's made a ring-tailed monkey of old Roll-Along Dorn."

"That's my hunch, too," pondered Rutherford when alone. "That would be Bundy's way. And

288

later on, if Bill finds such to be the fact, he can bite his nails all he wants but he won't get his twenty thousand back."

So, being the man he was and a friend of Dorn's and not of Bundy's, he went into prolonged and sober session with himself. In the end he slapped his desk, arose briskly and bestirred himself, demanding of the only man present—namely Roger Rutherford, banker: "What's the good of a power of attorney anyhow, if you don't use it?"

When Bundy arrived, dusty and curt, striding in hurriedly, Rutherford was ready for him. Bundy slapped down Dorn's check, saying in the tone of a disgruntled employer to some whippersnapper of a counter-jumper:

"Cash, Rutherford. Give it to me in the largest denomination of bank notes you've got. And I'm in a hurry."

"You look it," said Rutherford coolly. In leisurely fashion he drew the check to him and looked at it. "No can do, Bundy," he said, and shoved the check back. "There's no such amount of money as that in Bill Dorn's account."

"What the hell!" stormed Bundy. "Anybody that knows Bill Dorn knows that his checks are good. Look here, Rutherford, if you're trying to run some sort of a blazer on me you'd better pull your horns in. I want that money and I want it now—I've got to have it, and, by God, I'm going to have it!"

"Yes?" said Rutherford mildly, and slid his hand

under the counter. He somehow felt better when it closed on the worn walnut grip of an old friend. The last time he had seen Bundy the man had looked worried, hard-pressed; today he was harassed, goaded, maddened.

"You mean your damned bank hasn't got that much in cash?" asked Bundy, holding himself in check.

"We've got the money all right," returned Rutherford.

"Then you mean that Dorn, the skunk, gave me a worthless check?"

"No. The check wasn't worthless when he wrote it." Rutherford pursed his lips; he was beginning to enjoy this. "Bill, the son-of-a-gun, should have told me he was figuring on drawing so large a check. You see, the money was there when he was in to see me; in fact it was there until about half an hour ago. As it happens, Mr. Bundy, I hold Bill's power of attorney. I've been going over some of his papers this morning. A little while ago I found it advisable—strictly in Bill's best inter-ests, you know—to divert twenty thousand dol-lars from his account. It's just one of those things, Mr. Bundy. But surely to you a delay over so small a sum can work no great inconvenience?"

Slowly a congested wrath empurpled Bundy's face. Rutherford saw, and the seeing increased his enjoyment, that it meant a tremendous lot to Mike Bundy.

Bundy's eyes clashed with Rutherford's, started roving, came back to clash again, and Rutherford's whole body stiffened. For an instant he believed that his infuriated caller was on the verge of demanding his money at the muzzle of a gun. Then Bundy caught up his check and without a word went out. For a moment he stood in the road, his hands jammed fiercely into his pockets, his head down, a study in bafflement. Then he swung up into his saddle and spurred out of town.

"Headed back where he came from," mused Rutherford, no longer complacent but scenting trouble. "And going like hell was after him. Well, maybe it is. Crazy mad? He'll kill that horse; the fool didn't even have sense left to change."

It was perhaps an hour later that Bill Dorn came in, hurried like Bundy, demanding by way of greeting whether Bundy had called for his money. When Rutherford nodded Dorn lifted his shoulders in a high shrug. "I'm stuck again," he grunted, and stood for a moment scowling at the big hat he had set spinning on a horny forefinger.

"Squat, Bill, and we'll talk." Dorn looked at him sharply, saw that the tale was not yet all told, and slid into a chair. "Maybe you'll want to knock my head off, Bill; you'd be in your rights. Here's what I did."

When he had done, Bill Dorn made no gesture toward knocking his head off; instead a broad grin with a flash of strong white teeth was like a gleam of sunshine across his bronzed face.

"Roger, you old highwayman," he exploded, "let's play we're both of good old sunny Latin stock; come and let me kiss you on both cheeks!"

He went away in high good-humor. Having told Rutherford how things stood, having learned that Bundy had ridden back in the general direction of Palm Ranch and County Line beyond, Dorn went to the Liberty stable, got a fresh horse and turned eagerly homeward. Home, by thunder; that's what it was, what it was going to be. If a man wanted to live right close up to the threshold of Heaven, why, Palm Ranch was the place!

But this afternoon that same Palm Ranch was to have the seeming of standing on the portico of hell. For Mike Bundy, hell-bent, spurred a spent horse into the yard well ahead of Bill Dorn's return. He took the steps in two strides, he flung the door open without thinking to knock, he burst in on Lorna and Cap Jinks deep in talk, and shouted at them:

"Where's Bill Dorn?"

Lorna jumped up from her big chair and recoiled from him, backing away until her shoulders brought up against the wall, her eyes terrified. Jinks, too, stood up, bristling.

"Take it easy, Bundy," he snapped. "What's eatin' you?"

But Bundy couldn't drag his eyes away from Lorna's that were so eloquent of her abhorrence and fear.

"What is it?" he demanded sharply, though already he must have known, so eloquent of her thoughts was the look on her blanched face. "What's the matter with you?"

"N-nothing," said Lorna. Even to speak one word to the man, three times murderer, was difficult. She began moving still farther away from him, edging toward the door.

"Stop!" he commanded in such a tone that she did stop. He whisked a look at Jinks. "What's come over you two?"

"You look here, Bundy," retorted Jinks; "you're done for an' you know it. Take a tip from a feller that don't wish you any good an' dust to hell out o' here while you can."

"So!" said Bundy and slammed his big tired body into Lorna's chair. But something in his eyes held the girl from an attempt at headlong flight, a something that flared up hot and wicked and rooted her to her place. "So!" said Bundy. "Things have happened, have they?"

"You're darn' tootin'!" returned a vehement Jinks.

"The place looks deserted. Where's everybody?"

Jinks couldn't resist the temptation. "The boys are down by the dam, Bundy! Somebody blowed it up, maybe you heard? An' the runaway water done a right nifty job gougin' out the bank where the big bend is."

Bundy's expression did not change. He asked no questions about the gouged bank. He pushed his hat far back and ran a hasty hand over his wet brow. Then he asked in a voice which had abruptly gone quiet, staring fixedly at Lorna:

"Why do you look at me like that? Are you afraid?"

"I—I'm not afraid."

"You lie," said Bundy. "Where's Josefa?"

"She's gone with the others—to the dam."

"You'd think they never saw gold before!" he jeered. He knew now that they knew; no use denying. "The world's full of gold. It's easy to get when you know how."

Lorna stirred uneasily. "I am going—"

"You'll do nothing of the sort! *Look at me!*" She looked, read aright what was not to be misread in his eyes, and stood still. "Where's Bill Dorn?"

"He's gone to—"

"Never mind where he's gone!" cut in Jinks warningly. To Bundy he said tartly, "It's none o' your damn business."

"No?" said Bundy. "No? The yellow dog has double-crossed me, and it's none of my business!" He leaped unexpectedly to his feet and crossed to Lorna in two swift long strides. He clamped his hand on her shoulder and put his face close down to hers. "I asked you why you look at me like

294

that! Why are you afraid of me? You're all white."

Jinks rushed at him; had he had a weapon on him then he would have shot Bundy through the head.

"You get your dirty han's off'n her—"

With one great sweep of his arm Bundy hurled the thin, spare form across the room. Then, with terrible meaning in the gesture, he dropped his hand to his gun belt.

"You damn cowardly killer!" raged old Cap.

"Killer am I?" said Bundy. Again his voice changed; it was not raised, lowered if anything; it became unthinkably bleak and cold. "So that's it! Who has been here telling lies about me since I left this morning?"

Then Lorna blurted out the truth; had it dragged out of her, rather, by the sheer force of his determination to have it. "Sheriff MacArthur was here. Mex Fontana was with him. And we know—we know everything, about my aunt and—"

"Lorny!" cried Jinks.

"Shut up!" Bundy ordered him. "You two stand still. And keep your mouths shut. I want to think."

They looked at each other, then back at him, fascinated. Lorna thought in a panic: "He *is* a killer! It's written all over him! Why didn't we know all the time?"

There was not a sound in the room, save once when a board creaked under Jinks' boots and Bundy glared at him. Bundy appeared to have grown calm and cool; he was thinking, taking logical stock of prime factors, thinking fast but in a steady, continuous stream of reasoning which must, if he saved his neck, be without oversight or flaw.

"Jinks!"

Jinks started. "Well dammit! Here I am."

"I'm on my way. My horse is tuckered out. You go saddle me a fresh one. And don't stop to pick flowers on the way!"

Jinks needed no urging. He was at the door, his hand on the knob, when another "Jinks!" as emphatic as a pistol shot, arrested him.

"If you see any of the boys, keep your mouth shut."

"Shore," said Jinks, and had just started saying to himself, "He must be crazy or think I am!" when Bundy's voice gave him something else to think on.

"Look at me, Jinks; take a good look. Do I look like I just wanted to play drop the handkerchief or something? No? Well, now look at this!"

He drew out his belt gun, and thrust the muzzle against Lorna's breast. And now Jinks' face grew white.

"Do I mean it?" demanded Bundy. "Am I a killer? Would I hesitate a split second to wipe out this little she-devil but for whose coming in the first place I'd be riding fine and handsome right now?"

"I'll do it," muttered Jinks. "Take that damn gun away! So help me—"

"Sh!" Bundy half turned his head, listening. "Someone's coming. Open up, Jinks, but stand back. Who is it?"

It was Bill Dorn returning from Liberty. He pulled up in the front yard and ran up the steps. Both Lorna and Jinks called a warning to him, but Bundy did not seem to mind. Dorn stopped dead at the threshold.

"Take it easy, Bill," said Bundy. "This is my last play around here, and I'm going to make it stick. Keep your hand away from your gun; if you lose your head and go for it you might as well shoot this kid yourself. Let me away from here with a good horse under me and a head start, and no one will get hurt. Make one little slip and I'll drag Lorna along hell-bound with me."

Dorn moistened his lips but otherwise did not stir.

"Sure, Bundy," he said after a second. "Sure. You've got the drop on us. You can go."

Perhaps a trifle of Bundy's tension relaxed then; he seemed to breathe easier. When Bill Dorn said a thing, he meant it. Still Bundy kept his gun where it was.

"Shed your gun, Bill. Back up to me and let me take it. That's it," he said as he shoved Dorn's weapon into his own waistband. "Now, Bill, I guess I can trust you to do what's got to be done next. My horse is tuckered out. I want a fresh one in a hurry, the best on the ranch."

"Sure," said Dorn. "I'll go get it." He looked into Lorna's wide-opened eyes and managed a reassuring smile for her. "It's all right, dear," he said gently. "All Bundy wants is to get out of here."

"Yes, that's all I want now. To get out of here. Wait a shake, Bill! You'd follow me after I started—"

"No, I'll let you go."

"Your men would. There'd be a dozen of them. If I ran into bad luck, if my horse got a foot in a squirrel hole—No; it won't do. Saddle two horses for me. Lorna is going to ride with me as far as the border!"

"No! I won't stand for that, Bundy. I wouldn't trust you out of sight, not with Lorna."

"You'd rather see her shot right here before your eyes!"

"I'd rather kill her myself than have you drag her off to Nacional! That's final, Mike Bundy!"

Lorna, though as white as a sheet, said, with lips scarcely moving, without separating her teeth that were set so hard: "Bill—don't let him take me. He would kill me. I'd rather die here, now—"

For an instant Bundy seemed at the end of his rope. Then he saw the one way out. "*Bueno.* Saddle three horses, Bill. Lorna and I ride ahead. You ride after us, within shooting distance if you like. And you can have your gun back. The three of us ride friendly-wise to the border—and at every step I'll have this girl covered. Suit you?"

"Sure," said Dorn, and went to the door. "I'll get three horses."

He hurried out, ran the few steps to his waiting horse, toed into the stirrup to ride the short distance to the corral—but got no farther toward mounting. An enormous cloud of dust rose into the sky and under it, coming down the Blue Smokes road, he saw such a great, unprecedented crowd of horsemen that he stared wondering. He saw that they were coming swiftly; he saw through the dust the gleam of sunlight on many a rifle and shotgun—and the realization surged over him that here came an angry mob from County Line, and that they were looking for Mike Bundy. The sheriff had dropped a flea in the camp's ear, hadn't he? And if these men had made sure that Bundy had hoaxed them—

In five minutes they'd be at the upper gate. They'd be at the house before he could catch and saddle three horses, before he and Lorna and Bundy could get away.

He whirled and ran back to the house.

"Bundy," he said hurriedly as Bundy turned suspicious, hard eyes on him, "there's a crowd of men, two or three hundred of them, coming down the Blue Smokes road. They're almost at the gate. If you did salt those claims at County Line—

that's what MacArthur told them to look out for—and if they've tumbled to it, they're going to make cat-meat of you before you're ten minutes older!"

The rigid features of Mike Bundy's face turned a grayish-white. "Damn you, Dorn," he shouted, "hurry! Get those horses here on the run! Ours will be fresh—we'll run away from them—"

"They'll be here before I can—"

"Go stop them! Hold them up at the gate. Tell them anything. Stop them, damn it! Do you hear me?"

Dorn, fearing what might happen with those men gone savage through rage, was no less distressed then Bundy. The horses had to be saddled—the men had to be delayed—

"Jinks!" he rapped out as the only possible thing to do dawned on him. "Hot-foot for the gate. You can get there before them if you run. Grab up a chain and padlock on your way. Lock the gate. Hold those men off with whatever you can think to tell them; hold them every single minute you can. Then it'll take them a minute or two to break the gate down or cut the wires. Run, man!"

Bundy stood frowning but did not open his mouth. Jinks was off like a shot. Dorn again hurried out and to the corral. As he got the first horse saddled he saw Jinks, a clanking chain clutched in his hands, racing toward the gate. The oncoming riders saw him, too, for they shouted; but not knowing what it was all about they came steadily on.

Dorn, working as swiftly as he could, got the second saddle on, jerked the cinch tight and glanced again at the gate. Jinks, God bless him, was there first; Dorn could see him fumbling with the chain.

Dorn had trouble with the third horse; it fought the bit and his body was wet with sweat by the time he had forced the big clenched teeth apart and forced the iron in. He saw the mob at the fence now; Jinks had climbed up on the gate, the men had pressed close, he was haranguing them. His high-pitched voice floated back in a thin bugling; the words themselves were lost. The horse fought the saddle as it had refused the bridle. But the battle was short, the victory soon Dorn's. He glanced again toward the gate.

Men were shouting angrily; several were dismounting; they were set on breaking the gate down. Jinks jumped down and started running back to the house.

Dorn jerked the last cinch tight, swung up into the saddle and started at a gallop toward the ranch house, leading the two other horses. As he pulled in at the steps Bundy came out, forcing Lorna along ahead of him at gunpoint.

"Up in a hurry!" he ordered her. "They're breaking that damned gate down. They'll be in shooting distance—"

Lorna scrambled into her saddle. Bundy shot his toe into his stirrup.

Jinks had come in at the back door, had sped through the house, had come out on the front porch. As Bundy started to mount, Jinks took slow, deliberate aim. For an instant, scarcely longer, Bundy's gun had wavered. Jinks squeezed the trigger.

The one bullet was all that was necessary. It broke Mike Bundy's right shoulder. And as his weapon dropped from his useless hand old Cap Jinks made a glorious flying leap from the porch—and he brought down on Mike Bundy's head the heavy muzzle of a gun he had snatched from one of the riders' belts up at the gate.

When Mike Bundy regained consciousness and looked into the scores of faces about him, he read everywhere the same expression. Then he saw Bill Dorn leading Lorna away, the crowd falling apart for them to go, closing in around him after they had gone. It was a crowd of men grown ominously silent. But out of the silence he heard Jinks' voice piping up to say: "You fellers ain't got a right to hang a man for jus' saltin' a gold mine. But here's what Bart MacArthur told me: Mike Bundy kilt Jake Fanning account the real mine; an' he kilt One Eye Perez an' tried to get the sweetes' girl you ever saw, Miss Lorny, blamed for it; an' he kilt Miss Lorny's aunt, ol' lady Kent an'—Hell, by rights he belongs to me, 'cause I nailed him, but you can do as you think best. Only, account o' not messin' up a clean ranch, take him somewhere else."

The next morning old Cap Jinks and Lorna were sitting in the sun on the front porch, waiting for Bill Dorn to join them, when Jinks, out of a serene silence, became vocal.

"I was jus' figgerin', Lorny," he observed, "as how this no-'count Will Dorn person, what with chasin' back an' forth so much from the Smokes here, an' from here to Liberty an' back here ag'in, an' back an' fo'th some more—"

"He *has* done a good bit of riding, hasn't he, Cappie darling?" laughed a radiantly happy Lorna, and turned in quick expectancy, thinking she heard Bill's on-coming tread.

"Shucks," said Jinks, "he must of rid a thousan' mile—"

It was Dorn coming, and he came swiftly as she knew he would. "Darn you, Jinks," he grinned, as radiant in his own way as Lorna. "You're good to rest tired eyes on most times—but right now—Lorna, I've got to get you off by yourself, without old Cap horning in to listen."

"Hmf!" sniffed Jinks, and winked at the girl whose arm was tucked so affectionately in his.

Lorna jumped up. "Where'll we go, Bill?"

"Let's go for a ride!" said Sudden Bill Dorn.

Center Point Publishing
600 Brooks Road • PO Box 1
Thorndike ME 04986-0001 USA

(207) 568-3717

US & Canada:
1 800 929-9108
www.centerpointlargeprint.com

W